A PRESENT PAST

TITAN AND OTHER CHRONICLES

SERGEI LEBEDEV

TRANSLATED FROM THE RUSSIAN
BY ANTONINA W. BOUIS

NEW VESSEL PRESS
NEW YORK

www.newvesselpress.com

First published in Russian in 2022 as Титан
Copyright © 2022 Sergei Lebedev
Translation Copyright © 2023 Antonina W. Bouis

Library of Congress Cataloging-in-Publication Data
Lebedev, Sergei
[Titan. English]
A Present Past: Titan and Other Chronicles / Sergei Lebedev; translation by Antonina W. Bouis
p. cm.
ISBN 978-1-954404-18-2

Library of Congress Control Number: 2022950051
I. Russia–Fiction

TABLE OF CONTENTS

PREFACE

I REMEMBER the final years of the Soviet empire.

Even though I was a child, I remember the phenomenon of mystical feelings, elemental and ubiquitous, as sudden as a volcanic eruption.

The sense of the approaching end of an era also elicits mysticism. However, the Soviet Union was an atheist state, built on the doctrine of materialism. Soviet ideology—at least on paper—called for a rational view of the world and the only ghost allowed was the "specter of Communism" that Marx and Engels had prophesied in the nineteenth century.

That made it all the more astonishing how quickly the other world appeared, the "reverse" side of Soviet consciousness; a dark storeroom filled with everything that had been tossed, hidden, crossed out of life and memory during the seventy years of communist rule.

A new mystical folklore arose before our eyes, seemingly out of the air of the epoch.

It spoke of evil places, anomalous zones where the laws of physics did not hold.

About strange creatures, poltergeists who lived in houses

and apartments and persecuted residents they did not like, with knocks and noises and moving objects.

About children born with characteristic birthmarks on their bodies if their ancestors had been executed by firearms.

People's minds sought images, sought a language to describe the tragedy, and they turned to mystical allusions to make the evil past real and at the same time managed to become estranged from it, turning it into the subject of another world and another reality.

Well, ghosts are not born by themselves. They are born of a silent conscience. Dual moral optics. They are as real as the ignored knowledge of crimes and the refusal to accept real responsibility.

They are the distorted voice of the dead turned into mystical images. The voice of unwanted witnesses.

Throughout its existence, the Soviet state destroyed people and destroyed any memory of the destruction.

However, the archives of state security still retained millions of files. Millions of invented accusations. Millions of false interrogations built on a single artistic scenario: from denial to confession of nonexistent guilt.

These cases, this metatext with its standardized subjects and genres, may in fact comprise the most important and terrible Russian work of the twentieth century. The evidence of evil which remains unread.

JUDGE STOMAKOV

Judge Stomakov arrived at the dacha on Friday night, right after a protracted session.

Traffic jams in the city, traffic jams getting on the road, traffic jams on the highway. A red haze of traffic lights. Horizontal drizzle that poured into the vehicle's small ventilation window when you smoked. The road he traveled as a child, next to his father on the front seat, familiar with every turn, every foggy lowland. Now there were two lanes in each direction, sometimes even three, instead of traffic lights there were concrete loops of interchanges, instead of the woods—angular high-rise buildings and new neighborhoods. But it was his road, well-traveled, well-worn. How many thoughts had been contemplated at this speed, how many schemes and plots hatched. But now, when his most important plan, years in the making, was about to come to fruition, the road threw him an unpleasant curve: his car with its judicial plates and pass in the windscreen was stopped by a highway policeman.

The rookie didn't understand. His partner scolded the kid, groveled apologetically, and wished him a good journey. But it left a bad taste. The judge was angry and thought how in a month or so he would have a service BMW with a flashing light and then no bastard would dare . . . He should write down the name and call his bosses tomorrow, thought Stomakov. How had he introduced himself? Muzin? Kuzin? Zuzin? The name wouldn't come to him, as if the sergeant sensed the judge's attempts and was fighting to get away with it. Stomakov never did remember it and so he was in a bad mood when he arrived.

It was early and chilly. He wanted to go to the banya for a steam on the hot maple benches. Stomakov thought for a few seconds and regretfully denied himself that. There would be guests tomorrow. Special guests. Andrei Porfiryevich did not like the banya to be damp from the day before.

Of course, he could do as he liked now. His candidacy had been approved. He had completed his part of the bargain today, ruling as required, refusing to consider the case on its merits. Yet Stomakov always hedged his bets and never hurried.

The trunk was filled with food and drink. He had learned the tastes of all four guests and remembered nuances; for instance, Andrei Porfiryevich liked only Spanish olives, green and stuffed with pimento. He knew that all four men, higher up the ladder, would not consider his attentiveness fawning or extreme. They valued him because he did not miss a thing.

Deputy Chairman of the Supreme Court, said Stomakov aloud, relishing the sound. Here at the dacha no one would witness his self-admiration. The decision was made. Tomorrow they would drink to his appointment, confirming it with clinking glasses, and celebrate it interdepartmentally. Matitsyn was from the Procurator General's office, Voronov from the Federal Security Service, Golovko from the Military Collegium, and Lappo the first deputy of the Chairman of the Supreme Court, the heir, the successor. They had all been at law school together. Lappo was three years senior. They were friends who then went their separate ways. They met again three years ago, over the case that Stomakov concluded today.

Stomakov had taken note of the case long before it reached the Supreme Court, as it wended its way on appeal in the lower courts. He had his people on the ground in some regional and municipal courts who reported on promising trials. He read newspapers closely, watching and taking aim.

He had accumulated judicial influence this way, by knowing how to avoid unpromising cases and maneuvering to intercept those on which you could advance. The cases did not necessarily involve money, actually quite the contrary: You didn't make money or accept bribes from either side. But if you did everything correctly, you would not be forgotten. Only such cases led to the very top.

Stomakov picked up on this case after reading an article in a federal newspaper. It merely concerned a regional court refusing exhumation and DNA analysis. Way out in the sticks, a local story. But he noticed who was asking for the exhumation. Who was killed and when. He understood the forces in play: security services, diplomats, the presidential administration. He guessed the case would certainly reach the Supreme Court, the plaintiffs would not cease. The judge's candidacy would certainly be discussed with the FSB.

He weighed the case. He ran all the scenarios through his head. He realized: if the case came to him, given his previous achievements, it would propel him to the post of Deputy Chairman.

While the case was still floundering in lower courts, Stomakov started preparing. He talked to the right people to gauge which way the political winds were blowing. He greased some palms. Gave a few thoughts and suggestions. Told others that he would never want that case, it was too dangerous, a career breaker. Yet others were politely reminded of old debts. As a result, the case floated into his hands, dozens of volumes plopped onto his desk. The deputy chairmanship was guaranteed, both Voronov and Lappo hinted; it was essential to do everything neatly.

The neatness meant going to a lot of trouble. Over three years policies changed three times. Stomakov was forced to entirely reorient his judicial line three times.

First he leaned toward compromise, a partial admission of the responsibility of the Soviet Union, toward qualifying it as a "murder by prior conspiracy" and then referring to an expired statute of limitations. That is, to brush it off—but gently.

Then, after the anniversary speech of the foreign president, more discipline was required: a complete disclaimer, but still diplomatically expressed.

And the third directive, after the deployment of American missiles, was to respond asymmetrically, "spit in their face," as Lappo said. And it was Stomakov who came up with how to observe at least a minimum semblance of legal procedure—and inflict the heaviest insult.

In three years Stomakov got used to the thousands of victims in his case. And all of them had been dead for years. Executed by the NKVD over three days in a suburban pine forest. Sometimes he even felt an unofficial, superfluous interest in them, in the dead strangers, foreign officers, stuck together in the ground, turned by death into one whole, a human layer; they had left behind archival traces: orders to relocate the camps, train schedules, execution lists . . .

Stomakov knew that a judge has to protect himself. Both from the accused and the victims. Not for the sake of justice and the triumph of law, no. That was too stupid. For his own sake.

The judicial realm was a narrow caste. A closed circle with its own concepts, history, folklore, and knowledge that did not go beyond the initiates and was not shared with others. Prosecutors, police, state security, the presidential administration all knew a lot and gave tacit orders to judges, agreed on sentences, and naively thought that they all were stewing in the same juices.

But it was the judges who meted out sentences! And judges had their own means of perception, a secret art that cannot be found in any book. It was the same for the correct verdict and the incorrect one. A judge wrote someone else's fate. And a judge had to protect himself from any backlash. They didn't teach that in law school. It didn't even come with experience, but with wisdom.

Stomakov knew how to pass judgment without exerting any mental effort. To impose a sentence, seemingly without personal involvement. Rather than from him, the sentence came from the judge's table, the volumes of legislation on the shelves, the black Kasli cast-iron statuette used as a paper-weight—a soldier in a fur hat, overcoat over his shoulder, taking aim from his knee—the graphite pencil he used to correct his drafts, the huge court building itself, its chande-liers, stairs, corridors, the cloudy crystal ashtray, and, most important, the robe.

Other judges, young and foolish, changed robes almost every year, having new ones made of better fabric, took them home, hanging them in the closet with ordinary, amicable everyday garments—ignoramuses, what could you expect! Stomakov's robe hung in a special closet in his office, separate from his street clothes. When he left for home, he locked the closet and quietly said, "Good night, Your Honor."

Until this strange case, he never, ever allowed the victims to get inside his head. But these still managed to get through, even though he was on the alert. They pushed inside his skull like passengers into a metro car at rush hour.

He could have held off a few dozen. Maybe a hundred. But thousands . . . He was defeated by huge numbers. He was a fool not to have realized that quantity mattered even in posthumous cases—and how!

In a sense they did not exist, the officers of a foreign country imprisoned in 1939 during a brief, long-ago war and executed on the orders of the Leader. What did it matter how many: one or many thousands? They were gone, no more. "No" was a harsh word, final. But it turned out that they did exist: in Stomakov's thoughts.

He had glanced at their camp files only once. He needed to clear up one point that had procedural significance. He looked into a dozen cases, read their personnel data. He was curious and studied their photographs, ordinary faces, some of them you would never think were Polish, foreigners.

He started having dreams about entering the courtroom to pronounce his sentence on their case, sitting down in his familiar armchair, looking up at the public, journalists, diplomats, relatives, decoy agents, and seeing the dead men in their rotting uniforms and crumpled caps sitting on the chairs. In silence. Waiting for the judge to speak.

It did not scare him. He didn't waver. He didn't go to see a doctor: they would report to Lappo or Voronov, he would be taken off the case and forced to retire for medical reasons. He learned to sleep without dreams by taking pills. He turned in the final refusal to hear the case.

The descendants of the executed officers wanted the dead to be officially rehabilitated.

There were different ways to refuse. And he, having been instructed by Lappo to "spit," made the dead men pay for his troubled dreams. He found fault with procedural details, the status of the citizens of a prewar state that no longer existed, and the lack of authority of foreign representatives. And he made a deliberately convoluted, confusing decision, from which, in the end, it followed that only the victims them-selves could apply for rehabilitation.

"And how the dead men will come after you," Lappo joked, laughing, when Stomakov read him the draft before the session. "Aren't you afraid?"

"They won't be able to write a statement," said Stomakov admonishingly. "They are dead."

Lappo chuckled again and wrote his approval on the draft.

The faces of the family members when the embassy interpret-ers explained the court decision! Knocked the breath out of them! They couldn't squeal or groan. They reached into pock-ets and purses for pills, covered their faces with their hands.

So, their sobs were Stomakov's revenge for the stupid dreams.

Only one gray-haired woman, a mummy who sat in a wheelchair throughout the hearing, looking around with the wary grace of a bird, jumped up, shook her dry fists, and shouted in their language.

Stomakov allowed her to rant. He couldn't call in the guards; that would have been worse. He looked at her, not hiding his gaze, showing that he was not afraid, that he could distinguish the strictness of the law and the vulner-ability of feelings and was capable of respecting feelings. He thought he recognized her. Time, which deadened flesh, projected onto her face the features of her father, a cavalry officer who was the only prisoner in that camp to attack the executioners.

She has to be a hundred, thought Stomakov. He had a subconscious fear of the long-lived. Why had she lived so long? To do what?

Stomakov listened more closely. He felt a vibrating, multivoiced female force, as if all the women that this old one had been were yelling at him.

Stomakov understood.

The old woman, the lousy bitch, had known she would come to the courtroom to die. She thought she would die happy, after hearing that the rehabilitation would come. Now she was turning the power of her death into a curse.

Cold sweat poured down his back under the robe. Stomakov took detached note that he was sweating profusely during this trial. His robe began to come apart, to decay, as if it had been infected by the rotting clothes of the executed, by their underpants and shirts. And the old woman sat and leaned back, slid out of her wheelchair, and let out a final howl that sounded like a wounded animal.

Stomakov told his aide to call an ambulance. With somber dignity he asked the journalists and visitors to leave the scene of an unexpected tragedy. He promised that the court would make a special announcement the following week. The photographers had time for only a few shots.

He did what was necessary. With anyone else, things would have gotten out of hand, there would have been a huge scandal, press and TV, gossip, a real fest. But he outmaneuvered them: The decoy agents acted in time, surrounding and blocking access to the dead woman. There was a reason for their training, the instructions they had been given for emergencies, their rehearsals.

Stomakov saw Voronov, dressed in civvies, nodding at him approvingly from a far corner, as if to say: good job. Yet Stomakov suddenly felt terrible, as if the old woman had not just ruined the session but had pressed a secret spot on his body, one of the unremarkable points where eastern practitioners stuck their needles. Lappo had one, a master, a miracle worker, and Lappo promised to give him the number after his appointment, the clients were special, elite. She pressed the spot and started the countdown. The countdown to his death.

Reluctantly, Stomakov carried the groceries into the house and stuffed them into the fridge. He was hungry. But he didn't want to chew, swallow, wield knife and fork, have taste in his mouth. He stood by the open door, looking desultorily at the food, the logs of sausages, the multifaceted cheeses, illuminated by the butter yellow cave light of the refrigerator bulb.

It was a reflection of Stomakov's adolescence, when his father had finally managed to wheedle and manipulate himself a job as a legal consultant in the international division of the Central Committee. Compared to his managerial position at the Juridical Literature publishing house, it looked like a demotion. But in fact, it was a promotion in the nomenklatura ranks.

His father, lean, chipper, and not a great eater, no connoisseur of bounteous cuisine, began to fill their refrigerator to the brim with varnished sausages, gold bars of bullion-like butter, jars of caviar, cured meats, halves and quarters of cheese heads. These were his trophies, his overdue fortune. And he wanted his son to devour it, to fill himself up to the brim, charged with success, goodness, and stultifying mental health.

Stomakov could not eat his father's food. When he was a guest at other tables, he shamelessly gobbled all the delicacies. His father's food seemed to have the wrong taste. Not caviar, not cervelat, but some kind of cellophane, as if they were waxworks and not elite grub from special stores.

So Stomakov stood one evening by the refrigerator looking for something proletarian, like crumbly, slimy farmer cheese from an ordinary store. The house phone rang, and his mother, certain that it was his father calling to say he would be late, answered. He barely remembered her screams and weeping. He did remember perfectly how he picked up a plump link sausage with a piglet tail and popped it in his mouth along with the string and then took a bite out of the wedge of cheese with oval holes. He swallowed, belatedly accepting his father's communion, but could detect no flavor at all. Not even cellophane.

His mother never accepted the story of suicide that the police offered. She made up an accident, prompted by a widow's defense mechanism. A terrible combination of circumstances: the low balcony railing in someone's apartment, they never knew whose, and his father's poor vision. Yurochka forgot to put on his glasses, she said. You know what he's like without his glasses. As blind as a bat.

She easily disregarded external circumstances: army tanks on the capital's streets, the failed coup, the gray faces of the conspirators on television, the jubilant crowds in the squares.

But Stomakov understood. And he was astonished at his own impassivity, at his forced respect for the rules of the great game, in which his father was one of many figures who suddenly, in one day, became unnecessary, knowing too much.

He, it turned out, had brought about his own demise by getting a transfer to legal counsel. The sausage, the caviar, the *balyk*, the *basturma*—they had fed him his death in parts, in long installments, and now the time had come to repay the debt in one go.

Yes, he had thought of revenge. He brushed it aside easily, telling himself that he needed to wait until things settled down. Maybe there would be a follow-up investigation, justice takes a long time.

Later, at the institute, the head of the first department, the dry and usually unpleasant old man Mitradze, came up to him and expressed condolences. He wondered if Stomakov wanted to take an academic leave of absence: the rectors, given the circumstances, would meet him halfway. Stomakov understood that the system was still alive even though the state was collapsing. It would remain, it was even apologizing, and his father had bought him a future. Stomakov could rebel, give in to his anger, but then his father's unwilling sacrifice would be in vain.

"Thank you," he said to Mitradze, "but I will stay on. My studies will distract me. And my father . . . He really wanted me to go into law. To be a judge." The quick nod, like a tug on a fishing line, let him know that he had given the right answer.

Stomakov shut the refrigerator and went out on the open veranda. Scrolls of oak leaves rustled underfoot and the icy forest breeze touched his aching back. It was too fresh, that breeze, as if no one else lived in the area.

He looked around at the neighbors' dark houses. He felt that the area familiar from childhood was being transformed. The sparse forests trampled by summer residents, small meadows, miserable ponds, shallow hollows, copses, weak streams, and small fields seemed to have grown, closed in on one another, and the night had breathed into them something dense, menacing, wild. Stomakov hastily lit a cigarette and heard a dog whining somewhere nearby, it wasn't clear if it was at his place or at a neighbor's.

The wind let up.

The dog whined louder and then started howling softly. Not howling out loud, but as if suffering from unbearable horror, having pissed from fear, huddled in a corner, in a crack behind the barn, trembling violently.

The nocturnal canine voice seemed dangerously close to being human.

"Bitch," he said. "Bitch."

That was a password that opened the door of his memory.

Bitch. Male dogs don't howl like that. Only bitches. It's her bitchy, emptied gut, where the afterbirth was, that gives that nasty note. From the belly, from the womb, from the nipples oozing bloody milk, from the animal torment of birth, bitch, bitch!

Yes, that spring a stray mutt whelped under their old house. They got to the dacha too late, it had already set up a lair and settled the litter; the neighbors complained that the dog had dug up their garden plots and made a hole under the fence.

His parents decided that someone had to go under the house. But his father, who was usually very officious, hasty, hurrying everybody up, taking pleasure in his own, as he said, maneuverability—with the dexterity of a pickpocket he borrowed military words from conversations, articles, and encyclopedias, words like *glissade, raid, flank*, creating an aura of manliness for himself—was in no hurry to act.

He took a long time changing into work clothes. He sniffed them to see if they smelled of mice. He put new batteries in the flashlight. He gave the corroded contacts a thorough scraping.

Stomakov, who had just turned fourteen, realized that his father was afraid. Squeamish and afraid. All he knew was how to urge others to do things. He didn't know how to behave here. A stray dog, a pathetic creature, had direct power over his father.

His father would have called Miron, the handyman for the dacha community who was always called in to do chores like burying a cat or cleaning out the cesspool. But Miron was in the hospital, having spent the winter on a drunken bender. Father was mad at him, too, but most of all at the bitch that had chosen their house for her litter, as if she knew the owner's vulnerability.

Stomakov experienced a gloating sense of retribution. He saw that their roles had switched: the dog was forcing his father to act, and he was hemming and hawing, unable to perform. His father liked to drive his victims to this state of indecision and inability to act with his deft sarcastic jabs. Stomakov was grateful to the stray for the revenge. He was doubly grateful since this was the first time he felt he could predict the situation and manage the adults.

He watched his father spreading the small rug from the veranda, lying down on it with the air of a sapper preparing to remove mines from a building and cautiously crawling between the foundation pillars, the flashlight in his hand. He knew what was about to happen.

The bitch attacked silently and nipped at his hand. His father rolled over to his side, overplaying it, as if acting the part of a wounded soldier in a movie. The invisible dog began barking viciously in the dark, and Stomakov sensed his father was relieved by the hostility. It gave him a way out: He couldn't go where that creature was having a fit! Its fangs almost bit through his wrist!

His mother came running with antiseptic, smearing it on his skin that did not have a single scratch. Stomakov saw they were playing a duet, naturally, almost unconsciously, moving through life this way, helping each other out.

At lunch, his father displayed bravado, joking about the hound of the Baskervilles. He said the bitch would probably leave soon. Leading her pups away. Maybe even by next weekend. They wouldn't sit under the house forever, would they? Stomakov pictured how his father would appear to have forgotten about the dog on Monday and Tuesday. On Wednesday he would cheerfully say it must have run off by now. On Thursday and Friday, he would be anxious and angry, blaming the dacha cooperative board for allowing stray animals to breed on the property. He would have to call some dogcatchers, surely there was a service that did that.

Then, on the weekend, he would hesitate, fret, and suddenly hint: Son, could you help out your parents?

When they got back to the dacha the following week, opened the door, and stamped on the floor, there was no sound from beneath. His father said heartily, "Victory, comrades!"

"You should check later," Stomakov said with apparent innocence, feeling a sly and predatory joy: the clever hypocrisy, the accuracy of "later," which appeared to give his father a postponement but in fact ruined his whole day. His father frowned and shrugged—no rush. Stomakov had the feeling that the puppies were there, even though he couldn't hear them.

He and his father took the carpets out into the yard: they needed beating to get rid of the winter dust. As if attracted by the rhythmic blows, the bitch crawled out from under the neighbors' fence. It ran, limping, hiding in the bushes, to the house. His father did not notice, it ran behind his back.

Stomakov saw the dog in parts: sometimes one thing struck him, then another.

The pink, bare side, covered with festering, oozing cracks: It looked like it had been scalded with boiling water. A severed tail. The left hind leg, broken and healed crookedly. Eyes crusted over with sulfur. A slanting scar across the head. Burrs and tangles in its dirty fur.

And a huge belly, swollen and bleeding, dragging on the ground, marked with a red burn mark, tight nipples sticking out like little fingers.

The mutt was disgusting. Stomakov secretly imagined his father's stunned reaction when he saw it in daylight.

That in their closed dacha co-op, with respected residents, all leading staff of the Juridical Literature publishing house, who had decent, polite dogs with pedigrees, names, and veterinary records, there could suddenly appear this mongrel monster, this vile creature! Why didn't it go to the worker settlement by the railroad station, where equally vile little people lived? Why did it come to our house, his father would think.

Stomakov felt aroused, as if the rhythmic beating of the carpets had awakened his libido that had slept all winter. He was seeing the pink-and-red swollen teat full of milk.

He thought with surprise: Something had screwed that monstrous dog. Some cripple that matched it. Or, on the contrary, some fancy, pampered pet, like the stylish schnauzer Miki from dacha 16. He pictured sleek show-off Miki with the bitch—and got even more excited. He would have mated them, he would, just to see that live!

The bitch squeezed into the hole. The puppies started squealing under the house. His father heard them and lowered his carpet beater. He pretended that he couldn't make out what he had heard and was trying to figure out if he had imagined it.

"I've figured out what to do, Papa," Stomakov said. "We have to wait for the dog to go for food. Then bring the puppies into the woods. In a basket. The deep one for agaric mushrooms would work."

His father looked at him in astonishment, searching for and not finding the right sarcastic reply. Stomakov added: "I'll do it all myself. You and Mama don't have to worry."

His parents were a little confused that day, almost frightened. They kept repeating, "Take them to the woods, yes, take them to the woods . . ."

And the more they repeated it, the clearer it became what "take them to the woods" really meant.

Of course, they couldn't say outright that the puppies had to be killed, otherwise the bitch would find them by smell and drag them by the scruff back under the house. They both thought that their son, just a boy, truly was suggesting that they dump the puppies somewhere far away. And they did not dare hint, for example, to mention as if in passing that in the villages puppies and kittens were drowned, the villagers did not fool around.

Stomakov was pleased to feel their naiveté. He had already decided everything: where and how.

The bitch went for food Sunday morning. It must have figured out that the residents who come from the city on the weekend eat the food they bring with them at lunch and dinner and toss the remains into the compost pits. Stomakov liked seeing these patterns and knowing how to use them.

He waited for the dog to get far away. He put on a jacket, took the basket and flashlight, and crawled under the house. His parents took a position to block the dog's path if it came back. He knew that they wouldn't be quick enough, wouldn't even take a risk, even though his mother had a rake and his father a long-handled shovel.

It was dry and clean under the house. Stomakov had imagined a filthy lair and filthy and mean puppies, nasty like their mother. But the puppies were clean, sweet, well-tended. They stirred in the rags brought in from backyards. Large, with big eyes, and friendly. Alive.

He almost chickened out. He had expected them to be insentient creatures that would not understand what was being done to them. Maybe just squeak in confusion. What if they realized where he was taking them? Started to howl and scratch? A quarter of the way was through the dachas . . . Stomakov chuckled. The weaving of the tubby basket with a narrow throat, which he had set on its side in order to shove the puppies in it, made it look like a uterus behind ribs. The puppies, recently out of their mother's belly, were back in the tight belly of the basket by his decision.

That was amusing.

"Be sure to take them far away," his father said in parting, as if he had been willing to do it himself and his son had literally begged him for the right to deal with the puppies.

"Yes, yes, far away," his mother joined in. "Dogs have a good sense of smell. She'll find them."

"No, she won't," Stomakov replied confidently, feeling a physical pleasure, not unlike satisfying one's appetite, at the ease with which he understood the real meaning of the conversation.

"Far away," he said to himself. "Very far!"

He picked up the basket and headed to the gate, without looking back.

The street was empty. For years Stomakov had ridden his bicycle and played hide-and-seek with friends here, and now he walked like a stranger. He realized how odd it looked on a spring morning to have the kind of big basket they take down from the attic in the fall, when the woods are full of mushrooms. You don't go to the market with these. You don't carry garbage in them. Anyone who saw him would be surprised and ask in the dacha manner, where was he going, what was he getting?

He tried to come up with a clever reply and failed.

He walked and watched the dacha residents hanging laundry, washing cars, digging gardens. No one paid any attention to him. Stomakov realized that he had no need to worry: his intentions made him invisible.

He went out past the back road, to the thin pine woods and the railroad beyond it. As he passed the woods he looked longingly at the fire pit, weeds starting to cover it, and the pieces of railroad tie laid in a square: they baked potatoes and drank fortified wine here last year when his parents left him alone at the dacha for a week. With determination he clambered up the steep slope of the railroad, overgrown with fireweed, scattering gravel.

It was an auxiliary track, a siding for freight trains. Stomakov set down the basket and wiped the sweat from his face. The puppies were moving around inside but not yapping.

He looked back from the slope at the path he had taken and the roof of their house sticking up over the trees in the distance. At last he was alone. The shining lines of the tracks captured Stomakov between them, turning into railings, guidelines. He sensed the air disturbed by trains, the weight of the sagging wires, the vertical vigilance of the poles. The signal in the distance, flickering red, switched to green, an invitation to walk. A train would come soon, thought Stomakov, and picked up the basket.

The ties on this secondary branch were placed any which way, it was hard to walk on them, and people usually walked alongside the tracks on the gravel. But Stomakov quickly picked up the ragged rhythm and strode on, recalling with pleasure how simply and naturally he had found the place.

It was a pond covered in duckweed and littered with driftwood between two branch lines meeting at the point of a wedge, with the third side blocked by a swampy wood.

All the ponds in the water-starved area had names: Lipovka, Gluboky, Semikhatka. This one wasn't called anything. It was too small, too dirty, wholly unused. No one fished there, or swam, or had parties on the edge.

The nameless pond came to him during the week. Steep slopes, impenetrable swamp, thick dark weeds on the water, submerged branches—it came alive in his imagination, took on meaning, as if created for this, waiting for a sacrifice, pretending to be a stinking, useless puddle. Stomakov thought that there could actually be a bloody weapon thrown from a train window or an old corpse in the pond.

Stomakov strode along. The clearing of the pond was visible on the right, beyond the embankment's curving arc. He walked, testing his feelings, secure in the thought that he was carrying the puppies but sensed nothing in particular. His father would have suffered, not with pity for the puppies but from his own eternal uncertainty, hidden behind a veil of sarcasm, about what was right and what wasn't. He however really didn't feel anything. *Ezee*, as the dacha crowd said.

The pond, revealed from the slope, was just as he had imagined it.

Covered in scaly, shiny duckweed, a sinkhole. It seemed to have existed before the railroads, and ancestors had prayed to it, throwing bodies and carcasses into it.

He descended in a serpentine fashion, looked around: the slope obscured him, and now he could be seen only from the second track, but there was a freight train: smeared with grease, tanks like sausages.

The weeds were so thick he suddenly thought, what if the puppies didn't drown? Got stuck and struggled? He found a stone and threw it hard. The water made a glugging sound, the weeds spread, and the black and shiny eye of the water appeared.

Stomakov threw back the basket lid. He expected them to look at him in fear. He was waiting for that fear that would reflect his power over them. The puppies were cuddled up asleep, lulled by the swinging basket.

Furious, he grabbed one and threw it without looking far into the pond. Then the second, third, fourth, and fifth, listening to the duckweed slurp as it separated. He turned, expecting to see five windows drawing shut in the weeds.

The puppies were swimming. Paddling, using all four paws, heading for shore. Each swam separately, as if they understood that the shore was piled with dry wood, clumps of sawn shrubs, and if they all arrived at the same time, Stomakov would be stuck in the rubble and unable to catch them all.

Stomakov started running back and forth. He fell, tearing his pants leg, cutting his knee. The ground was stony, with sharp and heavy rocks, and he threw a big one at the fastest puppy with a white spot on its nose.

He was generally bad at anything that required accurate aim. He had the power, he was quick and agile, but it did not add up to accuracy. Soccer, fairground shooting range, slingshot: he always thought he had aimed accurately, but he always missed.

But here, when anyone else would have missed in haste, Stomakov was on target. The stone struck the puppy in the forehead, right on the white spot, the bull's-eye. The puppy sank as if the pull of the bottom and the weeds had finally won. Stomakov, selecting the heaviest stones, started on the rest. Of course, he didn't hit any of them on the first try. But he got them with the second or third. The puppies drowned one after the other, with the same unnatural ease with which the moving targets at a shooting range fall, all those bullet-pocked tin deer, rabbits, and boars.

The puppies were gone, but he kept throwing, crazed, wanting to hit them underwater, so they would not float up again, as if shooting a long belt of ammunition. Behind him, on the embankment, a freight train sounded its horn, a warning, squeezing its heavy articulated body into a turn. The wagons rattled and rumbled at the joints, like a machine gun. The power, the pull of the loaded train was transferred to Stomakov, and he pounded stones on the water, as if he wanted to wake the quagmire sleeping for decades so that it would accept his sacrifice.

The freight train slowed down, honked again, turning from the side branch onto the main line. And in the changed rhythms of the last cars Stomakov made out a steely, daring laughter: as if the blacksmith's hammers were dancing, having fun, hitting the anvil. The hammers were beating on his head, and he laughed with this metallic laughter, too. He couldn't stop himself, he laughed, jumped up and down, staring at the ruptured pond perforated by stones, like bullet-riddled garments.

"Took them to the far woods," he told his parents, setting the empty basket on the picnic table. "The one by the highway."

"What a job!" his father replied in his usual manner, distractedly, but without the habitual jab. "A shame, of course. But what can you do. It's life."

Stomakov washed his hands thoroughly, looking at them, so innocent in the stream of water, with neatly trimmed nails, thinking with feigned surprise: Could they really have thrown those stones? He painted antiseptic on his knee. His parents did not ask questions. They understood, of course. And they were uncomfortable.

The basket remained on the table all day.

That night he slept on the second floor. Even though they had roasted the blanket in the sunshine, the bed still gave off winter chill. His knee ached and burned. Stomakov woke after midnight and climbed out the skylight onto the roof of the veranda. He usually smoked up there, hiding the extinguished butts under the rolls of waterproofing material and then taking them away. But he didn't feel like smoking that night.

Childishly, he hoped for a sign that confirmed what he had done, something like a grade in his school workbook. He was sorry that he hadn't told his parents anything, his silence had deprived him of something important, the reason why he had done it. Recognition? Reward?

A shadow appeared in the garden. The bitch was there. It stood up on its hind legs and sniffed the basket.

Stomakov, watching from the roof edge, was grateful that it had come and put a final period to things. The dog, as if aware of his presence, backed away, vanished into the bushes, and left the lot—and out there, beyond the fence, it set up howling, disgusting, loud, with gasping hiccups, it must have been heard throughout the community.

Below, the lights came on in the veranda. A window lit up next door. Stomakov did not know what to do with himself. That bitch had tricked him, it was supposed to leave quietly, it didn't have the right, the bitch! He would find it tomorrow, find it and lure it, bringing along a heavy metal rod from the shed.

But the dog was gone in the morning. Stomakov never saw it again.

The judge clutched the veranda railing tighter.

His chest hurt as if he had been struck with a cleaver; he needed some Validol, the sedative so cool under the tongue.

It's just a stray dog, he said, reassuring himself. Just a stray. Maybe it was hit by a car and it crawled here. It's just three lots from the road.

The dog stopped howling. But he sensed that it was there, watching from the bushes. His anger and humiliation seemed funny; he laughed and wept, and the laughter tossed him up, the way his father tossed him over his head when he was a baby, so high that things went dark for an instant and his heart stopped in delight. Higher, higher, higher, toward the empty autumn sky, toward the icy stars—until it went completely dark.

ST. ANTHONY'S FIRE

Vitka Bolatov, aka Blotto, brought it to Batitsky. Vitka had stopped drinking long ago, he had a bad stomach, but the nickname suited him: he always seemed to be intoxicated by the chase. Vitka was small-time, a trickster, a scrounger, living day-to-day, but Batitsky appreciated him and paid him. Vitka didn't push crap, he didn't cheat, and sometimes Batitsky had the strange feeling that this petty, cranky, two-bit Vitka had the greatness of blessed pilgrims and holy fools.

In their dark and secretive work, luck was the highest prize. They tried to lure it, capture it. They tried to get it, the way you get fire by friction, by touching and caressing old things that fell into their sensitive hands. They hunted for brands, seals, and names—marvels and rarities that existed in the singular, things in which artistic tradition had exhausted itself and turned into monstrosity, sterility.

Vitka, art school dropout, had the light and accurate gift of finding things that manifest the instantaneous perfection of a historical style before it recognizes itself, before it matures. Such objects did not attract ordinary collectors, who fell only for recognizable, popular forms. Batitsky, not Batitsky the antiquarian but Batitsky the artist and later historian of design, loved objects like that, laconic and tranquil, expressing the spirit of the times as it formed.

Vitka, who knew how to troll anew places that seemed trampled and depleted, who was a regular at flea markets like the one by the Rabochiy Poselok station, where they spread out newspapers on the mud and sold useless faucets, candy tins, yellowed plastic prisms for chandeliers, chains of rusty, feral keys unused to keyholes, tubby tin soap dishes with a girl skipping rope engraved on the lid, dried-out rubber boots, one-toothed can openers, the remains of someone's miserable troubles—in those places Vitka had twice raised real pearls from the bottom of the rubbish sea.

Yes. The porcelain plate signed by El Lissitzky and the chased silver pitcher from the era of the Khorezm-Shahs, a work from the pre-Mongol period. Vitka brought them covered in filth, tormented, practically coated with blood and vomit. However, the filth and patina came off easily, and the objects were unscathed: not a single chip or scratch. That is probably why Batitsky paid him top price and then set these two things apart, as if recognizing their pride and chastity.

Batitsky was immune to collecting. Feeding the passions of others, he remained cold to their fetishes, secretly despising the animal-like peristalsis of accumulating and consuming; he had a seller's nature and enjoyed only the movement of objects and money, the play of prices. But the plate and pitcher did not make a collection. They were exhausted travelers seeking shelter, and the gambler Batitsky, who raked in money, never displayed them in the shop window.

This was something new. The items seemed to be visiting, remaining independent, and Batitsky studied them, mentally touching the borders of their alienation. Without admitting it openly, he gave them time, the protracted time of inorganic objects and materials that do not know the corruption of flesh, aging for centuries and rising in value over centuries; time to get used to him, to forget their suffering, to let go of their previous owners and give themselves up to him in the true connection between owner and owned.

The pitcher and plate, a ready-made still life. *Nature morte*. He was used to things that lived longer than humans, how else could it be in his profession? But they made him feel his age. The flow of passing life. The vanity of success. The beneficence of loss. Stubborn, he unconsciously sought a third something that was missing in the still life, an object of a different breed that could add inspiration, meaning, and mystery.

Then Vitka showed up again. He had been missing for a long time, having borrowed big money from Batitsky. Batitsky thought he would not return, that Blotto had been killed because the dope could have taken the bundle of cash to the flea market at the Rabochiy Poselok station. As he was counting out the euros, a thought flashed through his mind, that Vitka was asking for too much. It wasn't that he begrudged him, no. It was just that every person had a limit, a sum more than which he shouldn't have in his hands, because otherwise there was death, darkness, troubles would begin in the universe, and then the investigators would rack their brains over how it happened. Vitka had asked for more than his limit, a lot more, and for a second Batitsky felt like a murderer, but his curiosity was stronger: What if he managed? What if he brought something back?

Vitka did return. But now he was really drunk. His eyes radiated a dark, autumnal iridescence that very old pearls sometimes have before they crumble. Batitsky read in them that Vitka had been beaten, had been tricked, had smelled gunpowder, had seen the flash of a blade—and still he came back with something, had forced open a treasure box, a trunk, and came back alive from rotten corridors, black houses, and stood there crazed. He could not return the money but he would offer him something in payment, something he had carried out, tricking fate, lovely Blotto, the great hunter!

Vitka would not even sit down. He deftly reached into his pocket, like a magician. Batitsky barely saw the move and flinched. That was how bandits went for a knife or a gun; Vitka had already placed something on the table.

A holder for calling cards.

The cardholder lay on the table, carved ivory, just two colors: white ivory and ochre-red designs.

The white was snow, Batitsky decided. In the right lower corner grew a red tree, an eastern species, with a wavy trunk and umbrella-like leaves on the branches. Beneath it stood a man in a red robe, Japanese or Chinese, with a braid, looking at the whiteness, as if he had come to the edge of the human world, and beyond lay the deep kingdom of the elements. Joyless loneliness.

Batitsky could see that it was old, real. But it did not cost half of what he had lent Vitka. Yet he knew that he would take it and not complain, not mention their deal, because this was a gift; the trinity.

Vitka left the business after that, taking up icon painting: the guy must have really had a hard time, thought Batitsky, and yet he was happy because if he had not had a hard time, Vitka might not have brought him the cardholder, or having the money, might have kept it for himself; but Vitka had been beaten and threatened, and so he decided to settle his account.

* * *

Batitsky took the holder to show a colleague; Petr Petrovich Golovtsov was the highest arbiter, an expert on luxury objects: fans and snuffboxes, smelling salts flacons, cigar clippers, cigarette cases, pocket watches, matchboxes, tableware, hunting horns, inkwells, flasks, cuff links. The inanimate servants of wealth and etiquette. The words of a lost language of objects spoken by the nobility and the moneyed.

Golovtsov was known for his specific mindset, and his declarations were vague, like the drugged prophecies of the Pythia. Himself ancient, a fossil, covered in speckles, furrows, and cracks, he examined the cardholder, wiped it with a suede cloth, tapped his manicured nail along the side, studied the design through his loupe: the thin old man in a robe or kimono (Batitsky only then realized that it was an old man), the red tree bent left and right, like a pendulum, with sharp umbrella leaves, the napery of snow. He spoke with gentle sadness.

"Antosha, it's a holder for calling cards."

Batitsky listened.

"For calling cards, hmm," Golovtsov muttered absent-mindedly. "But not for one's own. For other people's," he concluded with judicial precision.

Batitsky did not understand.

"They didn't carry it with them." Golovtsov moved the holder so it was parallel with the table edge, and it became clear that it was meant to lie flat.

"This calling cardholder is not for making calls." Golovtsov pointed beyond the door at the corridor. "It's a cardholder for receiving callers."

"Is it rare?" Batitsky asked.

"You could say so." Golovstov again moved the holder with his finger, searching for the perfect spot on his desk, aligning its corners to the corners of the gray marble inkwell and the rim of the bronze lamp. "Received calling cards were rarely stored. What are they? Ephemera. A sign of what did not take place. A stand-in for the person who made the call but did not encounter the host. There is metaphysics in this, *mon cher*, a special subtlety: the card is a shadow, a symbol of presence, but fleeting, it was and then was no more. Those things were not kept, they had to go, what we call former people were sensitive to this, they had excellent pitch for the hidden quotidian, the grammar of daily life."

Golovtsov looked up at Batitsky, and Batitsky was embarrassed, as if Golovtsov had accidentally rebuked him for not noticing, not understanding the cardholder's essential feature.

"However, we can imagine," Golovtsov lectured. "We can imagine that someone out of vanity, for example, decided to collect calling cards. Not all of them, of course—you'd need albums for that. Select ones. The most valuable. A card deck of aces and kings, the powerful. Or a circle of friends, memory of first meetings, polite calls that turned into friendship, into interconnected ties. So he would have ordered a holder like this, larger, more substantive."

Batitsky was unpleasantly surprised to hear Golovtosv speaking that way, as if he knew his cardholder, and this acquaintance was of long standing and somehow undermined Batitsky's undivided right of possession. Golovtsov, as if confirming Batitsky's suspicion, asked, "If I may ask, are you keeping it, or . . ." as if they were talking about a woman, a courtesan.

"The object belongs to a client," Batitsky replied instantly. If he had said the holder was his, Golovtsov would have tried to persuade him to sell. This way, Golovtsov merely nodded: "I understand, too bad . . ."

On the way back to the store, Batitsky thought about the cardholder. Funny, he felt it had been flirting with Golovtsov, telling the old man what it would not tell him. What, are you jealous? he asked himself. Attached? Hooked?

The next day Batitsky set it out in a special, reliable spot in the window; whatever you put there sold. He was worried by his growing attachment, unnecessary in business, for if you love one thing and then another, what are you going to sell? He wanted to test its loyalty, play with price and luck: if it left him, that was meant to be.

The cardholder lay in the trusty spot, polished by success, and did not sell. It was as if no one saw it, or if they did, they didn't choose it.

Babitsky casually brought over two select clients, with money but also taste and understanding: Kaparidi, owner of a printing shop, and Malosolov, king of gold leaf, purveyor to the Patriarch's offices. Their eyes skipped right over it.

That happens when an object is marked by fate. It was used to kill or people were killed over it. Experienced people, even if they are not professionals, feel that and avoid it instinctively.

But the holder! Docile, simple! What could be fatal about it?

It lay there as if it had been forgotten, as if it still had an owner who would find it, buy it back.

Batitsky realized and took the holder out of the window, set it with the pitcher and plate, surprised that the holder had nagged him into putting it among its usual companions, its social circle; with objects of the same nature and rank.

Doing business, dealing with clients, Batitsky noticed that he was thinking of the holder. About the milieu in which it had functioned. House, visits, footmen. A myriad of objects gone from today's life. Special people to service and take care of those objects. And all that was gone. That world was gone. But it was here.

It wasn't a major thought, but . . . Batitsky did not believe in the memory of objects. Not only did he not believe, he knew for sure that they did not remember. If someone said they did, that was fairy tales, nonsense. Objects readily change owners, even if they are taken away forcibly, by deceit, are stolen or dishonestly obtained.

But he also knew this. There are things that should not be bought. Or sold. Just pretend not to notice them. That's all.

There were not many such objects. However, they existed. They did not necessarily have special value. They were like the first bright minds that appeared among the unenlightened Neanderthals and Cro-Magnons and drew deer and hunters on cave walls. Objects that have their own fate. It's better not to intercede, dispute it. It wasn't fate, or a curse, it was something else. It was itself.

The pitcher and plate, by the way, did not belong to that number. They had an undoubted aptitude for survival, to be preserved, but that was not equal to fate. But the cardholder . . . Batitsky could not sense its essence. He listened. He looked. He wanted to possess it, to learn its past and its secrets.

Possess not the way collectors possess things, with the absolute right of ownership while treating the objects as alienated fetishes, but to possess deeply, intimately, so that possession would not feel like possession, so that the line between body and object, mind and matter would vanish. So that alienation would be replaced by reciprocity. He had fallen in love, like a kid. If his colleagues had heard, they would've made him a laughingstock. And most important, why? What for?

Batitsky did not like the past from which the objects came to him. He kept the door shut on it. That had been a time of destruction, marauding, confiscation in the course of searches. No reason to keep that in your head. No reason to know what exactly had happened to their former owners. What their price was and who paid it.

His family had lived through that time with no losses or vile deeds. He was a commoner, what they called a herring son. His mother actually did sell herring from a barrel at the Ocean store on Baumansky Street, reeked of brine, saved up sticky rubles, and wanted him to work in the store. His school art teacher, the staunch old Musin, talked her into letting him go to art school: He did it by giving her a painting. He glued a page of the *Labor* newspaper to a board, poured lacquer over it, and painted a plump herring, a heel of airy bread, a shot of vodka, and a matte curl of onion: You just wanted to down the shot and chase it with a bite. He managed to flatter his mother's heart.

Batitsky avoided that past, but he was drawn to the cardholder. Perhaps because it did not want to tell him anything and did not expect anything from him, it was shut as tightly as a shell.

One day, when he'd had too much to drink, Batitsky decided that he could tame the cardholder by using it as it was intended. Fill it with his own cards, for example. Or following the instructions of the expert Golovtsov, with other people's cards. Fill it with new names, populate it with other people.

With determination, he took it down from the shelf, opened it . . . and stopped. The cardholder, light and obedient, lay in his hand, he could put in just his card, and be done. Batitsky sensed that it was, how to put it—occupied. Or rather, not quite empty.

He brought it to the light and peered inside with drunken persistence. He felt ill, as if he might faint, reason growing dim.

He cooled off. Lit a smoke. He looked at the holder anew. His expert eye, his ability to gauge size was off. Batitsky clearly saw a small, clearly defined object. He clearly felt an enormous space in it, as if the holder could hold, and did hold, a room, a hall, perhaps even a house.

Or, it was the house.

The house of those who were gone. A vault.

Batitsky touched it reflectively—and pulled away his hand. He thought the holder had scratched his finger. It was smooth, polished, but it had scratched him. He looked: it was clean and smooth. He remembered stories about poisoned jewelry caskets, snuffboxes with a poisoned stinger on a steel spring.

A powerful sense of fear, sharp as a blow, overcame him. The imagined bite of death sent a false fever into his veins, a streaking flame of venom. Batitsky understood that the holder was playing black jokes on him. Yet at the same time, he felt that he really was dying, turning black, burning up from inside after the prick of a hidden needle. This imaginary dying, the spectral flame fiercely scorching his flesh suddenly gave his body to someone else who had suffered this way and died this way, seared by the deadly heat of toxic blood.

Batitsky was now both himself and not himself; he and the unknown person had in common the cardholder, which was like a room that could be entered from two sides. Batitsky now knew who the other was: a nobleman, lawyer, collector of recommendations and connections, founder of friendships, creator of relationships, manufacturer of affairs and destinies who connected everyone with everyone, a bon vivant, conductor, intermediary, life of the party, counselor, confidant, favorite.

The cardholder, strange, intentionally eccentric, was his talisman, his house of success. He gathered them all in it, created a community, a network, a circle. Batitsky felt, as one feels a puff of air from a closing door, that this very association, this closeness was what doomed them.

The NKVD investigators followed those connections; relations, shared interests, closeness . . . They were like targets in a shooting range: set up to be shot. He had realized what was happening and hid at the very bottom—staying alive for a while.

This was his last object, Batitsky understood. What was left of himself. Batitsky saw everything he had sold, taken to consignment shops: cigarette holders, cuff links, watches, dinner services, officer's binoculars, parade spurs, pince-nez, Solingen razors—objects that made up the man and at the same time, objects of an era during which the era dies forever, having outlived itself.

Only the cardholder remained. No one wanted to buy it. It wasn't silver or gold. It would go for a trifle. The new, Red people needed watches and cigarette holders. They were constantly checking the time and smoked a lot; calling cards— who made calls now?

The NKVD did.

Batitsky felt he was lying in a deathly fever on a thin stinking mattress. It was Setun, some place called Setun, where was Setun, on the outskirts of Moscow, he guessed. Setun. Setun, surrounded by potato warehouses, and the night grew white potato eyes, oozed pus like sweet starch. A wet felt boot in the autumn mud blistered his foot, gangrene crept up his leg, broiling, he couldn't get up. The second watchman, Kornei, wiped his burning forehead with a wet rag, and muttered, "St. Anthony's Fire is in you, so you're burning, it burns." It was so strange to hear his rational peasant talk, that nonsense, because St. Anthony's Fire came from rye grain affected by ergot, and this was gangrene, and he thought that Kornei's mistake was leading death down a false trail. But death was not far away, it would not be fooled by Kornei's illiteracy, it certainly knew what it was and in what form it came. Kornei was honest, he would not take the felt boots or the sheepskin jacket, but he would take the cardholder hidden under the pallet. He had been looking at it for a long time. Had wanted it for a long time. He didn't know why. He just did, that's all, like a reward for his unwilling long labor as an orderly, for that wet rag over the burning forehead.

THE OBELISK

The Pokrovsky Cemetery was once on the outskirts, but the city had spread out and it now found itself in the middle. From the north, on the side toward the city center, it was touched by streets of former merchant mansions; from the southeast, the wooden barracks of the 1930s; from the southwest, the prefab apartment blocks of the 1970s and 1980s. Three faces, three ages of the city that could not keep up with its own growth, the hasty construction of military plants and defense research institutes, which was why its occupants were always crowded: in life and in death.

The cemetery was considered prestigious: it wasn't easy to get in. On top of that, it had its own special areas. Take Sector 17, called the Generals by local folk, where the plots were for major generals and higher, while the colonels and lieutenant colonels were buried wherever they could find a spot. Or Sector 23, called the Designers, where the rocket scientists, developers of multiple launch rocket systems, anti-aircraft gunners, ballistics operators, creators of submarines and radars rested—oh, the city had nurtured and brought many unheralded minds to glory and orders and awards! For some reason, next to Sector 23 lay Sector 4, known as the

University or Professors: the final resting place of the famous teachers of those designers.

Military. Scientists. Professors. The city's three main castes, who in life resided in the houses of the nomenklatura, shopped in restricted stores, and stuck together even in death.

The army families esteemed the broad polished gravestones with carved portraits depicting the whole upper body: the better to see the uniform and rows of orders and medals, the expression wise and confident as befit a commander.

The scholars preferred sculpture. A stone pedestal and a bronze bust, always with a large, open forehead to show the scale of the intellect. These bronze busts competed with one another, which was more significant, whose forehead was more prominent, as if continuing the rivalry among scientific institutes and schools; wags suggested that many of the heads could be switched around without anyone noticing; the sculptors developed the habit of using stock features and all the local Newtons came from a single breed: while their minds could master concepts of unthinkable complexity, their faces were hardly complex—they remained nondescript, devoid of any expression of uniqueness.

The laborers, factory workers, and lower classes were not buried in the center, naturally, but beyond the new city line, in the derelict, ravine-filled land along the high bank, with a view of the Zarechye forests, distant lumber camps, meandering narrow-gauge tracks, abandoned Old Believer hermitages, and the swift forest rivers, as brown as tea, flowing among the peaty swamps and light sandy banks.

Everyone else, the in-betweens who had achieved something of note but were not burdened by official positions, all aspired to the Pokrovsky Cemetery.

Of course, it stemmed from ambition and vanity. But there were also the superstitions of the residents who knew this city, a feeling that comes from the soil and tells you where the best place is to lie in peace, reliably, as if under the protection of the genius loci.

This sometimes led to amazing rapprochements and castling at Pokrovsky. People who could never have been neighbors in this world were tucked in next to one another here, or even changed roles; the cemetery had its own moves, pull, ways of getting things done, just as in the rest of life, in institutions, stores, and offices, but slightly differently. Certain things carried different weight here: position, connections, money were counted at a special, posthumous exchange rate.

Basically, that's how Grandfather and Grandmother Kosorotov got their plot. Grandfather, a dentist who specialized in difficult root canals, provided relief to the cemetery stone etcher, Mushin, a master of inscriptions, who suffered from perpetual toothaches: it must have been the stone dust. In gratitude, the etcher made it possible for the Kosorotovs, on the occasion of the grandfather's brother's death, to get a bit of land, a corner between two paths.

"We'll lie there like we're in a third-class train car," Grandmother hissed at her husband. "In everyone's view!

And you actually paid money for that! And there's no soil here, it's all sand and gravel. I'm ashamed to lie in it!"

But Grandfather put up with her complaints and did what Mushin, who had a plot nearby, had taught him. Every month he carried dirt he dug from his garden to the cemetery in a shopping bag on wheels. He sprinkled it on the path, reducing its width centimeter by centimeter, planting grass there. After two years the plot of land had expanded to a double bed, as Grandfather joked, and he put in an enclosure. As if it had always been there.

Kosorotov the grandson thought he had received an important lesson. His grandfather had not rushed, wasn't greedy, he didn't try to grab fifteen centimeters in one go. The cemetery workers or neighbors would have reported him to the administration. Now everyone could see that the plot extended into the path, but it had happened so slowly that no one would complain now, on the contrary, they would look on it with approval and envy: good job, they helped themselves, no embarrassment. That's the way to do it.

His parents did not approve of Grandfather's scheme. They were worried that someone from the administration would show up with a tape measure and make them tear down the enclosure: the shame of it all. They listened like martyrs to old Mushin's explanation, incredulous.

"You must understand, Alexandra Petrovna," Mushin told Kosorotov's mother. "It's not a crime, not theft! They sliced off some land. It wasn't even land, just cemetery slag.

No one will ever say a word. It wasn't pushy, it was done with understanding. It didn't even require a bribe."

His mother shuddered at the words "crime" and "bribe," even more certain that Mushin had dragged her trusting father into something sordid.

Kosorotov studied Mushin and his grandfather, seeing that they had something in common which neither his grandmother nor his parents had. Both were clever and precise, one a dentist, the other a stone etcher. Both drilled, dealt with hard matter. They brought peace and took away pain—one with fillings, the other with gravestones. Their cleverness and precision were not just professional skills. They sensed life, found the weak spots, the good material, and could figure out what to take from the bad material. That's why Mushin had given Grandfather the advice, he was a person who was clever and could use it properly.

Kosorotov grew up to be brawny. Not at all like his father or grandfather. His mother apparently had an ancestor who was either a drayman or a loader at the flour pier, a local celebrity who defeated all the fairground wrestlers, those who were native as well as visitors.

"Look at his size," Grandmother grumbled. "Try feeding the likes of him!"

He studied free wrestling at an Olympics reserve school where his parents sent him. He was already a regional champ. He knew that you could take a lot in life with brute force. The older kids in his courtyard feared him, his hotheaded father became polite with him, and not just his father, any adult he met grew meek and let him pass.

Kosorotov felt that this was just the beginning, more strength would come, even without training, without sweat and iron. Strength had chosen to inhabit his body. And allowed itself to be used reluctantly on the mat. But it had not come for wrestling. On the contrary: it had come to rest up, get a breather after belonging to someone who utilized it right and left, forced it to meld with his personality and feed his will. It had chosen Kosorotov because he was essentially kind and unruffled, hated arguments and competitions. Strength gave him smarts enough to never abuse it; smarts that were protective rather than inquisitive.

Kosorotov once overheard two school coaches discussing him. Mayevsky, the younger one, said that Kosorotov was lazy and needed to be pulled into line, taught technique and discipline, otherwise he would bury his talent in the ground. Rykunov, middle-aged now, and once the winner of national silver, replied thoughtfully. "He'll never be a wrestler."

"You have to build his character," Mayevsky insisted.

"It's not about character," Rykunov said. "It's not his strength. It's in him, but it doesn't belong to him. I saw that once. We once had an untrained guy in the army, he could turn over a tank. He was great in fights, he could take on a whole platoon. But he was laid onto his back at the district level. Why? Because his opponent was experienced, and he was fierce, not sporting, and turned the match into life-and-death. While the untrained guy's fuse seemed to blow and switch off the power. His strength was extinguished."

"That's just nonsense, stop spouting psychology at every turn," Mayevsky said with a chuckle. "However, you're his coach. You should know."

Other adults didn't know. All they saw was the body, the muscles. They regarded him respectfully, sometimes even with subservience.

Everyone, except Grandfather and Mushin.

Grandfather always took him along to the cemetery, to clean away the leaves and litter. He tidied up regularly, with a doctor's intolerance of dirt. Afterward, they went to Mushin's workshop near the cemetery wall, and Grandfather would say, "Go for a walk, Kostya. Petr Vasilyevich and I will have a talk."

Kosorotov would wander among the rectangular slabs piled by the workshop. Layered marble, blue-gray, like salt fatback. Black labradorite, sparkling with blue-green "eyes" on the edges. Crimson Shoksha quartzite, like raw meat. Mushin had taught him to recognize the stones.

He could have moved any of the slabs. But Grandfather and Mushin still looked down at him, like a pesky puppy.

He pretended to be taking a walk, as ordered. Actually, he watched the old men from afar.

Mushin was older than Grandfather, almost eighty. He hid his face in a thick gray beard that made him look like Santa Claus. But his body was still strong, agile, although his hands had arthritic bumps and bulges. And his eyes . . . His eyes belonged to a carver, accustomed to measuring and marking, using a forged steel chisel to make lines in unyielding stone.

Mushin was renowned. Everyone wanted him to do their monuments, but he was selective in accepting commissions, no longer interested in the money; he chose the stone and form and if the client did not agree, he turned down the job and passed it on to his assistants. His monuments were also renowned for their optimal positioning, never leaning with age, even though the soil on the cemetery slopes was sandy and unreliable. It was as if Mushin could sense through stone and through soil.

Kosorotov felt that Mushin could see that Kosorotov's strength did not belong to him. He saw and knew how that could be. And Grandfather knew, too.

Mushin had a granddaughter: Polina. Seven years younger than Kosorotov. Still just a girl. Mushin—her parents were divorcing—sometimes brought her to his workshop. The old man would then ask Kosorotov to play hide-and-seek with her among the stones. Kosorotov cheated without knowing why, peeking at the little blond figure in a dress of grown-up fabric—it must have been left over from when her mother sewed herself a dress—leaping between the stones. These bulged with natural chips and an elemental force—torn from the base by explosions, stunned, sullen, retaining the bedrock's grim and crude power. Kosorotov wanted to protect her from the evil boulders that had been awakened by mankind, their rough edges ready to squeeze and crush.

Grandfather died first. Mushin did his monument, which they had apparently agreed upon a long time ago. A severe slab of white marble with black letters spelling out name and dates with a simple inscription beneath: Doctor. Some people ordered facets, gilded letters, and all kinds of words. Mushin made a true effort for Grandfather, and the font was rarified but not ostentatious.

There by the monument, Kosorotov forgave Mushin for the ties with Grandfather from which he'd been excluded. He embraced the old man because he saw that no one could have done better. It was dignified. For a real man.

Flattered, Mushin said softly, so the others could not hear, "Thank you, Kostya, dear." Stepping back and looking into his eyes, he added, "We will lie next to your grandfather. If needed, keep an eye on us."

Kosorotov replied fecklessly and gratefully, "I will. I give you my word."

The old man ceremoniously kissed him on the forehead with dry, hard lips. Kosorotov imagined that he had pressed his hot forehead up against the ledge of a cold cliff.

His grandmother was buried without him; Kosorotov was serving up north at the time.

He wasn't supposed to be in the ordinary army. A sports platoon was waiting for him in Moscow, the Army Central Sports

Club, competition, prizes, medals, a fairly free regimen, girls in the capital, and then easy admission to the Physical Culture Institute's coaching department. It had all been arranged, and the institute recruiter, Lt. Colonel Kubikov, was supposed to pick him up in the morning at a municipal station.

Kosorotov got there the night before and settled in a corner. He caught a chill.

When Kubikov arrived, he was in the medical unit with a terrible toothache. Neither pills nor shots helped.

That used to happen to Grandfather. A dental wizard, he was also a dental martyr. In his youth he worked as a freelance dentist in the north and chilled the nerves of his teeth. When in pain, his body shook, sweat poured off him, and he lost control of his face which turned into a rotating gallery of horrible bizarre masks, images of suffering. Grandfather turned into a stranger, groaning and cursing—Kosorotov didn't hear that level of obscenity even in the army—and Grandmother was the only one to go into his room, bringing fragrant herbal mouth rinses.

Naturally, Kubikov did not end up taking him. Who needed an unreliable wrestler? The pain eased by evening. Still weak and stunned, he was grabbed by a naval officer. The navy was three years, not two, you couldn't lure people into the service, and they took him away with other wretches for training in the north, to the remote forestless hills, to the base of the Arctic patrolmen.

They went on long voyages, to the edge of the melting ice, to the blue frozen peaks of Novaya Zemlya; along the granite shores of the Barents and White Seas. When the unit received the telegram from home, the patrol boat was on a long voyage.

Back on land, Kosorotov was given ten days leave, and when he got home all he saw was his grandmother's name on white stone, written in the same severe font.

The neighboring plot, Mushin's, was untidy. He swept away the branches that had fallen over the winter, watered the lilies of the valley, and dropped by the workshop on his way home. The second etcher told him that Mushin had been in the hospital for several months.

In the third-class coach on the way back to the unit, listening to elderly female travelers talk about how many years one should conserve pickled tomatoes, he suddenly felt that he would not see Mushin when he returned in a year from the service. And he wondered, without reasoning why: What kind of monument would Mushin have? The old man must have thought of everything, left a sketch, a drawing, or maybe he chose, prepared, and cut the stone himself.

In the monotonous days of service, in the repetitive hours on watch duty, the thought of a monument helped him stay awake. Kosorotov conjured up different obelisk forms and stone types to see which fit Mushin's personality. It was a conundrum, a strangely alluring task with a trick solution. More than once Mushin had said, our craft is special, a tombstone tells more about a person than is written in books or that is known to friends. Kosorotov thought: What would

Mushin do? Would he reveal something about himself after his death through a monument? Or, on the contrary, would he conceal it?

One stormy night, black waves struck the ship's right bow, but he held the helm and kept on course. The worn machinery below was gasping, the propeller blades had weakened, and the hull was creaking. Both the crew and the metal had given up. Only his strength kept the ship intact, all its rivets and seams, bolts, nuts, valves. It was he, Kosorotov, who took on the blows of the sea, the rolling of the side, and the sea raged, as if knowing that the guard ship should have sunk to the bottom, and not understanding why the ship was afloat. Kosorotov wasn't dueling with the sea. He stood unshakable like a boulder. Stony faced. The ship rolled and heaved, objects slid, sailors fell. But Kosorotov stood firm, and the elements could do nothing but let go, and the storm released the ship, which at last took refuge from the wind behind a mountainous island.

Then, in the calm of the bay, Kosorotov suddenly understood what kind of monument Mushin, master of stone, had planned for himself. The shape, the kind of stone were secondary, that's not where the answer lay.

He would have a monument that would stand forever.

When he got to the cemetery, the monument was already standing.

As black as the polar night. Four-sided. Growing out of the earth like a bayonet. Culminating in a blunt four-sided pyramid.

The monument was tall and stood perfectly vertical. Two meters, at least, Kosorotov estimated. Even lieutenant generals did not get that much. Lonely as the pin of a sundial. Powerful as a stonecutter's hard-toothed, obdurate coring tool. It rejected, despised other monuments, other graves, as if it was the lone authentic one among the fakes, among mediocre, fleeting deaths.

Mushin belittled the rest of the deceased, including his grandfather. There was no calm perfection of skill here, but an arrogant, even disdainful challenge to the living and the dead.

And Kosorotov sensed that this new proximity disturbed him. If he could, he would take his grandfather and grandmother from here, rebury them somewhere far away, where this black bayonet would not be visible. He thought for the first time: What, in fact, did his grandfather know about Mushin? Where had they met? After all, it had happened long before the etcher had helped him get the plot. But when? How?

He went for a walk to visit the graves of his distant relatives. And when he returned, from afar, from the hill, he noticed two female figures at Mushin's obelisk. Polina and her mother locked the enclosure, stood looking at the monument, and went away along the path. Both were in festive colored dresses, they had probably dropped by the cemetery for a few minutes on the way someplace else. But it seemed to Kosorotov that there was no grief in their movements, no mourning; it was as if they were even rejoicing in the freedom that Mushin's obelisk conveyed to them.

He came back to the graves. And with his calibrated sense of balance, the sense of a wrestler and a sailor, he felt that something had changed. Mushin's monument, which had seemingly been standing straight half an hour ago, had lost its ideal verticality.

Just a tiny bit, but it was tilted.

He glanced around, comparing, checking the angles.

No. It was his imagination.

Kosorotov did not return to sports. It was too late, too many lost years.

His old friends in the group wore leather jackets and gathered at the river restaurant at the far landing point. They sent messages, inviting him to join the gang. He might have. They would have fights in empty lots and alleyways against boxers and karate athletes for the right to take protection money from the stallholders. But he knew that his strength would not allow it. If he went against its will, something ridiculous would happen, the sort of thing that occurs on the mat when an angry wrestler hurts himself instead of his opponent, a dislocation, a sprain, a trifle essentially, but that trifle locks his strength in an immobilized body.

His old coach, Rykunov, worried that Kosorotov would be drafted by bandits, suggested he do some work in the circus, replacing a sick athlete.

Kosorotov laughed, and the money wasn't much, either. But then he decided to try it for one night. The circus was decrepit with sawdust and sand reeking of horse urine.

However, in the arena his strength responded with nobility and gratitude. He tossed and caught weights, raised a platform upon which assistants were poised, and these corny old tricks suddenly brought things to life, jolting the bored audience awake and illuminating the air behind the big top with the simple magic of fleshly victory over inanimate weight.

Kosorotov enjoyed it. He discovered the hidden nobility of ancient circus acts. He did not compete with anyone, did not attack. Yet he still conquered the darkness that people brought to the circus from the streets, where his old wrestling pals had imposed the power of the fist.

So he stayed on with the circus. The energy of his performances was infectious. The ponies ran faster, the aerialists did more daring acts, the juggler stopped dropping the pins, the fakir swallowed fire with ease, and even the clowns, Dudya and Dum, pathetic weak drunkards, were occasionally funny and witty. They got invitations to tour, once even in Europe. It was there, in Germany, that disaster befell him.

The local entrepreneur, a shady crook, promised the director a juicy contract for at least six months and twenty cities, on one condition: that the evening would end with a wrestling match. Kosorotov against a local wrestler.

The entrepreneur, himself a runt, understood wrestling and understood Kosorotov's strength; he hoped that he had discovered a star who would bring in the crowds. He even came up with a stage name for him: Red Savage. Kosorotov wanted to decline, but the whole circus, performers and animals, expected him to say "yes"—then they would have good money for years ahead; they all had families, debts, the health complications that circus people endure.

So Kosorotov went for a good cause. It took two minutes to put the local guy flat on his back. But the local guy had time to shatter Kosorotov's ankle first. Kosorotov left the German hospital hopelessly lamed, and the ruined joint made him limp: how could he go out into the arena now!

He worked as a stevedore, hauling sacks of sugar and flour. He worked as a slaughterer at the city abattoir. But he found his place at the Pokrovsky Cemetery as a gravedigger.

That winter was terribly cold, the ground was frozen, and graves were not dug, they were hollowed out by crowbars, gouged with heavy sledgehammers on long handles. Kosorotov did the work of four men. There were many corpses that winter, as if the time had come for an entire generation to go.

A new alley of monuments for his former friends had arisen by the central entrance. Rows of stones depicting them life-size with their cars and in jackets and gold chains. The survivors, worn and wounded, got together for wakes, drank vodka, and did not recognize him in his work clothes.

Kosorotov now knew the cemetery the way an agronomist knows his field: which soil was where and its specific character. He learned the cemetery's darkest secrets, how people stole plots, how the dead were buried without official papers or corpses of murder victims were hidden in old graves, how bronze busts of academicians and designers were stolen and sold for scrap metal. But the more he learned, the more he sensed that there were still other secrets, secrets of the cemetery itself, that no one would ever know.

Mushin's monument was the best evidence of that.

In spring, when the earth awakens from its winter constraint, when the waters flow within it, many monuments misbehaved and leaned, especially if they stood on faulty, crumbly soil or over a water vein or if they were encircled and pressured from below by the roots of old trees. But roots could be chopped, trees sawn, soil strengthened, and the monument set on a reliable foundation, a broad concrete base.

Mushin's was set on solid ground. Yet it did not stand still, it danced. It tilted in every direction. Mocking the late Mushin and his mastery, all for naught.

The cemetery workers remodeled the infrastructure, raised the monument with a jack, laid rails. Outside builders came, measuring, tapping, drilling the soil, recommending special types of cement, leveling, promising it would stand for a hundred years—but it stood until the following spring.

In those years, various doctors tortured Kosorotov's injured ankle, X-raying, radiating, applying poultices and creams, making incisions—but it would not heal. In his mind, it all melded into one, the ankle and the monument that could not be set straight.

Surprisingly, the hassle with the monument did not evoke superstitious sentiment among the cemetery workers. So, it's unstable, so what, the better for us, easy money. Who was Mushin that the dead would trouble him? A stone etcher, a worker. Never did anyone any harm. If people only knew who's buried here—killers, butchers. And their monuments are fine and steady. That means it's just a random joke, nature's harmless prank. It happens.

Kosorotov could not imagine why this was happening to Mushin. But he watched the monument twisting in torment, drawing strength, drawing money, swelling like an untreated tooth in the gum. Polina had been advised long ago to take it down and raise a new one that was lighter or just a metal cross.

Polina was stubborn. Two husbands, who resembled each other, sturdy and tough, newly rich, had left her, tired of fighting with the sleepless monument. A priest misted it with holy water, and Nyushka, a holy fool, the cemetery stray, scratched her face and sprinkled her blood on the black stone, but it did not help. Polina called in another priest, another holy fool, other workers. But she did not turn to Kosorotov, a neighbor, a gravedigger.

Her stubbornness matched the earthly force that moved the monument. People saw the hardship, the work, the usual chaos. No one recognized that Polina should have broken down by now, given up long ago on the damned monument. But she did not break down. Neither patience nor family love could explain it. Nothing could.

One day Kosorotov had a toothache. Not like the one at the recruiting station, of course, just a cracked molar. He usually went to his grandfather's student, an old man now, who had an office in the cellar at the back of a cheap barbershop, where the thick black beards of Asian men were clipped. The old man worked with great delicacy, like a jeweler, and Kosorotov trusted no one else with his sensitive teeth. But when he showed up, the barber told him the doctor had died.

He went to the nearby clinic. Workmen were jackhammering the pavement, and his childhood fear overwhelmed him. He realized how much he had feared his grandfather, his shiny, ringing instruments, and that when he opened his mouth it was like entrusting him with his whole life, exposing his vulnerable innards.

At the clinic they sent him and his acute pain to the doctor on duty. It was Polina.

Even later, when they lived together, there was no moment more intimate and terrifying than that visit. She was a bad dentist, bloody, as surgeons say. The anesthesia did not take well, and she exhausted Kosorotov, drilling his tooth and touching his tense body with her small breasts, and he was torn between pain and desire. When it was over, Polina took off her mask and kissed his lips, dead from anesthesia, feeling nothing.

The obelisk obeyed him. Almost.

Kosorotov harnessed it, straightened it, tamped down the earth, and the black stone stood level—for four, five months, half a year. And then it leaned. Not as much as before, but it was still noticeable, and Kosorotov would straighten it out again. They were yoked together, he and the stone, his strength pacified the monument, and the strength of the diabase rock sapped the strong man.

He no longer asked Polina why it was necessary. He was like an ox, hardworking and subdued, obedient under the yoke.

The day came when he could not set the black stone back in place. The faceted boulder stood, leaning back, throwing a long dense shadow, and Kosorotov saw the same darkness before his eyes from the useless strain.

"I can't anymore," he told Polina when they were at home.

"Do it!" she replied.

He went to the entry and started dressing. Polina watched him without worry: she did not believe that he could leave, she was letting him go get some fresh air and reconsider.

Kosorotov went outside and decided to go back to his place. It was a bright moonlit night, quiet, like the nights of his childhood when no music from the infrequent cars reached the windows. He walked, limping, and suddenly realized that he truly could not do it anymore; he was strong but impotent. The damned stone had drunk him dry. There was only one way to save himself.

He unlocked the workshop at the cemetery and without turning on the light found the handle, polished by work gloves, of the sledgehammer.

He walked the familiar paths holding the sledgehammer right under its head. The cemetery was empty at that hour. Even the grumpy cemetery dogs slept peacefully behind the fence in the burdock plants.

Yet for the first time, he sensed that someone was there.

Dead people, the ones he had buried himself, whose graves he had dug. The deceased of recent decades, whose names were carved on tombstones. And the dead of long ago, forgotten, uncounted, expunged from memory; the ones whose graves have been used for other people, the ones who have been squeezed out, excluded, robbed.

The black obelisk that he could not straighten yesterday stood perfectly erect.

Now working in tandem with the force that twisted and shook the obelisk, he swung the sledgehammer at the black hulk. The stone moaned, the sound traveled over the cemetery, frightening the birds, echoing against the tombstones and fences, shaking off the silence of metal and rock as if it were rust or a scab.

He hammered away at it, leaving sugary imprints on the black polished smoothness. Any other stone would have cracked, fallen apart into shards, but the black obelisk stood, and Kosorotov called on all his and not-his strength, which appeared in full for the first time.

The black stone took the blows without yielding. But the ground was cracking, trees staggered, branches dropped, other monuments fell, and the writhing soil squashed fences into concertinas. The wintery graves sank, bones rose from the sand.

To stop him, the terrified cemetery spoke in hundreds of voices. The stones and cracks, the walls of vaults and tree roots, sand, water, flowers: nature protecting the dead and the dead who had become part of nature.

Through the black obelisk that had turned smoky and translucent, he saw young Mushin, barely out of adolescence, saw what he had done year after year: he stole monuments. So many had remained untended, after families disappeared, after people fled, were shot, had died—and Mushin chiseled off the names, polished the stone, and engraved new names; stealing from the dead, taking away the only thing they had left.

Through the black obelisk that had turned smoky and translucent, he saw his young grandfather, a dentist who served camp commanders in distant northern villages, for they, too, had toothaches, and he paid camp guards with spirit alcohol to buy the gold extracted from the teeth of dead men.

The obelisk again turned black. Kosorotov felt that just one more blow would topple Mushin's monument.

He raised the sledgehammer over his head and with all his strength, he smashed the monument into the ground between the graves.

The strength left him, flowed back into the ground from where it had come. He walked away, feeling the earth moving beneath his feet as Mushin's black obelisk teetered and his grandparents' light gray monument teetered, and knew that they would never rest again.

BARMAS BELOW

Kalyuzhny was a neighbor at the dacha. Not exactly a neighbor, his was the lot next to the neighbor's lot. At an early age, Mareyev had picked him out from among the adults, even though the old man barely exchanged a word with him as a child. He paid no attention to children. The other men sometimes took the boys along to catch crayfish in the silty pond, overgrown with sedge and horsetails, or to scoop up small perches with an old, patched-up net. They readily admired a new bicycle or played ball with the kids in a distant clearing in the forest, where two pairs of birches grew opposite each other—natural goal posts, except that one was half a meter wider, and therefore by a generations-old agreement of dacha residents, the team assigned that goal was forgiven more fouls than their rivals.

Mareyev remembered them, the simple, folksy, condescending adults, vaguely and as a bunch. But Kalyuzhny, who avoided kids, he remembered distinctly and individually. Two events stuck in his memory that he could not quite explain even as an adult. Devil's work? Magic? Something seeped through and was visible, like a watermark on paper. Not good, not evil. Different, something ordinary people did not have.

It enchanted him when he was a child. As an adult, it worried, irritated him, making him regret the rational, fundamental life of a professional he had chosen. If I had been capable of recognizing it in Kalyuzhny, he thought, that meant that I had it, too. After all the others didn't notice. And so what, he asked himself, so what? You're nuts, you're thinking about nonsense, mirages, who cares what you imagined as a child, you'd make a psychiatrist roll on the floor laughing.

Yet deep down, with the remnants of his lost abilities, he knew: it wasn't his imagination, it wasn't a lie.

What he remembered was true.

In those long-ago days, dacha complexes managed without dumpsters. All they had was a wooden bin near the gatehouse and highway exit, right next to the transformer shed with chess-like figures of insulators on rusty horns.

Grass and food scraps went into compost piles. Branches, windfall, and uprooted shrubs went into the old trenches in the forest. In general, they did not throw out a lot. Worn clothing was cut up for rags that were washed until they fell apart. Glass jars were saved for jams and pickles. Sheds held bits of metal, boards, and completely mysterious things— for every object, even unknown, will lie around for a while, come to its senses, and tell you what it is and what for.

But they had trash nevertheless. Ancient furniture fell apart. Chipped dishes broke. Rain and blizzards wore holes in rooftop waterproofing. Lichen-covered slate aged and crumbled. Tin cans and leaky bags piled up. Faded umbrellas with wooden handles, grotesque like a shot raven. Rubber boots that would no longer hold a patch. Unraveled baskets. Holey canisters, rust chewing through the chipped enamel. Threadbare bicycle tires like snakeskins. Grandfathers' coats of stiff, heavy fabric falling apart at the seams. Shards of windowpanes. Exhausted shovels and rakes with cracked blades and handles. Worn hoses suffering from aged incontinence. Torn, flyblown rag rugs. Brittle, burnt-out old cellophane for greenhouses. Discolored oilcloths rubbed at the folds. Ancient bins, dried-out tubs, corroded barrels.

Trash piled up, and the head of the household would load a wheelbarrow on the weekend, push it to the gatehouse, stop for a smoke with friends, and tip the garbage into the boxed-in bin.

Year after year the pile grew and turned into a mountain. The trash baked, compacted, as if it wriggled after nightfall in an effort to compress itself, groove to groove. The wooden sides cracked and fell apart, the trash spread over them and in a few years covered them completely.

The boy Mareyev took an intense interest in the trash mountain for some reason.

It towered by the gatehouse, in plain sight on the way to or from the city, like a border signpost. Every dacha family added something, and the mountain grew like its common past, the underside of dacha life, exposed here for all to see, smelling sour and foul, attracting burr-covered stray dogs.

In the spring, on their first return to the dacha, Mareyev would note an object that had just been thrown away—say, an iron bedstead or a barrel. He watched all summer how it would be swallowed and covered by the rising mountain: by autumn there wasn't a bit of it visible.

Mareyev thought that once in the mountain, things did not die but changed, becoming part of it, forgetting their former designations as tool, vessel, furniture, but remembering vengefully their selfless service to the people who abandoned them.

In the late summer twilight, after ten, his parents would sometimes let him ride his bike as far as the gatehouse one last time before bringing him inside and locking the gate.

He would ride slowly up to the mountain, which in the dark seemed like a monolith consisting of selflessness and hurt. He would stop with one foot on the pedal. He imagined that the mountain was standing on the legs of chairs and tables, reaching out with hose arms, pipe arms, rake arms, and pulling the bicycle out from under him . . . He would race away, swallowing the bracing night coolness, the whispers of leaves, feeling as if the mountain were watching him go, sighing disappointedly, bottle bottoms flickering, a scattering of greenish nocturnal eyes.

Mareyev was twelve when a special meeting voted to clear out the dump. The day before a new sanitary inspector had arrived unannounced, and she decreed: clear the trash in two weeks or the cooperative would be fined fifty-six rubles. They talked and thought and set the following Saturday for a *subbotnik*, an extra day of voluntary work, mandatory attendance for men. They gave twenty rubles to the villager Savka, who had a dump truck, for two trips to the big regional dump in a distant quarry; he charged a lot, the tightwad, but there was no one else to ask.

His father said he wouldn't take Mareyev to the *subbotnik*. It was dirty work, dangerous. Tons of broken glass, metal with sharp edges, it would be easy to get hurt and get an infection to boot. Mareyev knew that his father would say that. But he had a hunch that the ban would be lifted, and he would see time spinning in reverse, objects appearing from the bowels of the mountain that he had seen before, its belly would open and the grim spirit would vanish.

It was a sunny day and not very hot, just right for this business. His father came from the city train, changed into canvas trousers and jacket, put on heavy boots, and took two pairs of gloves, a rag in case he needed to cover his mouth and nose from the dust and stench, and a kit with plasters and iodine. Mareyev asked to accompany him on the bicycle to the gatehouse. He wore shorts and a T-shirt, so that his father wouldn't think he was planning to stay. But he had prepared his work clothes. Mareyev noticed that there weren't many people coming from the train stop, there should have been more, and they were mostly women with heavy grocery bags, pulling carts and chatting. No male voices.

The call was for ten. They reached the gatehouse at 9:49. His father always showed up early for *subbotniks*, which gave him the provisional right to organize and command, or at least to pick his own spot for work.

No one was there. His father looked at his watch and

spoke with forced confidence. "Well, that's it. Go back. They'll be here soon."

Mareyev understood that no one was coming. He had the knack of picking up snatches of conversations as he sped around on his bicycle past the wells and the line at the general store.

The chairwoman was not liked. The electrician Portnov had his eye on the job; half the co-op was in his debt, he repaired a torn wire for some, replaced a socket for others. Portnov prompted them all to skip out to make the chairwoman look bad. Only his straight-arrow father could have not noticed: after all, they had voted at the meeting, everyone agreed.

Mareyev pedaled slowly to the house. Suddenly he realized that his father knew everything. But it was beneath him not to show up, since there had been an agreement. He would stand there, like the last soldier of a runaway troop, unable to leave (for shame) and unable to forget the others and carry out the chore by himself: they had agreed to do it together, so it had to be together.

Mareyev pedaled harder, got home, dropped the bike by the gate, changed, and hurried back to the garbage dump.

His father was there, downcast and looking silly in his carefully selected work outfit. Kalyuzhny, whom no one had expected at all, was there, too. He didn't even go to the meetings. Short, solid, he was dressed in wide, patched trousers, a dirty flannel shirt, and clownish galoshes covered in gray goat hair. He was saying something to his father, joking, acting like they were pals and drinking buddies, while his father was glacial, not knowing how to get rid of him, waiting and hoping that Kalyuzhny would stop and leave.

"Here's Misha," said Kalyuzhny gently, as if he had arranged it that way. "That makes three of us. Let's start. We'll be done by lunch."

Bitterly, his father looked at the baked mountain, held together by a strange, mocking power that rules garbage and forces it to get tangled up in the most inconvenient way for dismantling. The mountain was the height of two adults. The best the three of them could do would be to take a bite out of its side, and then all the people who did not come would laugh at them. Savka the driver would laugh.

His father was about to argue, make a reasonable statement, but Kalyuzhny had already scrambled up like a monkey, without losing his wobbly galoshes, to the very top. His father turned away like a martyr. He did not see Kalyuzhny, balanced on the top, hop and stomp on the trash heap's head and clap his hands. Mareyev, chilled on that hot day, sensed the inside of the mountain release and unclench, and its power to connect objects that were, as they used to say, baked in, simply vanish. No longer was it a mountain, but a benign pile. It even seemed to shrink down, reduced in volume.

Kalyuzhny threw down an old bicycle wheel. Spokes flashed in the sun, the rim spun, shot through with sunbeams. His father shuddered, as if he had been assaulted by Kalyuzhny, uncertainly lifted the wheel, looked at it as if not quite recognizing what kind of object it was, laid it on the road, and stepped over to the pile.

Never—not before or since—had Mareyev seen a difficult job go so smoothly and easily, as if the task were performing itself. The three of them were merely transmitters.

At 11:00, Savka arrived and backed up his truck. And to his surprise, something that had never happened before—after all he was a driver, a big shot, plus a villager and it wasn't his garbage but the dacha residents'—he began to help, got into it, rolled up his sleeves.

Then Auntie Motylikha, who lived with a gatekeeper—she was also a villager but the dachas had taken over the land so as to surround her house, making her sort of a dacha person, and who had feuded with those dacha people all her life because of that garbage pit they stuck under her window—brought out a bottle of cool, sparkling kvas from her cellar along with glasses and served all four of them.

As people walked past and saw them working, they joined in. People came from their yards, as if magnetized. They went at it and finished by lunch, scraped the mountain's black underside with shovels and poured on clean sand. No one was wounded or scratched or had torn clothing or gloves.

The men were happy and sent someone to the store for beer. They forgot that no one had wanted to take apart the trash bin. Or that the reclusive Kalyuzhny had started it all.

Mareyev looked closely: Kalyuzhny was gone, as if he had never been there. Even his father, usually unyielding and scrupulous about sharing glory, honor, and rewards, did not notice; he had emptied a half-liter bottle of beer. They had put the bottles in a bucket and lowered it into the cold well water. It was only at home, at lunch, that he said in a bewildered and embarrassed tone, "We forgot to thank Kalyuzhny, what fools."

That night Mareyev dreamed of the clever old man, as gray as a wise ape. His divine stomp and clap—just like that, the garbage mountain released itself from within.

He wanted to be able to do that.

After that, he watched Kalyuzhny closely. He listened to the adults' conversations when his name was mentioned.

Kalyuzhny was an engineer. No one knew exactly what kind: something to do with construction, with boilers, with foundations. Or maybe with drilling or laying underground cable. Working with the ground, then. His wife died, and his daughter, an apothecary, was an old maid and did not come to the dacha. Mareyev was secretly pleased to learn that Kalyuzhny did not have friends or children; that meant he could try to become his student, his heir.

Kalyuzhny kept his property in order. Although he did not grow vegetables, not even potatoes or fresh herbs for the summer table, he planted all his land with wide-spreading apple trees, allegedly because the sun was bad for his skin. But Mareyev sensed that the shade of the trees was not there to shield the old man's skin. Something else, which was not on the surface.

One day in late autumn, he and father came out to shut the house down for winter. Everyone feared thieves, and they boarded up windows and hid valuables in the cellar, even though there were never any thefts in their community, not like at the neighboring one beyond the woods, where every spring they found three or four dachas had been broken into and grains and canned food stolen.

In the middle of the day, his father's temperature went up. Mareyev talked him into going back to the city; he would finish up the minor chores and return on the night train.

Mareyev finished up around 4:30, toward twilight. The train was at 7:12. He had tea and crunchy crackers. He walked along the creaking floors of the silent house. He realized that just one lot away was another empty house orphaned until spring: Kalyuzhny's house.

Mareyev went out the back gate into the woods. All the neighboring dachas were empty, there was one chimney smoking, someone planned to spend the night. He pushed through the yellowed nettles and crossed the ditch toward Kalyuzhny's gate.

Of course, this wasn't his first time trespassing. They stole strawberries and apples, you could always say your ball landed over the fence and that you were looking for it. But in the summer, when the foliage was thick, you had somewhere to hide. And the owners understood why the kids had come there.

But now, in the fall, when the branches were bare and the fruit harvested . . . Mareyev hesitated. The property borders meant something else now. What could he say if someone noticed? What story about a ball could he make up?

He began talking himself out of it. Why go there? He wouldn't be able to see inside, the windows were shuttered. He realized he just wanted to step on the lot's soil. Feel it.

Mareyev squeezed under the fence. He walked cautiously past the kitchen to the house. No one saw him, the only sound was the tired whine of a saw in the distance. But he felt someone was watching. He looked over the house and kitchen, the apple trees, the outhouse, the woodpile. He felt a strange touch, as if he had awakened the earth already caught in nighttime frosts and the ground would not release the soles of his feet and was pulling them down.

He bolted, and it felt like he had to pull out his feet and the soil was grabbing them with its icy hands.

When he got home, he fell into bed with a terrible fever. His mother naturally assumed he caught whatever his father had. But Mareyev knew that he had been chilled: by the viscous cold of another's land.

During the winter he decided that it had been a test. He liked the fact that the secret did not give itself up, protected itself, forcing his mind and emotions to work, leading him into the next age level. Studying became easier, as if the secret were helping, granting abilities to deal with life, and his parents started treating him with greater trust, seeing how he was succeeding in school; he's finally taken charge of his brain, they told each other, thinking he could not hear them.

His grandmother's health declined rapidly over the winter, but still she asked to spend the summer at the dacha. Just a year ago, they would not have left Mareyev with her at the dacha. But now they consulted and decided: It was all right. He had matured and he wouldn't do stupid things, God willing.

All his peers and playmates had been sent off to the first session of Pioneer camp and were not left with the old people at the dachas. It got hot, and his grandmother lay in her room, the heavy drapes drawn, settling into ill health and the burdens of the body, coming out only in the morning and evening to go into the garden and to cook in the kitchen; for the first time in his life Mareyev was left alone with the slow time of summer.

He had always had a passion for peeking. Attracted by half-open doors and keyholes. As a kid, he liked to imagine the life of mice under the snow—his father showed him the entrances into their dens on walks in the park. He was lured by binoculars, periscopes, telescopes, microscopes, cameras, loupes, eyeglasses, any optical devices that played with space. Now that attraction had turned into the ability to observe, to recognize what seemed to be on view but in fact was not what it seemed.

Mareyev learned to see the dachas as a single unit. To note the habits of the adults, to remember the days of each neighbor: hang out the wash, go for water, water the cucumbers, head to the store. Women, men, they were all predictable. Only Kalyuzhny knew how to be unobtrusive. To appear and vanish, as if he opened space or used underground passages.

Then Mareyev noticed that the old man played this game far from the dachas, too. He could appear at the station, for example, right in the middle of that long heat-frazzled line for eggs, when the nasty local women would never let someone into the line just like that: you couldn't persuade them even with a sob story. Mareyev, sent by his grandmother for eggs, had ridden his bike past his lot five minutes ago and thought he had seen Kalyuzhny in his garden, his striped shirt moving. However, Mareyev had no incontrovertible proof of a miracle; the shirt could have been hanging on the line, drying.

They had an unprecedented drought. The leaves on the trees died, and the rare breezes created a crunchy rustling.

The gardens were still turning green, all the water was being used for irrigation, pressure in the hoses coming only late at night. In the distance, fumes came from the big forests, the sky grew murky, and the sun set in a blue haze. As they smoked, men superstitiously spat on blown-out matches.

On Monday, when they adults went to the city to work, a fire broke out in the wide vacant lot beyond the outskirts of the dachas, where railroad workers had dumped piles of alder wood, cut down during track-clearing in the spring.

Only the grass was burning so far. But the rising wind drove a serpentine streak of fire toward the dried branches of the alder forest. If they caught, the flames would have intensified, spreading to the orchards and dachas.

They called the fire department from the gatehouse—all the trucks had already been dispatched elsewhere. They tried getting water from faucets and carrying it in buckets, but no way! The faucets either sputtered or sent out a weak yellowish stream, like an infant. For the most part it was women and teenagers trying to beat back the flames with twigs, shoveling dirt on them, but it was all haphazard and ineffectual. The fire seemed to sense their cluelessness and surged viciously, aiming sparks at their eyes, catching their sleeves, stupefying them with smoke.

Mareyev's parched throat grew sour with fear. He thought it was time to run home and lead his grandmother toward the highway. The dancing flames, which could have been put out with one precise salvo from a fire hose, were about to reach the alder and form a fiery wall, their tongues reaching for the houses.

And here, Kalyuzhny jumped out from the side, fearless and combative, the way small fierce creatures can be: weasels, skunks, martens. He ran with a dozen buckets on each arm, and these clanged and rumbled, chasing off bewilderment and telling the fire to retreat.

Kalyuzhny didn't seem to say anything, he just waved his arms around, but the crowd came alive as if it acted in unison. People moved, formed a long and therefore widely spaced chain to the village fire pond, which was almost dried up, overgrown with weeds, and dirtied by geese. Of course, they had thought of it earlier. But it seemed too far away, you couldn't carry enough water. And there wouldn't be much water there, anyway, in this drought, just on the bottom. And that wasn't even water, just rotten muck.

But the chain extended far enough and there was sufficient water. They poured it and put out the fire just as the alder branches were starting to catch. They stepped back, singed and confused, wondering how they had managed.

Kalyuzhny was gone. So were the buckets. No one seemed to remember him or say what a great job he did. Mareyev, sweaty and exhausted, looked around and realized that someone else, his father, for example, could have figured out what to do. Could have organized the crowd. But no, there would have been something missing: seconds, meters, an extra pair of hands, the last bucket of water. They would not have contained the fire.

From where did Kalyuzhny, like a magician, pull out those needed seconds and liters? Appeared here and there, filling in the dangerously stretched chain of bucket carriers. Splashed the fire accurately, economically, predicting where the flame would jump.

A storm raged that night. The rain smashed the roof like a liquid stratum. Half-asleep, Mareyev imagined it was Kalyuzhny walking in the sky. Buckets clanging, rounding up clouds to be milked.

The next summer, Mareyev no longer kept an eye on Kalyuzhny. From the first few days, the summer was filled with the flickering of girls' legs, knees, elbows giving him a nudge from a distance. He spent time at the pond, riding around the co-op community paths, finding out where they gathered, where they went for walks, and only rarely as he passed Kalyuzhny's property he wondered: Had he really spent whole days watching that boring old man? Now it seemed to him that this renunciation was the real process of growing up.

Then he finished school and entered a construction institute, not seeing the work of an invisible hand in that. After graduation, he spent a lot of time on projects in the north, building houses and industrial buildings on the treacherous local soil, fighting the eternal frost that crushed walls and foundations. He rarely came to the dacha, just to help his parents, to bring them there and back. However, as if the proximity to the land and his daily thoughts about it, its fluid dark character that sometimes confounds builders, made Mareyev start noticing Kalyuzhny again on his brief visits.

Now he lived year-round at the dacha: his daughter had found a husband at last and they pushed the old man out of the apartment. The dacha owners grew wealthier and were building more frequently. Kalyuzhny, though an old man, became the main digger, and he dug everything—ditches, wells, cesspools, recesses for concrete pouring. Deftly and quickly, as if he had studied the art of the shovel all his life, it wasn't something you learned in a year. He was muscular and strong, the labor had chased off debility. The dacha widows, who had buried husbands in their sixties, starting chasing him. He didn't drink or smoke and worked hard. But Kalyuzhny sent the ladies packing. A dozen of them took offense and retaliated by spreading rumors that he was sticky fingered and could pick up a few things while digging or appropriate the owners' tools, even though Kalyuzhny always brought his own. But how could you argue? Kalyuzhny lost his clients, and new diggers arrived, Asians who charged less.

His property was untended, littered, the apple trees grew crazily, and the house and kitchen looked dilapidated. Yet Kalyuzhny, still vigorous, attached a trailer to his rattling scooter, bringing home couches and television sets from the landfills. He brought wheelbarrows full of clay to the ravines in the woods, so he was digging something.

Again, it seemed to Mareyev that he was the only one who noticed the strange occupations of the rejected old man. He wouldn't have been paying attention, either, if it hadn't been for his childhood memory, that image: Kalyuzhny climbing the garbage mountain, stomp, clap—and the connection between things became clear.

That summer, Mareyev was offered a five-year contract in Africa. A German company, constructing hydroelectric stations, designing land stripping works. A higher level of remuneration. A different life. The soils were complex there, silty, engorged by the river, but if he managed it well, he would be able to move to Germany, join the engineering elite in great demand all over the globe.

His local ties were rearranged faster than expected. He decided to spend two or three days at the dacha: get things in order while his parents were on a Mediterranean vacation package bought last winter before the Africa job was offered to him. Actually, he didn't need to do this. The dacha was well maintained, he did not stint on money. However, he felt no attachment to it. It was too small for him, too crowded, and too daunting in its unchanging ways, the power of interconnection between objects that had outlived their time and were no longer used as intended by his parents but kept for the sake of stability in their lives.

Mareyev told himself that he needed to check everything one more time: It wouldn't be an easy trip back from Africa. His parents had grown anxious and expected consideration from Mareyev. They naturally would have preferred him to stay and start a family, give them grandchildren.

As he drove up to the dacha, he thought that his real reason for coming was to see old Kalyuzhny and say good-bye. The idea was ridiculous and therefore on the mark with an even higher degree of accuracy.

Kalyuzhny was at the dacha but did not appear in his yard. A window lit up in the evening and went dark by midnight. Was he ill? One morning Mareyev rose very early—he wasn't sleepy—and noticed from his veranda that Kalyuzhny's light was on. Had he gotten up, too? Or had he not turned off the light last night?

He immediately pictured the old man lying there, half-dead, unable to reach the switch and hoping that someone would notice and guess why the light was on. Of course, it was more likely that the old man had simply fallen asleep, forgetting about the lamp. It was a drizzly day, sleepy and gray.

Still, Mareyev put on a waterproof jacket and went to check. Kalyuzhny's gate was not locked, and he called loudly. "Hello! Anyone home?"

His voice dissipated, absorbed by the drizzle. Mareyev opened the gate and followed the path to the kitchen. He remembered how many years ago the ground here had grabbed his feet and stung him with cold. The ground stayed calm, lulled by the long rains.

The half-baked idea of helping the old man revealed the truth. He had come to learn his secret. He wasn't going to live here anymore and had no reason to observe niceties.

Mareyev went up the kitchen steps. The light was not on in the kitchen, and he had no reason for going there if his mission was to save Kalyuzhny. This was more of a search. But Mareyev opened the door and switched on his flashlight.

Kalyuzhny's kitchen was enormous, five meters square, an entire second house. In the past, Mareyev would look at the place and wonder why the old man needed so much space. What did he cook, what did he eat all alone in the emptiness?

The kitchen was stuffed to the ceiling. It was filled with headboards, tubs, pots and pans, barrels, window frames, pipes, bicycle frames, rakes, pitchforks, boxes, baskets, beehives, sieves, boards, chairs; trash. Mareyev recognized the boiler covered in peeling rust that he had taken to the dumpster himself two years earlier. There were things here from every lot, every family. The old trash mountain had assembled itself anew, as if back then they had invaded Kalyuzhny's real house, and he had taken it apart in order to reinstall it here.

It was his power that kept the mountain's component parts unified, realized Mareyev. That's why he could release it so easily, with a stomp and a clap. He lived there by the gatehouse, a second, invisible watchman guarding the properties because they were his, and he levied a tax on each one with trash, he had keys to every house. He rushed to put out the fire because the dachas were his to protect. That was why our dachas were never burgled, thought Mareyev: Kalyuzhny protected them. His power protected them even when he went to the city for the winter.

Mareyev shut the kitchen door. He was sure that there was no force here now. Not in the ground, not in the objects packed into the kitchen. Something had happened to Kalyuzhny. He would not be able to guard his secret.

Mareyev stepped onto the porch. The treads were dirty, the old man scraped clay from his shoes on them. He pulled the doorknob. The door opened.

"Anyone home?" he asked.

Silence.

He expected the same piles of trash inside. But no: It was spacious with little furniture. No one had lived here for at least a few years. Nor slept on the bed, sat on the chairs, touched the objects; the dust made that very clear. It was as if Kalyuzhny had died, and the house stood without its owner.

Mareyev walked through the rooms. He cast his engineer's eye around the house. He remembered the clay mud on the steps. He pushed aside a worn rug with his foot and saw the seams of a trapdoor.

The dacha houses did not have basements. Only shallow cellars under the kitchen. The thought of a maniac flashed and vanished. When he was a child there was talk about one called Viper who had a pit under his garage and lured boys in to help repair his car.

Mareyev, a builder, had seen bad places, had known evil houses. This was different.

Under the newspapers on the table he found a metal rod hook. He slipped it into the eyelet of the hatch and lifted slowly, trying to keep the hinges from creaking.

The smell of earth and fetid exhaled air rose from below. There was another scent, neither human nor animal. It wasn't the smell of the street or the forest but it wasn't the house, either, although Mareyev had encountered it before. He had encountered it in old buildings scheduled for demolition, the residents gone, leaving only a mess, bare walls, torn-out radiators, and blatant emptiness in place of the inhabited.

An earthen staircase. Mareyev used his phone flashlight to examine the steps: Was there any blood? No, it was clean.

He squeezed into the hatch and started down. It was stuffy, but it was amusing, because he realized what he looked like, and all his worries fled. God, he thought, the old man was nuts. He must have studied all those instructions on civil defense when he was young. Now nuclear war was upon us, every day there were stories on TV about NATO's missiles. This was just an amateur bomb shelter. Downstairs there would probably be a bed, a rifle, and food. A senseless bunker without an exhaust fan, where you couldn't spend more than two days. Kalyuzhny knew about engineering, he should have known. If he didn't that meant he'd lost his mind.

This clear explanation soothed Mareyev. He descended into the underground room. Just as he thought: concrete walls and homemade shelves: three-liter jars with grains, pasta, flour, sugar. A kerosene lamp burning on the plank table. Why didn't he run in the electricity? Did he think the apocalypse would shut down the electric stations? So, he was prepared?

The low ceiling, as if children had dug themselves a foxhole, forced Mareyev to crouch. In the far, dark corner stood a mesh bed with a pile of rags, quilts, blankets.

He lifted the flattened rags. In a sagging recess, as if in a hole or den, Kalyuzhny lay curled up, breathing faintly, reduced in size as if the digging had wasted him away; with overgrown curly gray hair, filthy, somehow no longer human, like a mole whose body was made for narrow subterranean spaces. He was the source of the odor that reminded Mareyev of abandoned houses.

Mareyev took the old man's weak hand. He looked at Kalyuzhny's nails, yellow, stone, sharp. He could barely find the pulse. But Kalyuzhny suddenly woke up, cried out, grabbed his right hand in a deadly grip and held their palms, etched with fate lines, pressed together.

Mareyev could not pull away, and their palms became one, glued to each other, and the other man's fate lines became his. They were seared into his flesh.

He fell into someone's memory, no longer that of a stranger. Into a cellar apartment, where through the dirty windows just below the ceiling, spattered with wet leaves, one could see only the feet of pedestrians. You lived underground, the passing trolleys sending tremors that shook the dishes in the hutch. Across the street was an ancient cemetery, and you were at the same depth as the coffins, in close proximity to the dead.

There was a small closet in the apartment, shuttered with a padlocked, homemade door. Mother kept old things in there, things that had been secreted out of sight, things that seemed illicit and even dangerous, forced into hiding. There was nothing wrong with them, though. A dusty couch. A carved shelf. A foreign-made bicycle with a nickel-plated bell. Leather cavalry boots with toothed spur wheels. A floor clock with the long, shiny tongue of a frozen pendulum, with thin, nervous hands that stopped at 6:33. Shiny cisterns for boiling medical instruments. A crumpled hearing tube. Bales of magazines in a foreign language tied with twine. Reindeer antlers. Elegant, thin-legged chairs without seats or backs.

Mother strictly forbade going into the closet without her. Or telling other children and even adults about the things kept in it. You asked why, and she grew angry and raised her voice: Because that's the way it is! Because I said so! Her face would turn ugly with anguish.

But you wanted to play with those treasures, you wanted to brag to your friends, especially about the grown-up bicycle with a crystal headlamp in front and a red signal light on the back fender; you learned where to find the padlock key. Then Mother, a master storyteller, entrusted you with a great secret: Barmas lived in the closet. They were his things. He was the owner of the cellar where you lived. A cranky, mean old man, he could kick us out. The closet was his room, and he did not let strangers in, especially children. He really didn't like children, noisy, disobedient, inquisitive.

You believed in Barmas once and for all. But you were also a storyteller, your mother's son. She had not taken that into account.

You rewrote the character. Barmas in your imagination became a creature of an innumerable secret tribe that lived beneath the city, dug tunnels between cellars, was ubiquitous, and could see everything from below; a severe tribe, but not without care for humans, protecting those they liked, and taking payment in the form of old things.

Mother grew hunched, ruined her eyesight doing proofreading, bringing home more work for overnight; you sensed how afraid she was, afraid to make a mistake, afraid not to meet the deadline, afraid of late night steps in the lobby, afraid of everything in the world.

You, planning a refuge, imagined that should Barmas give the command, cozy beds and various supplies would appear in the closet: sacks of grain, sweet sugarloaves, barrels of herrings in brine, boxes of chocolates. He could hide you there in case of trouble. And then make it impossible to find the door from outside.

Once, when Mother had to work the night shift at the printing house and a fierce wind roared down the street, shaking the loosened iron sheets on rooftops, you crawled into the closet with a kerosene lamp and asked softly, looking for protection, "Barmas, show yourself!"

Something rustled in the dark under the couch. Of course, it was a rat, but that movement was enough for you to believe: Barmas had responded.

For the next few days you saved bits of crust, grains of sugar, pieces of cracker from your dinner. There was no logic in it. Why would Barmas need your crumbs if he had unlimited supplies? But you sensed it was necessary. It was a sacrifice. Barmas would understand.

The offerings were eaten by the rat. You believed it was Barmas taking them. And protecting you and your mother. The whole house. Even the mean janitor, Chubak, and his aggressive dog, Maruska. Protecting and holding a place for you both in the closet if worse came to worst. Keeping his side of the bargain.

Then the war started. The trolleys stopped running, they no longer pushed the ground, did not move the bricks. In the cellar window all you saw were soldiers' boots striking the cobbles, then came feet in shoes and rags, and then the window was sealed: camouflage, blackout.

You no longer went to school. But your mother still went to work; yet she brought almost nothing home except weariness. You continued hiding crumbs from the table and bringing them to the closet, but your faith grew bitter. More than once, you asked Barmas to intercede for you, to feed you; but Barmas did not respond. Your mother complained that many adults had stopped helping one another. This made Barmas truly real for you. It turned out that your mother was right: Barmas really was simply a nasty old man, since he just sat underground getting fat stuffing himself.

Suddenly, you figured it out: His supplies were stolen. From people. That meant they should be taken back. And the thief should be punished.

Of course, you didn't change your faith right away. There were times when you hoped the old Barmas would return. He had simply left, he wasn't in the closet, it was the war, the war had scared off him and his tribe: bombs reach cellars, too.

There were no more crumbs. But you kept going to the closet to show that you remembered, that if any food appeared, you would bring it right away.

Winter came to the city, the streets were covered in snow, you could barely get out of the building. Before, Chubak the janitor would have cleared the snow. First Maruska, the janitor's bitch, disappeared, and then he vanished, too. The snow at the windows did not melt, it was piled up, threatening to push the panes and collapse into the room. Mother started burning things from the closet in the stove.

That was probably when you made the decision. The turnaround occurred slowly. Everything moved slowly then, as if pushing through a freezing wind.

First you chose the knife. Before the knife cut meat and vegetables, but now your mother was clumsily cutting kindling with it. She broke up the floor with a cabbage chopper and then she cut the pieces.

Now there was a hole in the closet. A hole leading down underground where Barmas must have run.

One day Mother was out. All the way across the city to see her best friend. Her husband was a military surgeon; he got a big food ration.

Weak, as if in a dream, you searched the room, looking for something edible. In the box with games like lotto, cards, and dice, you found a sugar cube. Long ago, when sugar still existed, you stole that cube and drew on it, putting black dots on its sides: one, two, three, four, five, six. Drew them and hid it in the lotto box.

You shoved it in your mouth and tried to chew, but the sugar was unyielding, it was the kind you hit with a hammer. An unpleasant voice in your head, sounding like Chubak the janitor, who liked to teach the older kids prison lore, said, "Hey, dummy! Put the sugar in the closet right next to the hole. And wait next to it. Your Barmas will come. He won't get away. They're hungry, too."

When something small and furtive moved in the cavity, you struck with the knife. Barmas jumped on you, and you tossed him away, stabbing, striking the floor, the ground, the living and sticky, furry and weak, but biting. Barmas tried to crawl away, to hide in his underground, but you grabbed his body and smacked him against the edge of the hole, against its sharp, broken boards.

Stopping, you realized that Barmas was gone. There was only a terrible emptiness in the spot he had held in your heart.

In the morning, Mother returned with a jar of dried milk; with a jar of the future that would last until spring.

She cut up and boiled the dead rat—and praised you for your courage.

You ate rat meat, and you thought that the emptiness in your heart was being filled with something disturbing and nasty, as if the murdered old man who had turned into a rat in death was mocking you.

... Mareyev, choking and coughing, pulled his hand away from Kalyuzhny's cold, unfeeling hand.

He felt a strange itching under his nails, as if something was cutting through.

He wanted to dig.

THE BARN

The barn stood deep in the hills, at the turn of the over-grown road that used to lead to the neighboring village—during the war sappers took apart its huts for logs to lay roads in the swamps. The wedges of three fields met at the barn: land that was runny, would not clump, would not stick to the iron of the ploughshare, shimmering with fine, light sand, heaving up stones to the surface every spring: the size of a chicken egg, a blacksmith's fist, a human head, a piglet... The stones, fantastically shaped by an ancient glacier, washed clean of dust by the rains, purple quartzite, pink with a sparkle of mica, granite, seemed—since they had shapes similar to vegetables—to be the bounty of the land, swollen muscles of abundant stone meat for the table of the swamp and forest goblins, the hidden giants that lived in the hills.

Atop the knee-high foundation of boulders, covered with lichen and crisscrossed by fatty white stitches of quartz veins, stood the barn. It was made of dark brick, as if it had been overbaked and starting to char, of an unknown sort, a bit narrower and shorter than usual; the work was calibrated with such a frightening excess of precision that it prompted one to ask: Is this a barn at all? Did people build it?

A simple rectangle. A gable roof covered in rusting iron. But the extreme severity of the brickwork created ideal corners, ideal angles of the rectangle, and that ideal, unneeded here in the bleak and impoverished region of hills and swamps, offended the eye, and the longer a passerby looked, the more he wanted to squint, to unsee the barn, as if the scrupulously drawn lines contained a stirring power, wielding lines and planes like a weapon, capable of piercing or stabbing or slicing in half; and also—capable of looking back in response.

The barn was too big. No matter what you sowed, you couldn't find a plant, fruit, vegetable, or grain that could be harvested from the three nearby patchwork fields in the hills to fill even a third of the space. So, it felt as if it had not been built for an ordinary harvest but for some festival of fertility, an unknown vegetal tribe, for marvelous seeds that would yield double, quadruple what ordinary ones do.

Long, stretched out along the axis of the valley, which made it look even longer. In the sunset hours, when the thick rays of the sun illuminated it from behind the saddle of the hill, the barn grew, stretched, expanded, while the local spinneys, thin and speckled, the low hills, the mossy bald patches of the swamps sank, squatted, cowered. And then—for a few minutes—it seemed that it was a treasure house in which the surroundings could be stored, neatly divided into parts, emptying nests and dens, and only the barn, enormous outside and limitless inside, would hang in the emptiness, without shifting, without registering the weight of the contents.

Idle experts, tramps, and people passing through, read the imprints on the bricks and figured that the builders were Germans. It was an old, prerevolutionary construction. They had planned to grow sugar beets by cutting and digging up more fields. But these ideas did not stick to the barn or fit into the folk biography. Birds did not build nests in it; woodworm beetles did not settle in the rafters; and only the timid, nimble, and swift roe deer came in the early mornings, when the foundation was covered in large dewdrops, to lick off the salt that oozed as a whitish crystal coating from the cement seams between the boulders—and then vanished, fleeing to nearby thickets, hidden by shadows and fog.

A blued padlock hung in the eyelets of the barn's gates, made in the form of an arch, tall, one and half times a man's height, bound with strips of pocked iron bearing the marks of the smith's hammer. The lock, as heavy as a bull's heart, was made of weapon steel, made to weapon grade; it was closely related to the smart, precise mechanisms of war; it smelled—the odor had not dissipated over the years—of the alarming scent of rifle grease. The padlock was also huge, the size of a birdhouse or dollhouse, and it seemed that a spirit could live inside it, the turnkey, the guard of the barn.

No one had the key. No one had ever seen it.

The padlock was part of the barn—and it did not belong to the barn at all. Everyone knew or was certain that the barn was empty, filled up with emptiness, thick, fermented to the point that it was no longer emptiness but the presence of absence.

The padlock, however, as complicated as a watch, as obvious and threatening as a seal, was evidence that there was something in the barn, something worth that protection.

Every building in the area had a job, every thresher barn, shed, hut, house, room, or cellar was used for something. But the barn by the distant hills was excluded from the circuit of peasant chores, it simply stood there, abandoned but not neglected, unneeded, inconvenient, too big for the small local doings. Sometimes, some newbie, appointee, hothead, proposed taking it apart for the bricks or setting up a section of the kolkhoz farm there, break through some windows, extend electricity, repair the road; but then he would put it off, forget it amid the routine work and bureaucracy, become local, grim, downcast—or leave for another region where he would recount the strange tale over vodka. Sometimes a random commission, with flown-in overseers, came across the barn and ordered it be opened, cursing right and left in fruitless, red-lipped anger upon learning there was no key, threatening people, sky, and hills, demanding a plumber who could cut through the lock with a torch, but by the time they looked for one, brought one there, the visitors' rage would dim, replaced by dull-witted weariness, and they frowned and left.

The locals did not consider the barn theirs, as if it stood beyond an invisible line of the habitable, tied by threads of succession and possession. Seeing it, they seemed to recall it anew, sensing its stature and character with a shudder—and then forgetting it until the next time. Children, free of the silent reproaches of their elders, could have been intrigued by its mystery, but children were rarely born in those parts, as if there was a hidden disagreement between masculine and feminine; the ones who did come into the world appeared, from infancy, as adults, enveloped by the smoky, bitter boredom of life.

But once, in a strange year when the region was flooded in August by hares, big gray hares that ate all the vegetation, scuttling for weeks in the bushes, apparently not hearing the thunder of hunting rifles and not counting the deaths among their tribe, the kolkhoz bookkeeper, Anna, had a baby boy. The father was not local; last fall Anna had taken courses in the oblast center and brought the child from there. In general, people reacted calmly, grown-up affairs, Anna was the best bookkeeper, you couldn't find another as good who could be lured to the kolkhoz; and she was thirty-five, practically the last possible age for motherhood.

Anna was fair, freckled, flabby, but big-boned; flesh of the flesh of the meager hills and fields where the undemanding cows, reddish brown with white cloudy patches, grazed. Slow, calm, she counted numbers, and everything always added up, as if through her bookkeeping, her counting, she quietly corrected life in the region in terms of possessions, money, and people, making ends meet.

However, the boy, Vanya, was different, not a local. Tanned from childhood even without the sun, dark-haired, active—he climbed out of the crib by himself, crawled out of the house by himself, stood on his feet before he was a year old . . . Something awakened in the locals, subtler than a chill: a wary interest, the detection of a draft. The elders, oldtimers, started watching him as if by accident, mentioning him in conversations as if by chance; without praise or condemnation, without emotion—but creating a certain electricity by the repetition, an accumulating charge.

Then, in his third year, it became clear: The boy did not talk. And he never would, the visiting doctor announced. Don't even bother, an operation would not help and therapy would not help, don't get into his head, it's not his head, it's his throat, not a muscle there. But the villagers, who said they sympathized with Anna, cheered up: the gloating flashed and went out, vanished in the sand.

Until he was seven or eight Vanya lived under everyone's eye; his mother was at work, in the office, while he wandered around the village, sometimes dropping into the gardens, into the houses; quiet, polite, but as stubborn as a beetle. Some were slightly happy to see him, others put up with him for Anna's sake, she was an important person, she could hold up your pay or, on the contrary, toss in an extra ruble.

But then they started noticing that he started going into the same houses more frequently. And looking at the same things.

He would just stand there for a minute or two and look.

At the dark blue enameled two-liter can.

At the broken cuckoo clock.

At the bottle-green ashtray.

At the rusted watering can.

At the burgundy velvet lampshade, moth-eaten and patched more than once.

At the whip, of rare, ringing leather that hung, coiled into a circle, on a nail.

At the shovel, the most ordinary shovel, leaning against the shed wall.

At the porcelain figurine of a ballerina with a piece broken off her tutu.

At the rag rug that lay on a shelf.

And the heavy, stifling coat of dark green prewar cloth.

At the tailor's wide scissors.

At the foot-operated sewing machine.

At the carved weather vane, a tin rooster on the roof.

At the long glass thermometer with a bright red vein of mercury.

At the dusty tapestry with reindeer.

At the table mirror.

At the sooty poker of forged iron.

At the chair with a carved back.

At a picture on the wall, a reproduction in a kopeck frame, *Morning in the Fir Woods*.

They did not notice this at first, because Vanya had a way of slipping away, vanishing from time and attention, but one time the cuckoo clock that belonged to old man Markel, the kolkhoz watchman, started up under Vanya's gaze after decades of not running.

Markel was distant kin to Anna, a third cousin once or twice removed. An insignificant man and seemingly lowly, ordered about by everyone, Markel this, Markel that, Markel fetch,

Markel find. But everyone seemed to know that Markel agreed to play this part and played it for his own satisfaction, but he could stop at any moment. That's why no one blamed him that the orders were not obeyed, that Markel went nowhere and looked for nothing. He slept late, past noon, the way no one in the village would dare. He hung around all day in the shed creating trifles, figures, look-alikes, of wood and metal, or cutting lures for fishing. Toward evening he got out his black pea jacket, cleaned his rifle, took a long time filling his lantern with kerosene, as if he were scrupulously calculating the length of the coming night to the minute; smoked a cigarette on the porch when twilight transfigured into dark, and left until morning; his bright lantern shone in the mist at the backs of farms, in the near pastures, at the boundary stones, by the wells, at the water mill in the brook, near the Black Ravine, where they dumped carcasses and garbage, near the pond, at the intersections of field roads—and at the distant barn, too.

Markel strode broadly, guarding many things, walking many versts over the long night. He didn't get sick, never ill, whether it was sunny, snow falling like a wall, or pouring autumn rain, the watchman went out with his lantern and military rifle to chase away the nocturnal evil. The younger ones wondered what exactly was Markel protecting? What was there in the village worth stealing? And most important, who would do the stealing? The region was empty, the barren kilometers grieved, no thieves or gangs of bandits, just old wartime foxholes and fraternal graves under modest silver-plated pyramids. But when they grew up a bit, they began to sense life and suddenly understand that Markel was doing a needed thing, to everyone's benefit, and from the windows of their houses they watched the flickering yellow lantern in the night with a double sense of gratitude and fear: gratitude to Markel who became the defense of the village and fear because the nighttime Markel knew something that the daytime one would not tell.

Markel came to Anna one the evening to talk before he started his work; the pea coat was belted, the rifle over his shoulder, and a cap without a cockade on his head; tall, taller than anyone in the village, lean, smelling of carpentry varnish. For the first time, as if awakening, Anna thought that Markel did not resemble the other villagers, he was of a special breed closer to her son, Vanya, and his fleeting father, about whom she remembered almost nothing, having been exceptionally drunk and merry.

"Hello, Anna," Markel said and dubiously adjusted his cap, moving it a millimeter to achieve the precise position known only to him.

"Hello, Uncle Markel." Anna had heard from the neighbor women that Markel's ancient clock had started to work under Vanya's gaze and at first she wanted to defend her son, to tell the watchman that he should be grateful, two clockmakers had refused to try, and here there was no need for money or fuss, the mechanism repaired itself. But Markel adjusted his cap again, lifting it a bit, and looked at Anna absent-mindedly but intently; Anna shuddered and sensed what she had kept hidden from herself rising to the surface: Vanya was not her son because he had nothing, not a drop of blood, from his mother, and she sensed it; everything in him was from his father, fleeting, random, but absolute. Or maybe not even from the father but from his scattered tribe, all his clans and generations, from all the branches living and dead. Her son was born of dust and ashes, of the night wind in deserted lands; he was not related to her and never would be.

That is why Anna said, "Vanya is sick, he has a temperature. Fever, he's imagining things. He'll spend a week at home, staying in bed on top of the oven."

Markel chewed his thin, bloodless lips, rubbed his temple with a fingertip, swallowed, and said, "Good."

From that day, Vanya rarely walked around the village and no longer entered people's houses. Anna had a big orchard, three dozen decrepit apple trees, surrounded by supports, wrapped in wire—to keep them from falling apart, the insides were rotten, inhabited by ants. The crowns were wild, like an uncombed mane, the apples small and scabby, good only for the hedgehogs. He settled in the orchard, built a shed out of rubble, found tools in the garden, in the grass. He began scraping the rotten bark from the trees with a copper brush, cutting out unneeded branches that only sucked juice from the trunk. By autumn's end the old orchard lightened up and breathed.

In the spring it exploded in blossoms. In a single morning it enveloped itself in pinkish white; not gauze, not a thin fog, but thick, solid, opaque clouds with an even, rounded edge, as if painted by an artist.

The newly blossoming orchard created a vague, fleeting confusion in the village. The picturesque beauty, the resurrection of the trees, and the promise of fruit did not arouse what they should.

Beauty—but there was something alarming in that beauty beyond its excessiveness and suddenness; it was too fragrant, too bright—as if it were not alive.

That is why they went about their daily business avoiding the orchard; not talking about it directly, not mentioning it, waiting secretly for the coming frosts, for the cold to attack the flowers so that the petals would turn black, crumple, and fall. But the usual cold did not come that May, even though it had every year for decades. Then the roundabout conversations began, how sometimes all the tree's force goes into the flowers: the flowering is lush, gorgeous, the ovaries set—but the apples do not follow, they remain green dwarves, freaks.

They watched secretly, and the ones with the best vision measured, are the apples ripening? Growing? Getting juicy? It looked as if the experts were right, the apples fell asleep on the branches in June, like a dead babe in the mother's womb.

They were not growing.

And everyone felt better, happier, as if they had been frightened by who-knew-what, some foolish joke that they took as a threat; they started talking the old way again, looking at the orchard with a smirk and using thumb and forefinger to show the size: no bigger than that!

They were not growing.

In the first days of July there was a storm. The area was windy, atmospheric rivers flowed among the hills, there was rarely a day that the wheat in the field stood quietly and the branches did not sway; there was always work for the weather vane and joy for the washed laundry; it did not quiet down at night, it blew and blew, moving and animating the shadows cast by Markel's lantern. The locals born here felt uncomfortable in other places—the air there was slow, thick, you breathe out, someone else breathes in, like eating out of the same bowl; back home, if you didn't hide your cigarette in your fist, the wind smoked it down, burned it, the sparks flying!

This hurricane was special. Usually the clouds gather for a week, fermenting in the sky as if in a vat, gestating a storm. Here, the sky turned gray in the evening and then darkened, as if something was pressing and pushing it from the other side. They ran around, gathering things, herding cattle, closing shutters, checking the bolts; they stayed inside, even Markel did not go out on patrol; the silence compressed them, their ears hurt, the windows creaked; it pressed and pressed, some of the young ones had nose bleeds, a cat birthed dead kittens, a bulb in an empty room burst, an icon wept resin tears.

Then it hit, that very night. The wind rushed down as if from a mountain, sometimes whole, sometimes ragged and torn, to be able to turn into every corner, beneath every eave, roaring in a hundred voices: shouts and groans, prayers, sobbing and weeping. The wind flew, pressing houses into the earth, and penetrating the logs walls, blowing out the fetid air, filling rooms, cupboards, cellars, commodes, boxes, pillows, and jars, it couldn't get into light bulbs or thermometers. The candles burned brighter and faster, the years of dust blown off and carried away, and objects creaked and jangled in response.

The dark was impenetrable, but they seemed to hear the crack of trees; the villagers listened closely to learn if the old apple trees were falling—as if hoping that the hurricane had been sent to destroy the decrepit trunks, and therefore they put up with it without complaint, like foreign troops chasing foreigners.

In the morning, the orchard stood unharmed. The fierce night wind seemed to have refreshed it, changed its haircut. The orchard was the same and yet not the same, as if it had grown up overnight, its roots finding a new source of water and drinking its full, and had become statelier.

The apples, apparently still the same, like stone green peas, looked bigger than the day before.

The voices in the wind had woken them up, given them a push, knocked off the stupor and sleep—in July the apples shot up, caught up in weight, in size, developed a gentle blush. The orchard calmed down, burdened by the weight of its fruit. The villagers talked, as if by accident, about the rotten trunks filled with dust, which meant that the branches were rotten, the core was spoiled, they would start breaking soon, no matter how much support you gave them; the yield would destroy itself.

The branches creaked, bowing lower and lower—but not a single one broke. The boy Vanya chopped y-shaped branches in the woods and adeptly placed them at the right angle, but the most sensitive people, Markel especially, knew that it wasn't a question of skill. There were so many apples, such weight pressed on the branches, that even the stakes could not help; they had to fail, break, there was always a weak point . . . But they did not break, as if something were holding them, beside the supports.

Markel started watching during the day. Yes, Vanya went out to cut grass, the grass was growing extremely high, as if getting strength from the apple trees; he spread the mown grass around the tree trunks, to decompose and fertilize; he hauled water from the well for the trees in a quotidian and disinterested way, like the other villagers. It looked like ordinary work, a blueprint of repetitive movements, muscle contractions. But if you looked more closely, the way only Markel could, for there's a reason he is the watchman, the seeing one among the blind, you would see that Vanya walked in a slight crouch, stooped: as if a weight had fallen on the back of his neck and he carried that weight around with him, or walked beneath it as if beneath a low ceiling. You could see that the branches had stilled, as if they had been glued, seized by the frost: the apples ripened and grew heavier, and the boy held them—and he grew, grew faster than kids do from summer work, from sunny summer days; the boyish was being replaced by the adult, the alienated.

Markel sensed that he had failed, the watchman; he patrolled for decades, guarding the invisible fence around the village, and still the shadow had slipped through and moved in; and what was he to do with it now? How could he root it out?

The apples in Anna's orchard ripened one night in August, all at once; yesterday they were still immature, and today, ripe. But that readiness was strange, unusual. The apples were colored in the range of the stones in the fields, from purple to pink; they glowed as if the shiny waxy skin did not contain white, sugary fruit but flesh, bloody meat.

And they began to fall.

Over the day almost all of them fell, softly thumping onto the dry straw the boy had spread.

They did not decay like apples, fermenting, turning brown, getting moldy; it smelled like a slaughterhouse, and the flies came as if it were a real one; but the boars, hedgehogs, hares, and domestic fowl, all who enjoyed windfall fruit, kept away from the orchard, and the neighbor's dog, a feisty mongrel, huddled in its shed and whined softly.

The boy got an old, rusty wheelbarrow with a squeaky wheel and started removing the apples.

Not to the compost or the Black Ravine, where they dumped garden trash, but across the field to the Moss Swamp.

The villagers did not go there, quagmire, weeds, a wasteland, no berries, no mushrooms, gasses bloated the swamp belly, coming up with a groan and a burbling; only Markel went in sometimes, standing on the mucky shore, looking distractedly at the humps and rust, the iridescent metallic streaks in the black peat water.

And left.

Now the boy was dumping the apples not-apples into the quagmire. Markel wanted to berate him, force him to take them to the ravine, but he held off; he didn't like what the boy was doing, but he sensed that it was meant to be, let him take them there, let him feed the swamp, already once fed, let him, let him . . .

Vanya removed them all in two days. And then he faded, grew quiet, vanished in the neglected orchard, in his shed. But you couldn't fool Markel; he knew what would draw the boy now, he knew and he waited.

So it happened, the boy started sneaking out of the village, wandering alone, and ending up near the barn that stood like an empty trunk in the bare and windblown harvested fields.

It was strange and sweet for Markel to watch the boy mooch about without understanding what forces were leading him, ruling him; he meandered, zigzagged, strolled, scuffed stones in the furrows, ate the late plums, purple and sour, in the plantings, stared at the scampering roe deer, their white rumps bouncing, and chewed meditatively on the briar, marked with red spots like the blood spatter from a point-blank shot; watched a pair of hawks circling above the field—and gravitated, gravitated toward the blackened barn.

At first, Markel wanted to hold the boy back, preempt him, as his watchman training demanded. But then, reluctantly, he changed his mind, anticipated how it would be: let him go, let him touch the padlock, let him feel what it is . . . Markel got carried away, although with some doubt, and his roused heart, having shaken off the years, trembled; he started bringing along an old worn flask with moonshine, sipping to move the blood, feed the inner fire, nourish the angry, arrogant hunter in him. It was early autumn, ravens had settled in the fields, and on the road to the barn where the old smooth cobbles lay like tortoise shells, they hammered chestnuts with their strong beaks, and other chestnuts, smashed, were scattered, reminding him of something; Markel relished the risky game, the interweaving of past and present, like the play of light and shadow in the fading foliage. He did not know for sure what exactly would happen when the boy touched the padlock—but he was absolutely sure that everything would change at that very moment, the barn would reveal itself—and so he lived in heightened anticipation. With greater frequency he saw that the boy was different, with the same figure, but taller, stronger, livelier. That meant he was alive, returned, the frisky rogue, and Markel superstitiously rubbed the docile, smooth rifle stock.

Vanya touched the padlock at last.

Markel thought it would kill him on the spot—but nothing happened. He stood there, picked up a metal rod and started digging around in the keyhole.

Markel sensed that the boy was shielded, he had

someone's protection, he sensed it but could not stop himself in his anger and disappointment that the barn did not defend itself; the old army boots that came from the barn's generosities—they never wore out, just changed the soles—started walking, marched his feet with a guard's gait. Markel followed the boots and shouted, "Stop, bastard! Stop, you son of a bitch, stop!"

On the way to the village, Markel hit the boy a few times; he didn't want to but had to for the sake of order, to put a scare in him, there's no other way with those smart asses. But his nose had to go bleed, he barely touched him, it was a bump, even if he had wanted to, who knew he had a nose as weak as a girl's . . . The boy wore a light calico shirt, the kind that looked like underwear; it was covered with bright blood, which kept dripping, without cease. Markel dragged the boy by his black locks, and he felt better, wonderfully better, for he had executed his guard duty, had not allowed loitering around the barn, and now he could exercise his own, personal, Markel interest.

There was a meeting at the kolkhoz, to discuss the water tower and use of water for personal needs, for gardens and watering cattle; the arguments were heating up between those who had cows and those who did not. The costs were shared equally by everyone, Anna was counting and saying that the administrative instructions were such and nothing could be done about it; yelling, noise, and some hotheads were getting ready to fight, looking around for sturdy planks.

Markel dragged in the boy. Everyone shut up, as if people had guessed what had happened at the barn would happen here, on the deserted lot by the office. They had waited their whole lives for this, preparing without preparation, dimly remembering that there was a part to be played.

Markel brought him over to Anna, explaining nothing to the silenced people he passed, and giving the boy a shove, said, "Take him. We go to the city tomorrow. To the school where he will live."

Anna took him, embraced him, and asked no questions, as if she knew this was meant to be.

Even though it was a clear, cold, late September night, it was stuffy in the houses, smoky, as if someone shut the damper too soon, and left behind the gasses; objects awakened in the dark: the dark blue enameled two-liter can, the broken cuckoo clock, the burgundy velvet lamp shade, the whip that hung, coiled into a circle, on a nail, the shovel leaning against the shed wall, the porcelain figurine of a ballerina with a piece broken off her tutu, the rag rug, the coat of dark green prewar cloth, the tailor's scissors, the sewing machine, the carved weather vane, the long thermometer, the dusty tapestry with reindeer, the table mirror, the forged iron poker . . .

The things, without moving, emitted the sounds of their work and existence: ringing, creaking, clicking, rustling; people awakened by the stuffiness listened, permeated with fear and anger, since they sensed unerringly which objects were making noise.

In the morning, the driver, dulled by insomnia, had a lot of trouble starting the truck; when he finally reached Anna's house, the whole village had gathered there. They stood in silence, almost motionless, drained by the night's wakefulness; but beneath the lethargy and the slouched posture lay the determination of an exhausted, cornered animal.

Anna led her son out of the house; Markel was waiting by the truck, the only one with a fresh head and a clear, hostile, and lingering gaze; but when they were two steps away from the watchman, the boy twisted away, quick as a hare, slid out of Markel's reach and raced down the road to the village, past the stunned villagers.

"Get him!" Markel shouted, straining his lungs.

He shoved the driver, "Turn around!" And told the men who looked livelier, "Get in the back, get in! Go!"

The crowd started, fell apart, and collected itself in movement; the men who fit rode in the truck, teenagers and the bolder women ran after the boy, as if that was why they had gathered, turned out with sour, craven sweat by their nocturnal fears; get him!—the words flew—get him, get him!

The truck caught up with the boy in minutes; another ten meters and he would have been crushed by it, but he turned into the field and ran, light-footed, along the freshly turned soil diagonally toward the barn. The truck turned, too, but got stuck in a ditch; the men jumped out and ran after him, but the soil was loose and held tight to their feet; they fell behind. But Markel threw the driver from the cab, got behind the wheel, backed up deftly and went around the field on the road and reached the barn right after the boy. By then the men showed up, grim, angered by the chase; their eyes attracted by the furrows, where lay stones churned up by the plow, red and purple, so smooth, so comfortable, just begging to be picked up . . . A man offhandedly lifted one, hefted it to test its weight, and another man followed, then a second, third, fourth, fifth . . . Behind them the women and children hollered, running across the field, and Markel blocked the road to the gates with the truck. He turned off the engine.

The boy waited for the adults to come closer, turned his back on them and faced the barn gates—and opened them with his gaze, the padlock shackle burst, it fell from the eyelets and a long echo resounded in the hills, the birds feeding in the plantings flew up in the distance, a motley boar herd dashed across the field; the men dropped their stones.

The clear autumn light, with an iodine tang, burst into the barn.

It was empty.

You could roll a ball through it.

But everyone shivered from that emptiness.

They sensed it was not empty.

It cried out about the losses, the victims; about those who were gone and would be no more.

Markel seemed stunned; he was remembering, for the first time in decades, how he had suffered with those voids; you go in a house and you can see right off that someone had been here, had lived here: voids. You can't fill it up with furniture, you can't hang a rug on the wall over it. That's when he invented the word: voided. He learned how to dig them out, so that life could reconnect over them, heal, regrow flush without a scar. Not with pliers or ax; not with iron, not with salt, only with live hands, strong hands; you pull them out, squash them, and then bring them here to the barn, where else could those voids go, this was the very place for them, this was the beginning and the end, this is where they came from.

That was why the others, the younger ones didn't remember, didn't understand that he had done his work; that was why the barn had to be so big.

Markel could no longer see that the villagers were there, downcast in confusion, hiding their eyes. He saw others, of a different human breed, tanned, dark, who had stood there, rounded up from the entire region, and also avoiding looking at the barn's gates.

The rest of his life seemed like a dream, a tale, and the truth was that one day when a dusty car drove into the village and a foreign officer asked if anyone spoke German there, he responded. He had been a prisoner as a young soldier in the imperialistic war, and he could *sprecht* a bit. He responded thinking that the officer would ask for directions, he wasn't the first, and would pay with a cigarette. But when the officer started asking about sheds and barns, he decided that he was a rear-guard officer, a quartermaster who requisitioned grain and cattle, moving the goods around, and readily said, there is this big barn beyond the village, empty, built for sugar beets.

He guarded it that night. Those were the officer's orders. They gave him a rifle, out of the weapons abandoned by the Soviets, a pea coat, and a lantern. He guessed what would happen in the morning, because he understood their talk. He walked along the length of the walls, lighting the way with the lantern, trying not to listen to what was being done in the barn; acutely feeling the cold wind, the dew, his life, which would have years, decades, if he could only stand through, walk through this night, the long night at the end of September.

Well, his life did turn out to be long; longer than many. It could have ended there, if that clever boy, who climbed out the ventilation shaft in the narrow round window over the gate, had escaped; he fell out awkwardly, hurt his leg, and Markel found him by his groans in the field, like a wounded baby hare.

"Where are you, little Jew boy, little yid kid; yiddie kiddie, come out, come out, wherever you are, I'll find you, and the kraut will eat you, salt and pepper, milk and honey, where are you?"

Markel remembered how he later locked the barn and threw the key in the Moss Swamp, to join them, mowed down by automatic guns and dumped into the peat bog.

He did not see that the villagers had dispersed, retreated, or that the boy had run off, or that he was not looking for the fugitive in the night field, muttering and whispering Jew boy, but had reached the Moss Swamp and was walking into the bog, the water up to his chest and soon the black stinking slime would pour into his mouth.

That evening, Markel's nephew, Markel Junior, took the lantern, pea coat, and rifle from his uncle's house; he gave the neighbors, the villagers gathered at the administration office, cautiously gabbling, a steady look and said calmly, "Go home, people. I will be on watch."

The village slept like the dead that night. In the morning they found the boy unconscious by the farthest fence.

It seemed to be him, but not him; he was faded, pale, white-skinned, and fair-haired, like all the locals. He still couldn't talk, but it was good that he didn't.

The old orchard froze to the roots that winter; they cut it down in the spring for firewood and burned it in their stoves. In the spring Markel Junior bought a new padlock in the city for the barn, stronger than the old one, foreign-made, thirty-six rubles according to the receipt.

A horrendous price.

THE LETTER Й

Click, click, click.

On the InterCity Express train, the fingers of a passenger were clacking on keys.

Click.

Click, click. Click, click, click, click, click.

Click-click.

Click-click-click.

Clickclickclickclickclickclick.

Click-click.

Click.

Ivanov got out his earplugs and squeezed the flexible plastic into his ears, blocking the sound with foam.

He could still hear it, but not as harshly. The ringing *c* was almost gone. Just the flat hiccup of the pressed keys.

It was a late train. The car was practically empty. He could have moved away. But he had failed to seize upon his initial indignation, the spontaneous reaction that he always allowed to dissipate. And now he sat there, angry for nothing, suffering over the passive, expectant, and amorphous feelings he had instead of the solid reflexes that generate clear and unambivalent actions in other people.

The clicking—she had long, hard nails—seemed to strike

at his joints, a secret, dormant acupuncture of the body. His body was dislocated, like a stifled sentence cut up into parts by chalk lines on the school blackboard.

Her computer screen showed tables and graphics. A business presentation. The words she was typing must have been the most clichéd, worn, and tattered ones, like profit-loss, debit-credit, percent, finance. Hackneyed, sullied words known to everyone.

But it was not the words that were striking his body, cutting it up and paralyzing it. It was the sound of nascent letters, all those audible scales and imprints: *click, click.*

It was the rhythm of his childhood.

He lay in the cradle, wordless, not quite here yet, seeking the first connections with the world. In the next room his grandmother clattered on the typewriter all day long—and sometimes through the night, if the work was urgent.

Loudly, then quietly. Quickly or slowly. Speedwriting, with descending piano passages. The audible imprints of letters filled the air like buzzing insects. Grandmother kept the windows shut so drafts would not scatter the pages, and he, an infant, absorbed the sounds. The tightly packed typewriter bars on metal arms that crisply struck the paper. Struck and embossed. Typed.

Red rashes appeared on him early. Intermittent, come and go, sometimes here, sometimes there—diatheses. His family thought they might be a reaction to dust or poplar fluff. To the fumes of nearby cooling towers, the stench of the paste factory. To the ubiquitous cockroaches. To eggs.

They were chafe marks, swelling from letters. His grandmother typed and retyped him, typed on him, as if he were a text that an editor kept correcting. Diatheses and rashes, yes, from letters. From the stinging metal letter heads. From the actual tempo and energy of the typing, because she did not compose and edit mere silly articles or penny-ante dissertations but documents that determined life and death.

That was how he entered life, grew up all rewritten, reworked: a creature with a dozen chrysalises and starts. Vacillating, wavering, and therefore endowed with a strange gift that revealed itself gradually.

A gift for imitation.

He was more than a simple parodist.

He did not repeat, he borrowed, he stole.

He stole other people's words.

It all began innocently. The philology department: he had followed in his grandmother's footsteps, she was an esteemed professor. Student skits at the theater studio, where they liked Aesopian word games, sketches with intimations of banned books. And of course, parodies, mockery, intellectual put-downs of the classics of Socialist Realism and Marxism that only they could understand.

He flourished there. He became the department's official jokester: one prank after another. Setting up meetings by calling from a phone booth using someone else's voice.

Pretending to be a rector and demanding grade changes. Once he even canceled a *subbotnik*, a Saturday workday, by mimicking the voice of the assistant dean. As for the amateur theatricals, the official anniversary celebrations, where toward the end of the evening he could sneak in something piquant with an anti-Soviet flavor, and the Party supervisor would shut his eyes, with a small grin, to say I understand, young people need to let off steam, just don't overdo it.

He was Lenin onstage. Dzerzhinsky. Marx. Even Reagan. And backstage, after the performance, in tipsy company—he was Stalin and Mao and Hitler and Brezhnev. A riot! The girls fell for him. One asked him to talk like Alain Delon in bed. He wasn't proud, so why not. He really did sound exactly like Delon, no one could tell it wasn't actually him . . . He was developing an act, performing in apartments, semiunderground clubs, getting paid, making connections.

Then he was called in to meet with the deputy dean for student affairs. He knew that was a complex post, one foot in the university, the other in the KGB. He went without anxiety, the dean wanted to discuss the new theater production that had been announced in the student paper. He was certain that other students called in for a dressing down were told to come in a different way. He was stopped in the hallway by the Komsomol secretary of their class, who said, drop by to see Fedyanin when you have a moment, he wants to congratulate you.

But there in Fedyanin's office, all his little jokes were compiled and presented differently: Article 70 of the Criminal

Code. Anti-Soviet agitation and propaganda. Especially the time he most cynically mocked the speech by the Comrade General Secretary at the Party Congress. Worst case—trial and sentence. Best case—expulsion from college and the draft. He would be sent on active duty. In Afghanistan.

"You were born into a Soviet family, a respectable family," said the heavyset, boar-like Fedyanin with feigned regret. "Look at you now."

He wanted to reply, "I wasn't born to anyone. My grandmother conceived me on the typewriter."

But he said nothing.

"It is only for your grandmother's sake," Fedyanin said, "that I will try to help you. But you have to help, too. Do you understand? Do you understand well?"

He nodded. Now he understood. He understood all too well.

He never met with Fedyanin again. He told his pals that he got lectured over his unsuccessful act in the October Revolution anniversary celebration.

"We need more Soviet content. More!" he said in Fedyanin's voice.

Everyone laughed.

He met with the agent at a safe house apartment in a residential building. His handler, Major Demyanin—Fedyanin and Demyanin, they rhymed, like a bell—first questioned him thoroughly, calmly: how did they joke, how did they parody, who participated, who organized, who laughed, who didn't.

Don't be afraid, don't be shy, it's just between us, this is work. For some reason Demyanin needed to know whether it was professional parody or just amateurish? Could it be qualified as artistic or just homemade?

Well, he gave him the General Secretary.

Demyanin could barely control his laughter. His eyes showed that he appreciated the brazenness.

He asked, "Can you do me? You've heard the General Secretary a hundred times on TV. You've had time to rehearse."

Ivanov replied, "Can you do me? You've heard the General Secretary a hundred times on TV. You've had time to rehearse."

Demyanin shuddered. He grew pale, he flushed red, breathed out and asked politely, "Can you do it again? For example: Peter Piper picked a peck of pickled peppers."

You could tell the man had graduated from the philology department. Had a flair for words.

"Can you do it again? For example: Peter Piper picked a peck of pickled peppers," Ivanov replied and continued in Demyanin's voice, "In the name of the Committee on State Security I thank you, Comrade Ivanov."

Demyanin sagged. The major was overwhelmed.

It's scary, uncanny, to meet someone with absolute pitch for voices. It's like smashing into a mirror and drawing blood.

That was Ivanov's secret stake in the game. He sensed that the hammer letters had worked over the major, tapped on his joints, bones, and tendons, and the major had been turned, conquered, even though he didn't know it.

Soon after he was dialing a number that Demyanin had written on a piece of paper from a phone booth on Pokrovka. It was a familiar trick: just recently he had phoned the class beauty and pretended to be the goofy Kostik madly in love. He knew Kostik's voice. Demyanin had played a good recording of the new voice in which he had to say a few words. And handed him a roll of two-kopeck coins, wrapped in heavy paper, the coins clean and bare, straight from the mint. Ivanov smiled at this niggling accounting seriousness—the cheap price of human destiny. Two kopecks—a box of matches. Two kopecks—a pack of aspirin. Two kopecks—a round at target practice. Two kopecks—an envelope.

Two kopecks swallowed by the coin phone, *click, ring, ring, ring, ring*, then a calm voice: "Hello."

Ivanov said in the fake voice: "Hi! Come at eight. Bring the agreed. See you."

And hung up.

Exactly the phrase "the agreed," not quite grammatical. Two kopecks—a phrase. He still had forty-nine coins.

Later they took him to an institute outside the city, recorded him on tape, making him use other people's voices to speak loudly and softly, whisper and half-whisper, moan, howl, weep, scream, and stammer. It turned out he could mimic everything except singing. He could not sing in someone else's voice. The vocal cords couldn't take it.

He was also studied there by graphologists, masters of forged handwriting; specialists in meanings and intonations, whose work was not only to imitate penmanship but the manner of speech, the linguistic portrait. They discovered his second gift: writing.

The theoreticians clashed in battle, which was primary, which secondary, sound or letter. He said nothing, feigning ignorance, even though he knew that for him the letter came first, his grandmother had hammered letters into him, letters, letters, letters consumed him.

Sound—in his case—was secondary. Even though historically, sound came before sign.

Thus his new life began.

Officially, following his grandmother's example, he went to graduate school and sweated at the department writing his dissertation. But once in a while he was asked to say a few rehearsed words into the phone. Or write on a piece of paper a paragraph or two selected by technicians as suitable for the planned mise-en-scène.

The papers changed: a lined sheet from a notebook, a scrap of newspaper, a form. The words changed: confessions, accusations, last words. He turned fate lines, changed biographies, and his natural alibi.

If life were such that it was possible for him, a sorcerer who destroys the original, to exist as a phenomenon, then also possible was another person, who would of his own will say or write the words needed by the KGB. If there was no original, there could be no truth. And there was no guilt over forgery, since there was no forgery. There was only the primordial, extramoral, natural power of the gift, which was given and therefore had the natural right to express itself.

Click, click, click—the neighboring passenger was in a hurry, banging away. Her earphones were probably playing pop nonsense, a contemporary compote of sounds, *boom-boom-boom.*

Music like that was not dangerous.

Sometimes it happened: in the middle of a concert, in the blizzard of a musical movement there would sound a sad little hammer as counterpoint, the only instance in the whole symphony, and in the midst of the consonant, intertwined flow of notes Ivanov would suddenly hear the striking of the typewriter's lever, the brief cry of a letter being born, its existence still whole, undivided into graphic and phonetic, and Ivanov would be pierced by a sweet shock in which punishment and caress combined into a single blow.

Click, click.

The computer's plastic keys.

Their sound was a tickle, an itch, playing on blunted nerves.

The layout was Latin script, QWERTY. Foreign letters were being born. They were not subject to his power. His gift existed only in his native tongue. Foreign letters mocked him, would not submit, would not be memorized, would not be printed. Even the alphabets would not stay in his head.

This was his leash and his brand. He was a tributary of the Russian language, and therefore he was doomed to serve the power of the Russian word, and through it, the Russian government.

Here, in a foreign country, in a foreign language, his gift weakened quickly if he did not feed it.

In the first few years he basically begged for scraps. He ate in émigré restaurants, all the Kalinkas, Moskvas, and Hermitages, reading the menus, listening to his countrymen speak. He shopped in Russian stores, slowly going through the products, reading the ingredients, veal, fat, salt, water, pepper, bay leaf, onion, preservative number whatever; his ears took in the chatter of the staff, Manya, Vanya, ring it up, bring this; wandered in libraries, in the pathetic Russian literature sections that had mystery novels with worn covers and two or three volumes of Tolstoy and Dostoevsky; checked used book stores where one could find émigré editions from the 1920s. Or, he would tag along with Russian tourists on excursions, joining the human hive, catching their simple "looka that," "wow," "no really," digesting the rough provincial phrases among which once in a while a pure linguistic emerald would glimmer, crude and poetic, low and life-giving.

He sat close to them in tourist restaurants, enjoying over a beer their moans and groans, burping and lip smacking, the primitive and familiar sounds of feeding.

But that wasn't enough food. Just a snack. If he had been able to walk down a Moscow street and swallow its voice, he would have been sated and intoxicated. Forget hospitable Moscow. Moscow had sent him here. Here was where he was to live. Here he would get orders and perform deeds.

He discovered how to eat his fill, get the nourishment he needed almost by accident. A doctor's prescription.

Yes, a doctor, his own physician, a ceremonious old man, an old doctor.

"The waters," said Herr Ostermeier. "You need to take the waters, it's beneficial, invigorating, you will relax, your sleep will normalize, the tactile effects."

Ivanov almost burst out laughing. The waters. Greetings, Turgenev and Dostoevsky, greetings, nineteenth century, greetings, Russians in Europe! Impossible! What am I, a literary character?

But at home, he reconsidered. Off he went, like the damned, to Baden-Baden three hundred kilometers away—to soak.

He had never liked water. He liked stone.

And in fact, the pools did not impress him. Water, splash and splish, it flows, it washes, and so what?

Shabby hotels. Rheumatic doormen. Elderly pugs on the leashes of elderly pugs of the human breed. In damp grottos, greenish marble masks with mouths deformed by calcified growths spat out not volcanic streams but merely warm, slightly steaming water. Boring. Dozens of costly gold watches in the show windows of the commercial streets ticked out the same empty, useless time of the aging wealthy.

As if to counter the quiet and prosperous ennui, Russian toxic goose bumps, hair bulbs filled with swollen bubbles of horror that the Russian organism breathes from within, covered his body. His grandmother had awakened them in him when she typed. He had a bright, painful rash, like those in his childhood from the hammering of embossed letters.

At first, he thought he had picked up a fungus, some vile disease, and hurried to a dermatologist. But as he stopped on the bridge over the river with the ridiculous name Oos, he heard a Russian party picnicking on the shore and automatically stopped to listen and charge his strength . . . He realized that his gift was charged and as strong as it had been only in Russia.

He later guessed the secret, he read the landscape. He learned that this whole area from Karlsruhe to Basel was the Upper Rhine Graben, a rare scar in Central Europe, the imprint of tectonic activity not stilled since ancient times.

Oh, how he was struck by the word Graben, *grab-grob-grub*, both Russian and German at once.

He read some geological articles and pictured the rift in cross section: a seam, a hidden fault, a zone of chaotic compressions and stresses of the earth's crust.

The rocky foundations of Germany and France repelled each other along the Rhine line, giving rise to tectonic trembling, stone cracking, noise, and confusion.

Hence the geothermal springs, hot, salty waters that rose up through the cracks under pressure and poured out onto the surface: excess, excess from the hot hell's kitchen of the depths.

And Russian writers, vampires, sensitive to the gaps in reality, to the abysses under the fragile cover of existence, felt the hidden mechanics of this place, and were drawn to it.

The local water, oversaturated with salt, thick as broth, fed and watered the city, pouring out in thermal baths.

The tricky element of water turned into a constant game with fate, into the flickering of cards and the rotation of the roulette wheel, like a water mill wheel. And beneath the earth, under the foundations of the gambling houses, the gears of tectonics spun, the impulses generated by the stretching of the earth's crust burst and faded away. The water carried upward, into pools and bathing places, the echo of the netherworld, the hot voices of the underworld, and the clatter of underground hammers.

That was what the Russian language fed on.

The passenger had stopped typing. Now he could hear the muffled beat of the train wheels. She wore a white mask with a valve pin. She looked like a scientist in a lab (everyone now looked like a scientist or a bank robber). The mask created the sense of mystery and danger. Yes, exactly that mix, mystery and danger. It was always hovering over Grandmother's desk with the typewriter.

Other children wanted pets, a cat or dog. Ivanov wanted the typewriter, a mechanical creature.

He was drawn to the slit on its red metal surface, which gave him a view into the dark, graphite-scented womb where the mechanical stamens of the levers, topped with letters, were gathered in a crown. Having only a vague idea of the mysteries of sex, he nevertheless unmistakably identified it as a bud, a place of copulation, of pollination. The color of the machine itself was scarlet, frivolous, disturbing, like lipstick; and this only added to the seduction of the slit.

When no one was home, Ivanov would peel off the gray fabric cover Grandmother put on the Yugoslavian machine that turned the beauty into a hideous swollen mushroom without a foot. He caressed the corners and surfaces. He touched the keys. He pressed, carefully bringing the arm with the letter right up to the paper.

He simply could not understand why the letters on the keyboard were not in alphabetical order. Why were they mixed up? Was it a code? He had never seen any other typewriters and thought that they certainly had normal keyboards in accordance with the alphabet. Grandmother, a professor and editor, must have a special machine for special writing.

He had seen that the texts came out of it in the most ordinary language—but was it? Was there a second, false bottom, a code, a secret message? There must have been a reason why she often locked the door when she was working and would not let him in?

The alphabet began with the letter A, a simple, open letter imbued with innumerable exclamations.

The keyboard with Й.

Й—What kind of letter was that?

Not even a letter, more of a misunderstanding. A hiccup. A squeak as if someone were being squashed.

But Grandmother's machine, red like blood, like the Kremlin stars, like the country's flag, proved that Й had primacy in the alphabet, mysterious and inaccessible, like a person reaching up.

Once he recognized it, he noticed Й nodding to him in school dictations and textbooks, on store signs, in notices on lampposts, on newspaper stands, posters, schedules. Followed him in crowds, in the Metro. A figure in a gray hat, into which the small line atop the letter had turned.

He sensed no danger from his follower. He did feel a powerful connection between them. Й-Man had become part of him, and he wanted to represent him on paper, not handwritten but printed, by the typewriter.

Grandmother did not allow him to even touch the machine, as if it was a precious musical instrument.

If it had belonged to anyone else, his mother or father, he would have done it long ago. But the typewriter belonged to Grandmother. And her things were untouchable, that was the law at home.

His grandmother was a mountain. Her bulk was not the sponginess of cakes, the puffiness of featherbeds, but the heavy bulk of flattened limestone, of mountainous layered folds.

It seemed that if she stood up abruptly she might shake the house. She was cramped everywhere; every garment was too small for her. The fat people in his picture books were always bad: priests, capitalists, bursting with gluttony and greed.

But his grandmother ate little and modestly. It was all Lenten, tasteless, boiled. Her mountain body grew not from food but on its own, like tree fungus or tumors.

Her face did not belong to her body. It seemed to be taken from someone else. A miniature head: spectral gray hair pulled into an elegant knot. Thin, with the skull bones showing beneath the skin like fragile porcelain. Pointed bird-like features. The head of an ethereal, weightless creature, capable of turning into a sylph, of flying as if there were no weight or gravity.

Grandmother, a heavyweight, loved the ballet. She went to the theater or watched on television. He peeked. A strange thing happened in those minutes. Her real body, young, buried in the mountain of flesh, would awaken. It trembled, repeating the dance movements, shaking the deposits of fat.

Ivanov was afraid of her. She talked without opening her mouth, whispering words, spitting them out with her lips. Sometimes she forgot and revealed her steel teeth.

He sensed the close resemblance of that mouth with rows of dull steel crowns to the dark slit in the typewriter where the arms with letters formed a crescent smirk.

His father had begged her so many times to change to gold crowns or get false teeth, smooth, white, chic!

But Grandmother, who loved fashion, lipsticks, updo hairstyles, jewelry, refused outright. She smiled in an ugly way, like a snarl, baring her steel teeth with a mysterious pride, as if they were the most important, precious, and supernatural part of her organism.

Bewildered, his father would retreat.

He sensed that Grandmother's teeth had a vulpine biting power, related to the biting mechanical strength of the typewriter that embossed letters on paper.

More clicking. Infrequent bursts, short sequences. The passenger was correcting her text, that was clear.

She thought that if no one could see her computer screen, her writing would remain a secret. Live, breathe into your mask, sweet thing. Ivanov won't be able to read your scribbles by ear.

They were almost at the station. Before the station there came the bridge over the Rhine. Pause. A great blank.

You don't have steel teeth, dearie, and you are typing ordinary letters, just one of myriads that exist.

You will get out at the station and go down into the U-Bahn or take a taxi. No one will follow you; you won't slip by like a shadow; you won't appear in the crowd wearing a gray hat of a breve, the curved diacritical mark hovering in the upper reaches of the letter Й.

God bless you with ignorance, my girl.

Here was the bridge, and the hulk of the cathedral moved toward them on the left like a horned clot of fog.

It wasn't visible in the dark of a December night, but Ivanov always saw and felt it.

Its two peak towers reigned over the city. Two sharp cones jabbed into the skies, hardened lava of the inferno like the volcanic stalagmites, "black smokers," that grow as they are belched out of the tectonic breaks on the ocean bottom.

The whole city was pierced through; Gothic spires grew out of its fruitful riverine soil like the clawed tails of sleeping underground dragons.

The cathedral was a stone sponge. It blackened, it absorbed fog and rain. It was built so that the unspoken majesty of the Word could breathe inside. But the Word had penetrated its stone pillars, penetrated its buttresses, and it towered over the city like a giant letter: Н or Й.

Ivanov knew it was Й. From his balcony, he could see the very top, the two axes without the crossbar.

But it was there, of course. It was understood.

The chimeras screamed into the night in high-pitched limestone voices. That was why herds of letters roamed the city at night. Their metal-shod shoes clattered on the ancient cobblestones.

It wouldn't do to run into their gang, they would give you a good beating, count your ribs for you.

You would wake up and you wouldn't be you anymore, your life rewritten, a new name in your passport, and another face in the dancing reflection of the store window.

But he was not afraid of them.

He was protected by Й, who came with him from the homeland.

Й was the most Russian letter, the most Russian sound, something compressed in the throat, an unborn, rotten, swallowed moan: Й.

He had learned to find strength from the shape of the cathedral; he had started being followed around the city.

The fate of language. Someone in a hat.

Й.

He. Masculine gender.

Ivanov loved walking along the Rhine.

Large rivers gave birth to cultures. They gave them their first gods and whispered the first letters of their languages.

He was happy there by the rushing water, even though he did not like either the poetry of Heine or *Das Rheingold*.

He went there to observe.

The Rhine barges, as long as German compound words, traveled up and down the river. They carried gravel, grain, metal, sand. And some, with black sides and the lowest draft, carried letters.

He learned that secret of Europe almost accidentally.

He was renting a remote little house in the Alps for a month. Demyanin, a major general by then, had ordered him to create a suicide note and plans for two telephone calls, which their subject was supposedly going to make before writing the note and killing himself.

The subject lived in a mansion in a village not far away. Ivanov had seen him a few times in the restaurant in the square. The refugee Russian banker was hiding here and writing his memoirs. Ivanov was slowly, in great detail, writing his death.

The note would be read by graphologists and linguists. They would analyze the handwriting and turns of phrase. They would certainly recognize a forgery.

But he guaranteed authenticity.

Whatever a computer program that simulates voices can generate, another program can recognize and expose.

But he guaranteed authenticity.

There in the Alps, he wrote in the morning and evening and spent the day in the mountains. He wandered in the crevasses overgrown with dark pines and breathed the cold of the snow. Й, his constant companion, did not bother him there; Ivanov met him only on the streets of Geneva, where he had gone three times to meet with his handler. Oh, Geneva streets, the trodden paths of Russian revolutionaries and Russian spies! Й was in his element there, doubling, tripling: a little man in a gray hat.

However, Ivanov sensed that even in the remote spot, he was not alone. Deer dashed across the slopes, owls hooted, eagles circled overhead. But there was someone else as well. In the cliffs themselves, in the roots of the mountains.

He listened closely, putting his ear to the cracks, and he heard the stone flesh, thawing after the winter, crackling.

Beyond that was another sound, hidden, distant, muffled. Like a miner's chisel tapping the rock. Or a typesetter.

Having lost his way in the evening, he decided to follow the brook and found a cave. A heavy mountain brow overhung the water and beneath it, surrounded by ocher spurs, its mouth showed darkly. He entered without a light, feeling that he was in man's first home before he knew how to build huts. Here, in the womb-like dark, speech was born and hands drew the first signs with pieces of flint on the limestone walls. He pressed himself against the clay wall, softened by spring waters, as if he wanted to become disembodied, to return as inanimate clay into the womb of the earth—and he saw into the cave's darkness.

He saw the sullen, wordless little kobolds working in the old drifts. They chiseled out stone and carved letters, the old Fraktur letters of the now defunct typefaces with which Germany proclaimed its will to Europe, with which orders for the execution of Jews and certificates of racial purity were printed eight decades ago.

This was where the primary ore of language was mined. The source of its power. But those letters were no longer used, for the swastika shows in their spidery features, and the meanings of the words for which they were created no longer counted. The new, eco-friendly letters were made from recycled plastic in a factory near Bonn.

Since the new words were not identical to the old ones, no one could pronounce the old spell, unlock the gates under the mountains, and free the kobolds from their labor. There under the Alps, the old language was still produced, because it takes longer to die than humans, and the kobolds had no understanding of history. The gates opened in one direction only, and the kobolds handed over the only thing they knew how to produce.

That was why the secret service barges carried those dangerous letters along the Rhine to sink them in the North Sea, creating artificial reefs that help tame storms.

As he fell asleep in the cottage, he listened to the wind and the quiet hammering of the kobolds in the roots of the mountains and wondered: How did this work in Russia? Surely the old forest spirits died during the Civil War, as did the enchanted forests where they hewed the old tsarist letters, *yat* and *er*, from linden and oak.

The new ones, he thought, what were they made of? He answered his own question: metal. Black cast iron. There was a factory in the Urals built in the 1930s that was not listed as being part of any department. A heavy press on its own stamped the letters of the new age, the new Bolshevik alphabet.

His university studies flashed through his mind. He remembered that Й, even though it existed in the prerevolutionary alphabet, did not have the full rights of a letter. It was merely tolerated. A sponger. It was not always included in the alphabet. Sometimes it was recognized, sometimes it was deleted. It was squeezed by its relatives i, и, and the *izhitsa* descended from epsilon.

In 1918 the Red reform of orthography did away with the iota and izhitsa for being relics of the past, like priests, capitalists, and kulaks. There was room for Й! Й was put in all the textbooks, it took up pride of place. In 1934 it officially entered the alphabet.

Yes, thought Ivanov, that was quite a letter. Just like my grandmother, a girl from a peasant family who grabbed her chance! Little letter, you took advantage of the moment and won the pot! If not for the revolution you would have stayed playing bit parts, you would have worked in newspapers or books.

But you figured it out, you originated in commissar semen. By 1943 you were a Soviet Letter, you were immortal! Everyone had to learn you, and no text could do without you now, excuse me, let me through.

Yes, 1934, thought Ivanov. Just in time. On the eve, so to speak. As if they were waiting for you before starting the arrests, writing transcripts of interrogations and sentences for execution by firing squad. How would the investigators and prison wardens have managed without you, Й?

And what have you become, Й? You are now as truncated as memory, an echo of the age, an echo of all the cries of pain and horror, all the screaming and weeping. You are what is left of the interrogators' "Hey" and the prisoners' "Aiee" and "Oy" and now you have recognized yourself and wander restlessly.

Back home, Ivanov had dinner and sat on the balcony with a glass of wine and a cigarette. In the distance, beyond the rooftops—thankfully, they did not build skyscrapers here—he could make out the twin cathedral towers in the moonlit sky. He was waiting for the moon to appear exactly over the towers. At that moment, the present and past combined for him.

In his childhood apartment, he could see two factory chimneys from the window. The moon would sometimes hang above them this way, with the lunar disk filling the gap between the two structures with silver light. That glow hypnotized him, imbued him with anxious determination, and once, when no one was home, he followed the path of moonlight into his grandmother's room, removed the cover from the typewriter, sat on the edge of her broad armchair, glanced at the silvery matte whiteness of the paper, sensed the coordinated readiness of the mechanism, and boldly struck the outermost key:

Й

Letter? Person?

Letterperson?

Й Й

Й Й Й

Й Й Й Й Й Й

Й Й

A line?

A column of people?

Who were these people?

The rhythm of typing turned into a march, and all those

letter people walked while he typed, lived and breathed while he typed, and it was important to type

Й Й

their life and fate lines, their marching rows

Й Й Й Й Й Й Й

Й Й Й Й Й Й Й

Й Й Й Й Й Й Й

Й Й Й Й Й Й Й

The page ended. He loaded a second, third, fourth page, banging out line after line.

The key fell off the arm. It bounced along the table, rolled on the floor, and grew still somewhere.

As if it had escaped.

First Ivanov thought he would find it easily. Big deal—turn on the light!

But the key was gone. He felt every square of the parquet floor, turned his flashlight on distant dusty corners; in vain.

The Й had run away and the clock was nearing eight. He hid the ruined pages under his mattress, he moved the typewriter ribbon so the Й's would not be visible, adjusted the armchair, replaced the cover. He had completely forgotten the ecstasy of typing, the letter people. His pathetic hope was that Grandmother would think the key fell off by itself. He knew he was kidding himself. You couldn't fool her.

The next day, when his parents were out, she gave him a whipping, using his father's army belt. She struck without energy, but the heavy belt did the work, thrashing his buttocks, and he felt terrible that his ass, a dirty place, was being touched by the five-pointed star on the buckle.

His grandmother did not tell his parents. The fugitive key never did turn up.

Years later, when he was a graduate student and already knew Major Demyanin, knew his gift, he went into her room to collect the papers and books she asked him to bring to the hospital; barely recovered from her heart attack and contrary to doctors' orders, she was desperate to get back to work.

"The file on the right corner of the desk, bring that for sure," she said on the phone. "That's the most urgent and important editing."

She was certain that he would not open the file. But he was a different person now, one who had learned Demyanin's lessons. Ivanov overheard careful conversations at the department. He remembered the deputy dean telling him: "For your grandmother's sake."

Grandmother, grandmother, why do you have steel teeth?

He loosened the strings on the cardboard folder, tied with a cunning double knot. Inside was a thin stack of sheets. He took the first one from the top.

He still remembered it. His memory for letters was perfect.

Typewriter system (name): "Moscow" No. 37645
Name of the institution: Experimental Plant of Sanitary Ware

Address: Lentvaris, Charno str., 15.

Keyboard via ribbon:

§ № – / « : , . _ % ? !
й ц у к е н г ш щ з х ъ
ф ы в а п р о л д ж э)
я ч с м и т ь б ю ё
+ 1 2 3 4 5 6 7 8 9 0 =
Й Ц У К Е Н Г Ш Щ З Х Ъ
Ф Ы В А П Р О Л Д Ж Э)
Я Ч С М И Т Ь Б Ю Ё

§ № – / « : , . _ % ? !
й ц у к е н г ш щ з х ъ
ф ы в а п р о л д ж э)
я ч с м и т ь б ю ё
+ 1 2 3 4 5 6 7 8 9 0 =
Й Ц У К Е Н Г Ш Щ З Х Ъ
Ф Ы В А П Р О Л Д Ж Э)
Я Ч С М И Т Ь Б Ю Ё

The Lithuanian Soviet Socialist Republic is one of the Baltic republics that is part of the multinational family of our Motherland. The Lithuanian people have passed a long historical path in the struggle for freedom, equality, and independence. Many conquerors, Nazi occupiers tried to change the historical development of the Lithuanian people, to impose their will and order upon them. Currently,

Latvians, Estonians, Armenians, and other representatives of the peoples of the USSR live in the Lithuanian SSR next to Lithuanians. Thanks to the wise Leninist national policy pursued by the Communist Party of the Soviet Union, all the peoples of our country live in a friendly, cohesive family.

OUR TIME IS RICH IN IMPORTANT SOCIOECONOMIC AND POLITICAL EVENTS: THE STRUGGLE OF PEOPLES FOR PEACE, FOR NATIONAL AND SOCIAL LIBERATION, SOCIAL TRANSFORMATIONS IN DEVELOPING COUNTRIES, AND THE DEVELOPMENT OF CONTACTS IN THE SOCIALIST COMMUNITY, THE STEADILY INCREASING EXCHANGE OF CULTURAL VALUES BETWEEN PEOPLES AND THE EMERGENCE OF A NEW SOCIAL COMMUNITY— THE SOVIET PEOPLE—ALL THIS NECESSARILY INVOLVES MILLIONS OF PEOPLE OF DIFFERENT NATIONS IN MUTUAL COMMUNICATION.

Sample taken "_____" _____ 1988.

He picked up other pages.

The Estonian Soviet Socialist Republic . . .

The Azerbaijan Soviet Socialist Republic . . .

The Moldavian Soviet Socialist Republic . . .

What was this nonsense? What gibberish about the struggle of peoples for peace?

Then he understood what she was composing.

It was the template for testing typewriters. He knew the KGB did it. But he had never thought about their algorithm.

He pictured thousands of typewriters repeating the text

dictated by a KGB operative and written by his grandmother, a doctor of philology.

First, a warm-up, a simple movement of the keys.

Then the lesson. Dictation.

Apparently, it wasn't enough to take a sample! Every machine had to repeat the mantra, the spell. Not a random collection of words but: THE STRUGGLE OF PEOPLES FOR PEACE.

Absurd. Irrational. And therefore delightful.

That was the power of language.

His fingertip touched the new Й key. For the first time he felt a direct relationship with his grandmother. Not in the sense of closeness or similarity. In the sense of a curse.

She worked for them. And so did he.

She was first, and that somehow excused him, turned his contact with the committee by a quarter or third into a farce, a family comedy, gave him the indulgence of recidivism, heredity, even some kind of inevitability.

But he sensed it was all in the letters.

In that fugitive Й, which was the key to their secret.

The letters were the ones ruling their fate. Letters that Grandmother had loyally served all her life.

She lay dying in the same room, near the same typewriter that stood by the headboard.

She had been sick for years and years. The disease gradually consumed the fat of her body; on her deathbed she was a little girl sewn into a wineskin of bloated skin.

She was leaving and taking the secret with her.

Her breathing, ragged and hoarse, suddenly evened. Only her fingers, the thin and nimble fingers of a typist, did not calm down, twitching as if they were typing.

"Breve, breve, breve," she whispered. A password, entry to the other world.

She passed away, with "breve" on her lips.

Closing her eyelids, he thought maybe she said "bravo"? Had he misheard? No, he could still hear it: breve.

Before calling the police and an ambulance, he circled the room looking for some message, sign, trace, even though he knew his grandmother would not stoop to the tackiness of a posthumous note. She could have said it. But she did not.

He mechanically touched her glasses, pills, inhaler, the last and closest things to her.

He saw something forgotten, turned smaller: the typewriter under its cover, silent for many years.

He took off the cover, sat down and placed his fingers on the keys, closing his eyes.

And it, confidante and servant, began to speak.

He felt a fine, ant-like prickling in his sensitive fingertips. The typewriter was dying along with its mistress, turning into just an object, metal, and the keys rattled in death agony under his fingers, typing spectral letters through the dried ribbon:

LONG LIVE THE SOVIET UNION

He looked at them, as if regarding them from a height, and decided that the letters were composed of female and male bodies dressed in white T-shirts, shorts, tights, put together like parts of a rebus.

Made from the bodies of gymnasts who froze in positions, straining their muscles, on the cobblestones of Red Square.

He was the Supreme Viewer on top of the Mausoleum looking down at them. They were sacrificing their young bodies to become the sacred slogan for him.

The strains of the march resounded. The parade columns moved on.

The phrase stood and there were no more bodies, only letters:

LONG LIVE THE SOVIET UNION

ДА ЗДРАВСТВУЕТ СОВЕТСКИЙ СОЮЗ

And yet he could distinguish one body, the smallest one, bent into a crescent: the line above the Й. The diacritic mark breve indicating a short vowel. He remembered it from the case of sorts in the underground printing house.

The girl was a feather.

The girl was a petal.

It was he, the Supremo, who saved her even though he had not given that order.

He saved her because he did not like typos. Everyone knew that very well. He had taught them that.

They had already taken that girl, the breve. They had knocked out her teeth during interrogations, torturing her for information about a Trotskyite student circle. Then it became clear that there was no replacement. There was no backup breve who had rehearsed the number. There were other girl gymnasts but they could not be held with out-stretched arms for the necessary length of time.

The word Soviet, СОВЕТСКИЙ, sovetsky, would not have the line over the И.

Someone smart down below had the breve girl released. And the interrogator arrested. There she was held high by men's hands, swallowing blood.

She truly was the breve. Exactly what was needed.

He was pleased.

He looked into the future and saw that they all, all the letter people, would be no more. They would burn like matches. But the breve girl would survive. The only one. Because the others could not turn completely into letters.

But she, the sufferer, could. She was a profound sign.

She managed.

He would reward her.

He would give her a long life and loyal service.

Ivanov took his fingers off the keys, but it was too late.

Without wanting to, he had learned everything the keys had typed.

Linguistic analyses of anti-Soviet documents.

Linguistic studies of anonymous denunciations, leaflets, and letters intercepted by the postal service.

All of Grandmother's works.

He sat on the balcony listening to the tireless squirrel scuf-fling around the tree—didn't they sleep at night?

The moon had left and December darkness hid the cathedral. Not a sound in the street, except for the *putt-putt* of the late-night pizza delivery moped.

Behind him in the room, a red typewriter stood on a special table that had belonged only to her.

He would go over, strike a key lightly, so the white paper would show:

Й.

THE NIGHT IS BRIGHT TONIGHT

The illuminated evening sky expanded, twisted, and spread serpentine corridors, curtains of incredible light, lemon, violet, grass green, aquamarine: a spectral rainbow, stranger, more illusory than a mirage.

It was as if a different world had spilled into ours, slipped in, hovered above us, preserving its shape and slowly dissolving: bizarre aerial molts, pearl icon covers, animated fogs from the other side of the firmament, colonies of cloud corals.

The shining veils grew heavier, clouded, joined with our matter and germinated in it; conception and birth at the same time, the painful conjunction of worlds, from which emerged a homeless matter, belonging to no one, ensconced in its own sphere, sought by invisible and disembodied ghosts and spirits to clothe themselves.

The sky arched, clinging to the scanty soils of the North: the desolate gray coasts of the Arctic seas, the hilly tundra lemon yellow with reindeer moss, the green larch hummocks. The radiance descended from the heights—into the earth, stone, and water, into the flesh of trees.

In those parts, yellow gas torches blazed from tall pipes, pointlessly illuminating the polar day and polar night: that was how surplus gas by-product was burned during oil production.

Thousands of torches simultaneously seemed to go out and then blazed anew, but the flames were the color of the radiance.

The workers on the pumps and drilling rigs froze, hearing the pressure rocking and banging underground, the shaitan rushing upward to break all the valves and emergency locks: the earth opened up.

The tundra wept with all its streams, and the humble reindeer cried, and the shepherds ran to the great-grandchildren of earlier shamans to find out what these spirits were that were coming out of the earth.

The radio stations of the Northern Sea Route resounded with wandering voices, hundreds of voices in different languages, sliding over all the bandwidths; the second mate on the bridge of the icebreaker leading a convoy past Neupokoev Island saw a flock of strange birds just ahead flying in a line, rather than in wedge formation.

The miners going down in elevators for the night shift heard the supports creaking within abandoned rocky faces far away, stones falling from the ceiling, and then a strange sound, like sludge on the river; someone was moving through the thickness of the bedrock.

The fishermen on a seiner sailing from Novaya Zemlya hooked something on the bottom with a trawl; both heavy and alive, it dragged the ship off course, and the experienced boatswain gave orders to drop the trawl.

Astronomers in the Pamir Mountains, above the clouds, saw star showers, which should not have been there, they were not listed in the guides, and yet in the North and East the stars flew from the sky, sparking like phosphorus match heads.

That night, icons wept and bled, memorial candles lit themselves; migrating storms of music, not written by anyone living, unborn music, were delivered and vanished in concert halls. In train stations, long-gone locomotive horns were heard; at distant railroad halts, at train crossing barriers in fields, strange trains were seen that were not on the schedule, trains of old cars no longer in service that must have been collected at distant depots filled with rubbish; in the Moscow Metro, especially in the old lines constructed in the 1930s, late-night passengers imagined that the empty platforms where cleaners were washing the floors were actually filled with people, as in rush hour; it was crowded, people were breathing, whispering, coughing, weeping, deciding the best route, wondering at the new lines and stations; in the tunnels, figures crossing the tracks could be seen through the windows, and the passengers sobered up and hastened to get off at any random station to breathe some air.

The air of the cities was also filled with the same whispers, as if monuments were talking to one another, and it seemed that the boulevards were full of people, and that the illumination burned with a ghostly, icy, northern light.

The Kremlin

Lt. General Burmistrov, commandant of the Kremlin, decided to sleep in his office; the parade rehearsal was scheduled for early morning. Of course, he could have slept at home, it wasn't far. But he particularly liked the Kremlin at night, empty, when only the overnight staff was there. The tourists were gone. The officials had left. The president, too. Just the Kremlin itself remained. The sacred seat of power. The place itself was a deity, the only one Burmistrov served.

He strolled along the river wall, listening to the whispers of the chatting fortress towers coming through the muffled noise of the city. Cold rose from the Moskva River, even though a warm night had been forecast. The general grew chilled and could not fall asleep. Out of the blue, he recalled how he had hated the Kremlin when he was young. He was sent to serve in the Kremlin's elite regiment. Special marching, winter guard duty by the Eternal Flame, an eternity before your shift ended, a cursed icy eternity, while before you there were free people, lovers who came to Alexandrovsky Park, carrying whiffs of home cooking, perfume, cigarettes, champagne . . .

Then, on the eve of demobilization, he was called in for a chat and offered the chance to enroll in the school. Of course, he accepted. There was no choice. He had hoped that future work would take him somewhere far from the Kremlin; he had studied languages.

But Burmistrov did not get into intelligence. He became part of counterintelligence. The Second Main Directorate. He was sent abroad only once, to Egypt, where Soviet specialists were building the Aswan Dam and hundreds of other industrial projects.

Officially, the KGB was not there, naturally. They couldn't even bring in the *Pravda* newspaper. His colleagues in construction organizations and geological contingents were called "deputy managers of the contract on general questions." He was considered responsible for the recreation of the workers, and so his cover at the embassy was in the cultural department.

It was there in Egypt that he changed. The "Soviet friends" were generously shown ancient temples and necropolises, tombs and quarries. Some were curious, enjoyed the exotic locales. Others were stifled by boredom, heat, and dust—to hell with those pharaohs! And Burmistrov, a pure-blood Russian, nothing Oriental about him, suddenly felt something . . . familiar. Alien, but close. He did not understand a damn thing about hieroglyphs, mummies, or statues, but easily remembered the names of deities and rulers, and when he looked at the sarcophagi and pyramids, he smelled their dead life, their afterlife power, so familiar to him, a former Kremlin sentry.

After all, Red Square also had a stone pyramid, Burmistrov told himself. And there was a mummy. He had protected it himself, standing guard at the door of the Mausoleum.

The general kept a box of slides at home. Sometimes, he would shut himself up in his study, turn on the projector that smelled of ozone and dust burning on the hot lamp: it was the scent of the desert. He would be transported there, where Osiris and red-nosed Horus carved in granite reigned, where young and golden Tutankhamun lay in the gold sarcophagus; where every wall was covered in hieroglyphs.

When he was due to leave Egypt, his Arab vis-à-vis, acting as an obscure official in the Ministry of Culture, an undercover counterintelligence officer (trained by fugitive Nazis), suggested a trip to the Valley of Kings. Burmistrov agreed and got approval for a counter recruitment. But contrary to expectations, Farouk did not try to recruit him. He brought him to a new excavation site, started two months earlier. The main chamber had been cleared out by robbers back in antiquity. But the side chambers were untouched and Egyptian archeologists were carefully bringing up ritual animals of the dead dignitary—embalmed cats, dogs, horses, cobras, and even a Nile crocodile.

Wrapped in rough gray sacking, the animals resembled creepy dolls that could wake up as soon as they were untied and the bandages unwound.

Farouk was impeccably polite. He explained and gestured, as a ministry official ought. But Burmistrov could not get over the strangeness of the event.

For members of modern society, supporters of Nasser, Egyptian antiquities were important but still secondary symbols of Egyptian nationalism. For many Muslims, they were pagan filth in the face of Allah, the true God.

Yet Farouk—and what a name, the name of the overthrown king!—spoke of the burial chamber and the late dignitary as if he was an Egyptian from an idealized Egypt, a country in which the line of successive kingdoms had not been broken to this day. Burmistrov thought that it might be a recruitment move, but then laughed—nonsense, why create such difficulties?

Yet he felt that he was being recruited. Not by Farouk. The agent had merely brought him—but to whom? The spirit of the dead dignitary? The ragged fellahin digging in the dirt? The archeologist Dr. Kasem, a professional, a polyglot, and Sorbonne graduate? This cruel and dry land?

There at the site, Farouk gave him a farewell present. He whispered with Kasem and then brought him something in his fist.

"This is for you to remember Egypt," said Farouk. "They just found it. The Gods love you."

The Egyptian opened his hand.

It held a bronze scarab with gilt wings and turquoise eyes. It had not been washed, merely wiped with a brush, and it was covered by the dust of eternity.

Burmistrov knew this had to be a provocation.

Egyptian antiquities could not be taken out of the country. However, he certainly knew that important people were sending some interesting things to Moscow.

His baggage would be searched at the Cairo airport. They would find the beetle. That's when the recruitment attempt would begin. But it was all absurd. You recruit on the quiet, and the Soviets always traveled together in a group, everyone in view. There would be a scandal.

He thought that Farouk was acting mechanically, just to tick the box. Except that did not jibe with the wise Farouk that Burmistrov had observed over three years.

No, Farouk wasn't acting. This was really a gift. Not a random one, though. There was a plan, there was a hidden compartment.

Burmistrov wanted to refuse politely and in a friendly way: the ban and law applied to everyone. Then he pictured himself setting the scarab on his hand on a blizzardy, icy winter day in Moscow and remembering the blinding Egyptian sun . . . scarabs appeared from dead flesh . . . scarabs rolled the sun toward morning . . . Hepri was its name.

Burmistrov shook his head. He realized that he was already holding the scarab. The bronze beetle's sharp legs pricked his skin: if he tried to hand it back, it would dig in till he bled. Burmistrov saw how beautiful that ancient beetle was. He, as an officer of the KGB, had nothing of his own except for the shirts and trousers in his leather suitcase. The state gave him a uniform, pistol, and apartment, and he gave them an oath, he gave himself. But now he would have the beetle, his scarab, his only truly personal possession; a treasure.

"Let's get in the shade," Farouk said. "It's hot."

Burmistrov, who had gotten used to the climate, realized that it was stuffy in the valley, that the slopes were broiling and giving off sticky heat, that the sun was making him dizzy. He put the scarab in his pocket.

They drank tea in the shade, in the archaeologists' tent. Burmistrov washed and freshened up, Farouk drove him to Cairo. The beetle seemed to vanish on the road, quietly hiding in his pocket, and Burmistrov remembered it only when he was packing. Stick it under the lining? Leave it here? Throw it away? Give it to someone else, here's a souvenir, a trifle?

Burmistrov had almost decided to throw it out. He had even figured out where—in the garden of the cultural center where the scarab would disappear in the greenery, returning to the earth from which it had come. But he couldn't. Not out of greed, no. Out of fear that the beetle would vanish and he, Burmistrov, would stay the same, mediocre, would never be promoted beyond major. But with the scarab . . . He couldn't explain what would happen if he kept the beetle. Reason demanded that he throw it away, right now, but still Burmistrov wrapped the scarab in cigarette paper and put it in the inner pocket of his jacket.

No one stopped him at the airport. On the contrary, he had the feeling that Farouk was nearby, giving him cover, opening a corridor.

A few days after his return, the deputy chairman, head of counterintelligence, called him in.

He wanted to risk asking for a move to intelligence. Back to Egypt. But the moment he saw the boss's face, he knew his fate was sealed.

"There is the opinion that you should be transferred to the Ninth service, Comrade Burmistrov. As the deputy commandant of the Mausoleum."

It was so sudden that Burmistrov thought: this is the beetle's doing.

Thus he returned to the Kremlin he had dreamed of escaping; the great precise turns of life.

He came to love the Kremlin. He learned to respect its power and strength. Rather, the scarab taught Burmistrov. Another person existed inside him now: the one who served not the rulers of the country, there had been four in his life-time, but the Kremlin itself.

That other person was given otherworldly senses: the scarab's hearing and vision.

The bronze beetle that was always in the left pocket of his uniform transmitted the sighs and whispers of the ancient walls, the squabbles of ghosts.

There were nights when he felt the walls closing in on him, squeezing his ribs, breaking his bones, and he would wake in a sour, disgusting sweat.

There were nights when he soared above the Kremlin, like a spark flying over a campfire, and he saw that the old fortress *was* fire, the great insatiable flame of an altar raising up the red tongues of the towers. He walked through the corridors and sensed how close the other world was: press a little and it would seep in, like black mold on the wallpaper, damp spots on the ceiling, the horror's gray hoarfrost, blood stains on the carpet runners. In those moments he felt an itch beneath his fingernails, as if invisible icy needles were being pushed under them, and he would get a youthful erection, his penis pushing against his braid-ornamented uniform trousers.

There was only one place where Burmistrov never took the beetle: into the Mausoleum. The scarab did not hint or urge; it just waited, the ways the ancients could wait. Burmistrov sensed that it should not be done. He imagined with great clarity how inside the Mausoleum the scarab slipped out of his pocket, ran down his leg to the floor, and Burmistrov could not catch it. The beetle ran to the sarcophagus, climbed the pedestal, and ended up, impossibly, inside the bullet-proof glass. It clambered onto Lenin's forehead, paused, and then squeezed into the mummy's mouth. Burmistrov stood, stunned, petrified, the mummy looked unchanged, but something had already happened, vile and irreversible, and there was nothing he could do.

The first time he had the vision, Burmistrov separated himself from the scarab—or the scarab from himself. He left it at home on a shelf. That lasted only three days. He desperately needed that otherworldly perception, that supernatural link to the Kremlin that the talisman gave him. He realized that the scarab would demand payment one day. But he consoled himself with the thought that the bronze beetle knew how to wait. It had waited for thousands of years in the pyramid. He had the tech guys check the scarab: it was pure metal with no hidden features.

There was only one thing now that Burmistrov did not like in the Kremlin.

The children's festivities at New Year's.

He hated them and that was that.

Two weeks of nerves. Dozens of performances.

The little bastards came from all over the country with their Little Octobrist troops. The Palace of Congresses, a glass box, alien crystal; they had razed the old building, the true Kremlin, to build it. Presents, tens of thousands of presents, hundreds of thousands of chocolates. The same idiotic villain Koshchey abducted Snegurochka, the

Snow Maiden, and dragged her into the darkness; the general watched the rehearsals and the performances, as the rules required.

Every year a child passed out. The parents thought it was the excitement, delight, the stuffiness of the Palace. But Burmistrov knew: these were different faints.

The juvenile scoundrels saw. They saw what no one had the right to see. The Kremlin in its natural form.

Faces. Ghosts.

They had a special ambulance on duty by the Palace, the 11th department of the Military Medical Division. The parents were always told that this was the manifestation of a dangerous psychiatric illness and the child needed immediate hospitalization. What happened next did not worry Burmistrov. It wasn't his job.

He had realized long ago that he would be commandant until he died. Such was the will of the Kremlin. Such was his loyalty.

But that evening as he strolled along the towers, for the first time, almost accidentally, he thought about retirement.

Retirement! Impossible!

Just yesterday, he would have been furious with himself. But now he thought he could simply remove and shed the Kremlin, like a formal uniform weighed down by medals. Take it off and leave by the secret underground passage to the Moskva River bank.

Change clothing in a special underground room. Put on a worn gray raincoat from the agents' wardrobe, take an unobtrusive suitcase like the kind people take on business trips (money, weapon, set of documents) and come out into the light as another person, say, Valery Timofeyev.

Raise his hand and get a taxi. Look at the Kremlin across the river for the last time. Wearily tell the driver to take him to the Three Stations. The driver would be just right, not an agent, not a spy, just a hack, there were still a few left in the garages, not everyone had been recruited by his colleagues, not everyone.

Suddenly, the face of the imagined driver seemed familiar. From an old agency photograph.

Burmistrov recognized him.

There was this little Jew in Egypt. Smart, a good geologist. But Burmistrov sensed there was something off about him. He was much too active.

Back then, Burmistrov had just recruited a Russian, also a geologist. The agent quickly told him what was wrong. Their contingent was searching for useful layers. The cunning Jew cheated with the drilling samples, fiddled with the drawings a bit, and on paper it looked as if the layers went off toward the Gulf of Suez, which meant that their contingent had to move to that area to explore. He had apparently decided to go to the Promised Land. It might have worked. Ah, yes, his name was Mikhail. Changed from Moses.

Burmistrov could have stopped Mikhail-Moses. Call him in for a chat and send him back to the Soviet Union for treasonous intent. Let them deal with him.

But he wanted to catch the fool attempting to flee, to prove the fact of his intentions. So he let the little Jew get almost to the shore. But then there was a mishap. He got away from his guards. The Pharaoh's soldiers, damn them, messed up in the dark and shot the fugitive.

Burmistrov never thought about Mikhail-Moses. Yet now he was thinking about him. It felt like the scarab was scratching him near his heart.

Burmistrov reluctantly reached for his pocket. It was amazing, he thought for the umpteenth time; the pocket should show a bulge. The uniform was tight, he had put on weight. But it didn't, as if the beetle flattened out in it, changing its shape.

The general did not like that thought. He stopped his hand. He thought again of the heat in the Valley of the Kings. The clever Farouk. The inscrutable Kasem, imbued with eternity. And yes, it was only three months after the clumsy border guards had shot Mikhail-Moses. Strange. He had never put the two events together.

So that's what it was, thought Burmistrov, that was it.

His hand moved on its own, took out the scarab and set it on the desk.

The bright turquoise eyes glowed from within; blue with a tint of green.

The general pulled his hand away.

The scarab scuttled across the desk, ran down a leg to the floor, and slipped under the wardrobe.

Dazed, Burmistrov breathed out and breathed in. The air

seemed purified, fresh and icy, as in winter when you fling open the balcony doors of a smoke-filled apartment.

He sensed the agitation and whispers of the imperial relics in the Faceted Chamber: clusters of gold and precious stones, clots of strength, power, and fate.

Previously Burmistrov had heard their subdued, twilight rustling only a few times, when the rulers of the land were dying.

This time the relics moaned and groaned. Burmistrov felt the diamonds, rubies, and sapphires dying, waning. The pearls faded and the soldered metals fell apart. Precious stones cracked, exploded, stinking bile pouring out of them, the sediment of imperious greed accumulated over the centuries.

The scarab had vanished. Burmistrov could see the beetle descending along the cracks in the old walls to the underground labyrinth beneath the Kremlin, and it would go even lower, lower than this world, to passageways of the dead that know no borders.

The scarab was saving itself.

The general rushed out onto the balcony.

The Kremlin ravens, the grumblers, were circling above the towers and flying away, up the course of the Moskva River; to the source.

The stars!

The stars on the towers!

They used to be ruby, but now they were shining green and blue, lemon, violet; unearthly colors.

And the desolate night sky seemed to light up from them; it flashed with blossoming wreaths of northern lights, forming illuminated arches, corridors, and burgeoning scars.

A roar and a flash, and Burmistrov could see through the Kremlin's red brick, raging flesh to its true skeleton: instead of majestic towers there were prison camp guard towers, instead of the walls there were threads of thorny barbed wire.

The sky burst into a storm, a wild mixture of elements. Rain and hail struck the Kremlin like shrapnel, the windows rang out, the rooftops shuddered. The raindrops and bits of ice turned into stinging snow, the blizzard winds shook the walls, the Ivan the Great belfry let out a deep and shocked peal.

Green and blue lightning bolts pierced and gutted space, illuminating the whole city.

Tornadoes tore panels off the roofs; the spirits of the air acquired iron wings.

Burmistrov did not hear a living soul around him. Everyone had taken cover. Everyone had run off. The sentries were gone from their posts and the guardhouses were empty.

It was just him and the Kremlin.

The last remaining guards.

The old hardened fortress, fused with the roots of the earth, still stood.

He had a moment of hope.

Then onto the black cobbles of Red Square, washed by the rain and reflecting the sky's glare, came people.

Translucent, like swirls of fog.

Burmistrov saw what they were carrying and shuddered at this incomprehensible detail: pine cones.

Huge cones, their scales bristling and splayed. Burning, as if in the belly of a samovar, with pure green flames.

An instant, and the walkers were inside and outside the Kremlin, on the riverbank and in Alexandrovsky Park.

An instant, and they were at the walls, at the cathedrals, at the towers.

An instant, and kneeling they lowered the cones into the earth, as if they were planting seedlings.

Burmistrov shook his head. He understood who had come. The ones who never could have returned.

The dead from the taiga camps. Prisoners who had felled trees, cut away branches, sawed and floated logs. Those sent by the Leader to overcome the great coniferous forest of the north and had died, becoming part of it, surviving in the roots and crowns, finding new life in the branches and needles.

He rushed into his study, fell to his knees, praying that the Kremlin walls, the crown of red frozen fire, would overwhelm the green might of the forest. And suddenly he noticed that the room smelled of . . . foliage.

Fresh foliage.

The half-dead, sleepy palm that dozed in a pot had stretched to the ceiling. It threw out sharp juicy leaves. The pot cracked and its roots spread across the floor. They grabbed and entwined Burmistrov's ankles.

A palm . . . There had been palms there, he remembered against his will. The Egyptian border patrol had brought

Mikhail-Moses's body to the outpost, and the palms rustled in the dark, angry, the searchlights reflected on the edges of their leaves that looked like the edges of swords.

Burmistrov tried to run, sensing how the arboreal power was overwhelming the Kremlin's brick and stone.

The roots kept him in place. A green blade struck his back and sliced through to his heart.

He did not see the glowing pointy seedlings breaking through the cobblestones. Or the branches and roots piercing the stone, weaving a net, tying living knots. The old Kremlin was destroyed, leaving only flashes of weak light, that of the builders' enslaved talents finding posthumous joy in the emancipation of their creation.

Lubyanka

Colonel Shevkunov, the commandant of Lubyanka, was held up at work that night. Actually, he had not wanted to stay late. On the contrary, he had planned to leave early. His wife was spending a week in Murmansk with her parents. His colleagues invited him to spend the weekend hunting, promised they would get a boar, but he refused. He needed to be alone. To think. Marina would be back in a week and he had to tell her something.

Marina was sure that he had a mistress. She had the idea that he wasn't spending all his time at work. She said, I can tell you're involved with a woman. What could he tell her? How could he prove that there was no one except the old woman Lubyanka? Swear to it?

She would write to the Party committee, the colonel thought desolately. In her irksome teacher's manner. Shevkunov had no doubt that the higher-ups would accept the letter. He was in good standing. No one envied him his job, because it was dark and thankless. But he had no defenders, either. Lubyanka would not defend him; it liked watching people devouring their own.

He needed to sit. Think.

But things got backed up and kept Shevkunov at the office. Work, work . . . A rotting building. He knew that. He never said it out loud, but he knew. Outside Lubyanka looked magnificent, its façade was delightful and imposing. But inside it was rotten. Beams, ceilings, pipes—all rotten. You never knew what would break next. They repaired, replaced, used the latest materials, but it was like patching a corpse.

Even in small things: You oiled the door hinges, the next day they would creak again. Lightbulbs burned out two or three times faster than in the adjacent building. But no one paid attention, they were used to it. He was the only one. He had graduated from construction college, he understood these things.

Shevkunov wrote to his superiors that the old building had to be totally rebuilt. Or razed and built anew, instead of repairing the facades. They had already spent double, maybe triple, what it would have cost to start from scratch.

The response was, naturally, that "funds are prioritized for the construction of the Main Computer Center." Right, in that stupid building opposite, across Kirov Street.

Shevkunov felt that they simply did not hear him. Did

not see what was written in his reports, as if the letters floated away on the page. Did not sense what kind of building they were working in.

Just now, as he was planning to leave—a sewer pipe burst again. And not in some cubicle, but directly over the boardroom. A disgusting brown stain spread on the ceiling.

The next meeting was set for Monday. Shevkunov pictured an angry first deputy yelling: What is this crap, Comrade Shevkunov! Shovel it away! Wash it off!

At first it didn't stink too badly. But then the odor spread through the whole floor. Who had such disgusting shit? First it smelled like shit, but then it was like rot, decomposition— what was that? Dead rats? The worst part was that the plumbers couldn't find the source of the leak. A shitty puzzle! And those assholes from the First Chief Directorate would joke about it.

"We have a leak somewhere."

Damn the place! The bitch!

He stopped himself. Bit his tongue. Yes, in rare fits of fury he called the Lubyanka a bitch. An old whore. He knew it heard and remembered.

Bitch. Trash. An old woman trying to look young, having buried many husbands, people's commissars, and chairmen. A long-lived piece of scum, a spider! Oh, you're bursting, too, Shevkunov, it's flowing out of you . . .

He caught his breath. Looked around.

Something was missing. Something was gone from his office.

He hastily scanned the familiar surroundings. Cupboards, safe, desk, lamp, chairs. Everything seemed to be in place. Use some imagination! Shevkunov went to the window and looked out at the square. No cars. No pedestrians. Everyone was gone. Was there a storm coming?

The statue was gone, too.

He blinked. It didn't help.

Iron Felix, knight of the revolution, the first boss of Lubyanka, was not on his pedestal.

Shevkunov jumped back from the window. Crazy! The workload, the reports had really gotten to him; he was losing his marbles worrying about the upcoming conversation with Maria.

The colonel peered cautiously out the window, hoping that the statue would appear.

But it was gone.

The god of Lubyanka, its Primate, was gone.

Taken away?

Stolen?

Planned renovation? They'd forgotten to inform him?

Shevkunov really, really wanted to go home.

I am going to leave now, he told himself. The exit is on Furkasovsky Lane, you can't see the square from there. I'll walk to the Kirovskaya station. The Metro is still running. I'll come back tomorrow. Sleep. Sleep. I'll come back, and Felix will be on the pedestal. For sure. And we'll repair the leak.

He wanted to spit on the seal to attach it to the office safe and keep it secure. But his mouth was dry. Not a drop of saliva. Shevkunov took a sip from the decanter and vomited onto the floor.

The water tasted like a toilet puddle. The same stench as the sewage leak. The stench of decay.

The phone rang on his desk. The red light started blinking.

I'm not here. I left. I'm gone.

It was the security guard.

Shevkunov picked up the phone.

"Hello," he said, not the regulation response, trying to keep his voice steady.

"Comrade Colonel?" the guard asked, not recognizing his voice.

"What's up?" Shevkunov gulped. Damned voice. He sounded like he had a cold.

"The alarm went off. In Comrade Chairman's office. This is Captain Vikentyev reporting."

Shevkunov felt relieved.

They had installed the new system two weeks ago. There was a false alarm almost every night. Pulling electrical stunts. More trouble from Lubyanka.

"Have you recorded the incident?" His voice was back.

"Yessir," Vikentyev said.

"Call the technicians on duty and those responsible from the Central Research Institute," Shevkunov said vindictively. He didn't like these clever developers with blind faith in their machinery who didn't understand anything about old buildings. "Let them fix it."

And he added, "I'll go up there right now. Make sure."

"I understand, Comrade Colonel," Vikentyev replied rather too freely and hung up.

Shevkunov put the receiver back neatly.

The red light went off.

Why had he said that? Why didn't he send some men from the security office? What was going on?

Shevkunov felt that he had an explanation. But it hadn't quite formed. Something beckoned him upstairs. It had to be connected to Felix, Shevkunov thought.

The colonel hurried to the elevator. I'll just take a look, he thought. He felt like a child: they lived in a communal flat, and the last room at the end of the hallway belonged to Irka, Irka-Cream, a full-bodied vendor in the dairy row at the market, who was visited by the men from the market at night, and then there were sweet, drunken cries coming from her room, and Shevkunov, panting, eavesdropped and looked for a peephole.

The elevator came to an abrupt halt. Those Lubyanka elevators did not bother with niceties. Shevkunov came out, still half in his memories, and took a few steps.

The corridor reeked of bad tobacco. Tobacco from his childhood. The door to the Chairman's office was ajar. A ray of yellow light fell from it in a diagonal slant.

Shevkunov should have jumped back into the elevator and raised the alarm, so that armed guards would rush in, so that the exits would be manned, so that cars with operatives would arrive on the square.

But Shevkunov felt a strange weakness, as if from hunger. His builder's intuition, sensitive to construction flaws, told him that the alarms would not ring, the telephones would not connect. This was not an accident or a diversion. Something else. Unknown.

Sticking close to the wall, he slowly walked to the opened door. He sensed no direct threat. He calmed down and mentally addressed the building. These are your tricks, eh? Again with your tricks? Can't you let go, old woman? You'll get yours, you will!

He imagined the old building surrounded by construction crews, a huge rusted metal ball swinging on a chain right into the façade, and calmly noted, as if checking a list, how much he hated Lubyanka, for that old bitch drank his strength every day, drank it like an alcoholic.

But why are you tiptoeing? he asked himself. What are you afraid of? Her? You know her character, no need.

You fear whoever is in the office, he replied.

The entire floor was absolutely still. But it was the stillness of presence, of a trap.

He should have turned back. But the cracked door lured him, sucked him in, like a ghost in a draft.

Shevkunov looked in.

A fire burned in the white marble fireplace, red, flaming, its tongues leaping out. Only one lamp was turned on, providing a dull yellow light. The huge map of the USSR on the wall, usually covered by curtains, was also glowing—violet, blue, and green lights moved around on it, as if the map were showing what was happening in the country—or in the skies above it.

Maybe the Chairman was here? thought Shevkunov. And the guards missed his arrival?

He shut his right eye. Looked only with his left.

And he saw them.

They were all over there by the desk.

Those who had died their own deaths and those who were executed. Fallen into oblivion. Elevated to heroes. Thrown into exile. Those revered and those excised from encyclopedias. All the dead bosses of Lubyanka. All its dead lovers.

Bronze Dzerzhinsky, toppled from his pedestal.

Clinging to him, like the monument's shadow, Menzhinsky in sparkling round glasses.

Confused, emaciated, gray Yagoda.

Elegant but devastated Agranov, who had outlived himself in his cell.

Yezhov, gray, broken like a puppet on a string.

Meaty, with a shaved head, Frinovsky looking like a human pig.

Pale-faced, balding, with thin sensuous lips, Beria in a civilian sweater and broken pince-nez.

Merkulov with his heavy jowls.

Chubby cheeked, sweet boy Abakumov.

Kruglov, sliced in half by a train but still holding himself together.

Thick-lipped, big-eared Ignatyev, responsible for the Doctors' Case and exiled to some Tatar hinterland.

Pale, immobile Andropov, still stunned by his recent death.

Twelve.

Twelve what?

Shevkunov took a backward step.

He could hear that the corridor was no longer empty.

Voices behind every door. Tense. Anxious. Frightened.

Shevkunov understood the timbre and tone of that fear. He recognized it. He was once that scared.

After all, he had gotten there from the bottom. From the construction department of the Ministry of Internal Affairs. He started out managing prisoners at construction sites. They built housing for the agency workers in a northern city.

The prisoners worked well: They were experienced. But there was one, Bumblebee they called him, who was a joker.

Shevkunov had informants, he knew a lot. But they never could tell him anything useful about Bumblebee, or they were lying. He swiped small things, he could get lime for someone, or vodka, small sins, well known. They usually turned a blind eye to it, to keep the convicts working hard.

Yet Shevkunov felt that the trickster could cause big problems. Then he found him with his pals in an unfinished building. The prisoners were crouched around Bumblebee: they were probably going to brew up *chifir* tea or had gotten some weed. But no, they seemed to be arguing about something, and then Bumblebee took out a spoon, an ordinary aluminum spoon. He put it in his palm. Turned his hand over.

The spoon did not fall.

It just hung there!

Shevkunov had seen enough prison camp tricks, there were fakirs who were better than anything at the State Circus.

But this scared him. It was nothing: the spoon stuck to Bumblebee's hand like glue. A trick, sleight of hand. What made the fear worse was that he could tell that it wasn't a trick. He felt it and he was helpless. He was given the answer, but no protection.

Later, of course, he calmed down. Shevkunov decided that Bumblebee was planning a breakout with his gang. He'd seen it done: he would fill their heads with nonsense and they would follow him through fire and water and the guards' carbines.

He called for Bumblebee who arrived grim and slippery, but he greeted him respectfully.

Shevkunov wanted to pretend that he knew about the planned escape, that someone had snitched, but instead, like a fool, as if the devil had pulled his tongue, he blurted, "What are those tricks with the spoon? A vaudeville performer! Can you tell fortunes, too?"

Bumblebee slowly looked up: the disdain in his eyes could not be permitted in a convict. Shevkunov made a fist but could not raise it, while Bumblebee's face grew gray and old, and he spoke unwillingly, as if forced to do so, as if he had to respond since it was the law.

"You're green, captain. Lubyanka is waiting for you. The building . . ."

And broke off. He dropped his head on the table.

Shevkunov, on the contrary, grew tense, tight, his muscles ached as if he had been given some kind of shot, and then collapsed as well, and Bumblebee's words receded.

Shevkunov deemed it a good idea to send Bumblebee to the logging camp. When the construction was over, when the commission approved the building, they offered a transfer to Moscow. He felt a pang in his heart: Bumblebee had predicted it. But he pulled himself together, and anyway, his wife, Marina, would never have let him refuse, she had always dreamed of living in the capital.

And now Bumblebee's words came back to him, resounded once again. Shevkunov backed up, understanding that he had to leave, leave quietly so the people in the offices did not hear. He remembered what no one liked to talk about: how they fatally tortured their own people, Chekists killing Chekists. Then still others killed the former torturers.

He remembered and realized that he had given himself away. By that very thought. He turned and ran. The carpet runner suddenly crawled toward him, tripping him. They got him from behind, twisting his arms and whispering in his ear: "Got you, bastard!"

He wanted to shout imperiously, "Let me go!" but merely squeaked stupidly, "I'm one of you!"

"March, bitch!" And they laughed behind his back.

The shoulder boards vanished from his uniform. His ID disappeared from his pocket. His body ached, hurt unbearably, swelling with old bruises. His toothless mouth whispered, mumbled the mangled sounds that used to be his name. They dragged him down countless stairs, and he heard the rumble behind him—spy, spy, spy, and he wanted to go down there, to the bottom, to the abyss, for there it would all end.

But it did not end. They tossed him into a cell and shut the door. When sand and stones crumbled from the ceiling, when the building shook to its very roots, he jumped up, pushing at the low ceiling, trying to save himself and it, beloved and cursed Lubyanka, and held on, held on until the upper force overpowered him and stones fell on his head.

Stalin's Kuntsevo Dacha

Lt. Colonel Tishchenko, commandant of Kuntsevo Dacha, was completing the evening rounds. Actually, this was not part of his duties. There was a chief guard who was the one to check on the posts. But Tishchenko knew that he had to do it. It was required. He was in his twelfth year of service here. He understood a few things about the place that were not spelled out in the manual. That even the old-timers might not articulate.

Tishchenko had quickly noticed that the dacha had its personality. The officers and warrant officers were chosen by the personnel department, and it was very selective. Recommendations, questionnaires, service records, everything had to be top-notch.

But it was the dacha that decided. The old house got rid of the people it didn't like—some slowly, some quickly. The house had a cruel sense of humor.

Dog handler Sergeant Nefedyev, a teetotaler, became a drunk and was fired—his own dogs had bitten him.

Captain Malofeyev, head of finances, a precise man, left his briefcase with secret payroll information in a taxi. That would have earned him only a reprimand, but the next passenger to ride in the taxi was a known agent in the French embassy.

Major Pozhigailo, caretaker, graduate of the Energy Institute. A hard worker who adored the dacha and managed to get hold of paint, cement, glass, and furniture (supplies were not easy to come by even in their department), received an electric shock when he plugged in a new kettle in his cubicle. Paralysis, life as a vegetable.

Lieutenant Kirillova, in charge of the maids. A general's daughter, by the way. Plump but beautiful. Chic dresser. Tishchenko tried to put the moves on her but it didn't work, he wasn't in her league. She died in a car crash right by the Praga restaurant, on a government road that connected the Kremlin and the dacha, with some black marketer. Even her father couldn't hush it up.

Or, more recently, three months ago. Senior Lieutenant Andreyev, an athlete, height 189 cm, a vice-champion of the KGB's Ninth Department in the triathlon, master of sports in sambo, and a crack shot. He wanted to calm down some drunken sailor in the Metro, a vagabond, as it turned out later, deported to the hundred and first kilometer. Not a criminal, not even close to gangs. Andreyev caught a penknife in the artery and bled to death at Partizanskaya station, before an ambulance could get there.

After Kirillova, by the way, Tishchenko realized that it wasn't just the dacha. He loved the dacha, the promiscuous trollop, that's why he felt its preferences. He was a village lad, from a remote area, he fought his way to the top, went to a pedagogical institute after his service in the border guards, and was offered a secret service position. He still remembered his woodland home, his hungry childhood—there were many abandoned villages in the region and he and his friends entered a lot of empty houses to fool around. There were lots of creepy things that scared them, but the evil forces knew their place and their small power. Good for scaring kids, no more.

It wasn't the dacha.

It was the Boss.

The Boss who had died here.

It was his manner. His style.

His power.

They had been afraid to destroy his dacha, thought Tishchenko. They had removed him from the Mausoleum, taken down his statues, flogged him at the Congress, rewritten the textbooks—he had studied to be a history teacher, so he knew—but they did not touch his beloved dacha.

They must have left it just in case he came and demanded space, a room for the night, shelter. There were so many nomenklatura dachas around Moscow, enough for a regiment, a division! Yet they preserved this one, which the Boss had left forever, had turned over the power to them.

But the Boss was not gone.

For years, Tishchenko secretly wondered what the principle was. Whom did the Boss accept and whom did he reject? He calculated, he built hypotheses. He took into account hair color, features, age, gender, nationality.

Then he guessed. And the guess made him accept the thought that the Boss was here.

There was no principle.

There was just sheer power.

Whim. Impulse. A moment's desire.

He could no longer rule over everyone. Perhaps it wasn't even him but just a part of him. A shard. A remnant.

Imprisoned. Attached—not to the body or the grave but to the place he died.

Waiting for something.

Could they have known, Khrushchev and the others? Guessed? Those materialists, cynics? Or had they simply sensed, like curs that had not forgotten the whip? Instinct? Tishchenko thought they had sensed it.

That's how he learned about the rules. The real rules here. If you sense that the dacha and the Boss wants it this way—do it. You didn't set it up and it's not for you to change it.

That's why he did the evening rounds, checking the fence, searchlights, barbed wire. Then he checked the fire hydrants, the hoses, the fire extinguishers. He had accepted the fears of the building. He dreaded blazes, smoldering cigarettes, lightning, decay, termites. He quit smoking. Actually, no one smoked here. A healthy place.

There was nothing obviously supernatural in the building itself. The Boss did not humiliate himself. No strange whisperings, creaking floorboards at midnight, silhouettes at the end of the corridor, or things moving from place to place. No. Not even on the day of his death.

Only occasionally did he make his presence known, his cruel attention to details. Once, Tishchenko saw that one of the new soldiers had hung a bird feeder made out of a milk carton on a naked lilac bush: March was freezing, trees in the dacha woods were cracking from the frost. They had never had bird feeders at the dacha, and Tishchenko wanted to tell them to take it down, he wasn't going to do it himself, but he forgot. The next morning, he got to work and was stunned. The fluffy soft snow beneath the lilac was scattered with frozen dead bullfinches, red brushstrokes on the white.

Sometimes—rarely, rarely—Tishchenko received signals, nonverbal orders to do something: for example, rake the fallen leaves from the main path, or do a second polish of the floors, or cut the birch tree knocked down by wind into logs.

Once a year in December on the eve of the Boss's birthday, Tishchenko felt that the dacha was preparing for something; expecting important guests, as in the past.

Those nights were the darkest of the dark, the sky was hidden by clouds, not even a single star's light reaching the earth. Disturbing, graceless winds blew, the winds of tramps and vagabonds, the winds of wastelands. The Boss's power seemed to expand beyond the dacha territory.

On those days, Tishchenko felt even more acutely that the Boss had not left the world. There was a lot of him on the roads of the earth, in its houses.

There he was, an old shepherd walking down from the mountains, and he would raise his hand to stop a truck, and he would smile upon seeing his photograph in the cracked windshield.

There he was, a cheerful elderly hunter striding in a logging area, raising his hand to stop a truck for a lift, and the petty thief driver, son of exiles, would curse the managers and say that there had been order under Stalin, and he would smile and wink understandingly.

There he was waiting on the platform for a train, and he would start a conversation, and across the road they were taking down the factory chimney, wrecking it but the crane couldn't handle the ball, and someone would say, oh, they built things much better in Stalin's day, not like now, and he would nod in agreement and offer him a cigarette respectfully.

He would add all those words and signs into a piggy bank, a great big one that could never be filled, but he wasn't afraid. There were many of him walking the roads, spending the night in random houses, talking with people. Many were waiting for his return, many gave a handout for an old man's health without knowing that they were donating to him, thinking that they were speaking their words into the air, throwing their curses into the flowing water, burying their hatred into the ground. But he would find everything that was his, find it, take it, catch it, snatch it out of the flow, dig it out of the ground.

That was why he wasn't at the dacha, Tishchenko thought glumly, he was busy, doing his work, and only a small portion of him was left to be guarded. In December he—they—would gather. Confer. Talk about business. And go their ways. But one day the whole Boss will return. With a full piggy bank, a heavy sack filled with the human harvest. Until that time, Tishchenko had to protect his house.

The lieutenant colonel would have retired a long time ago, he would have found a way, but he sensed that the Boss would not release him. The Boss knew all his thoughts and intentions. It was too late to run. But the Boss would also protect him from his superiors. He had chosen him for his orphanhood, his rustic thoroughness, and it turned out that Tishchenko deserved his trust. He would be rewarded when the Boss returned.

Tishchenko completed the rounds.

Time to go home.

Suddenly there came screaming and shrieking in his head: he couldn't make out the words, it was a roar, like water in river rapids. His half-mad, paralyzed grandmother, Fenya, had mooed, roared, and screeched from her bed when she was thirsty or thought that they were outside, the terrible ones who came to take away icons and grain.

Tishchenko listened more closely and began to make out creaking sounds: lock the gates, lock the doors, shut the guardhouse shutters, shut, lock.

He guessed that the one who lay paralyzed here was attached to the dacha by his spasm and paralysis. And he felt a fear that only immobile paralytics could feel. He guessed and then feared that the Boss must have read his mind. And would not forgive him.

Tishchenko looked up at the sky.

A storm was moving from the north.

Lighting flashed in the distance over the Oktyabr meadow. Branched, multitoothed.

Its light was reflected to the south of the dacha, in the river valley that was damp and foggy at night. It flashed in the ponds and remained there, extinguishing: like signal flares burning out.

Tishchenko looked harder.

Something moved. Something familiar, old, forgotten.

Long ago as a child, Tishchenko had seen ball lightning. The gang was rummaging around an abandoned village, looking in the corners of log houses for the coins traditionally laid under the first row. Sometimes, they found silver tsarist rubles. But this time they didn't find a single coin, even though the village looked prosperous, big houses that had belonged to kulaks. Senka Motyl, their leader, went crazy.

He found a pole and started smashing everything rotten: fences, the well, doors, window frames, he knocked down the old banya. Tishchenko wanted to shout: Don't, leave it, let's go, it's getting dark, but how could he stop their ataman, their leader! The others thought it was great fun and picked up stones and sticks.

That's when it appeared. It floated up from behind a tall, black shed in the distance. Yellow, violet, blue, lemon, iridescent. A breeze rustled the grasses, even though the trees remained immobile, and there was a hint of storm. Everyone froze, and the horrible thing approached Motyl—it seemed to look him in the eye. Then it let go and floated back behind the shed.

Motyl became feebleminded. The schoolteacher, Petr Mikhailych, a tiresome old man, told them in class that it had been ball lightning: a known phenomenon. Tishchenko listened and thought glumly that even though the teacher had studied at an institute he was still stupid, because he did not understand what had occurred at the village at all, he was just droning on about science. The force had let them go. Just that once.

Now Tishchenko saw flashes in the Setun valley where the Kiev-Matveyevskaya line lay. Those were just sparks on the railroad line, he told himself, but he did not believe it. The flashes had that color he remembered: blue and lemon and yellow. He had never liked the Setun River, dirty, rusty, steep-sided, with indistinct, ancient burial mounds along the banks.

He turned around and went back to his office, trying not to run. He picked up the special Lubyanka telephone, an ancient apparatus that remembered the Boss's guards. And froze.

There was silence on the line. Just the whistle and howl of wind.

Tishchenko rushed to the window.

They were coming from the Setun: dozens, hundreds of flaming spheres. Tishchenko's heightened senses told him that each was a creature. Don't stand in their path and they won't touch you. Like the other time.

But a lieutenant colonel had to, was required to be in their path.

He had sworn an oath, not to the state and not to the party: to the Boss. At that moment he fully felt the existence of that oath; the Boss pulled on it like a leash, demanding that he come to his senses and act, save the dacha, wake the guards, turn on the searchlights, release the dogs, roll out the fire hoses.

Tishchenko reached for the speakerphone. Then he remembered how he had wanted to stop Senka Motyl, how scary it was in that unpopulated village, and how clearly he felt, the only time in his life, that they were doing a bad thing, they should not be searching for coins. They should not even drink water from the well.

He sidled away from the phone and slipped into the yard.

The fireballs were at the nearest trees.

This was the death of the Boss and the dacha, Tishchenko knew. Their time had come.

But that was not what the Boss thought.

Space seemed to yawn and the Mustache appeared in the middle of the courtyard. A huge Mustache, big enough to block a street. It huffed and barked, but in vain: the terrible lights were coming closer.

Tishchenko heard the Boss's silent shout: What are you doing, my slaves, you bits of grime! Have you forgotten my fury and my caress? My sharp word and the whip? Bow down, slaves, chips beneath my ax! Serve me, and I will raise you from the camp grime, the road dirt, the stink of the mines and swamp logs!

Tishchenko fell to his knees and wanted to serve him, he pulled at his holster. It would not unsnap and he could not get his gun.

The leading ball shot out blue lightning, and the Mustache turned to ash, dissolving in black smoke.

Tishchenko felt that all the iterations of the Boss all over the world were dying, the hitchhiking old men, collectors of knowing smiles, dealers in stilled feelings, greedy and terrible beggars. They knew the night belonged to them. But the night was bright, and the living lightning bolts were searching for them, catching them, turning them into heavy ashes, burning their heavy boxes filled with soiled feelings, leaving scorch marks on the sides of the road. The Boss was dying in his multitudes. He was no longer the Boss, not the ruler but only an empty name in the wind.

The dacha burst into blue fire. The logs of the house groaned, the metal roofing whirled and burned, the windows burst, and yet the dacha stood, even though dry wood could not stand in a fire, yielding slowly, burning but not burning down, tolerating it.

It was as light as day, and Tishchenko saw one single hair,

stained red by tobacco, a fierce hair of the great Mustache.

Like a doomed man, he reached for it, to preserve it, like a holy relic; he heard a whisper, plant the hair in a pot with human fat, and it will grow, sprout, and then the Mustache will return. He reached for it, and then he was struck by something heavy and sparking, it struck him to death, ruthlessly and painlessly; at that moment flames—green, yellow, blue—consumed the dacha.

That night there was neither time nor distance on earth. The living slept soundly. They all had the same dream, some more vividly, some less.

The dead northerners rose from the execution ravines, untouched, dark, voiceless, forgotten—and marched into the land of the living, to the villages and cities, heard by the night roads, sensed by trees and animals, seen by nocturnal birds; the wind rose, a strange wind, blowing backward, into the past, into the region of loss.

TITAN

It was right here, on the corner of the empty square by the red-and-white church, that I had a special feeling as a child.

You were walking home from school. Looking around out of boredom. Suddenly you realized you could not, simply could not set even one foot in the tracks of the man walking in front of you.

He was absolutely ordinary, the pedestrian. Baggy gray coat, wide black trousers, scuffed black briefcase, a loaf of white bread peeking out from it. He did not elicit fear. But you could not step in his tracks. It wasn't about him.

Danger clung to him, small and inconspicuous, like a flea. And like a flea, it could jump from one person to another. Just one mistake, just one shoe in another's footsteps.

I would immediately turn to the back courtyards, and the bad feeling would go away, the day would settle back in its groove. My footsteps echoed as a slushy reverberation in the archways and counted the stone treads of the entry. Yet that fragile feeling remained in my heart, like the echo of my father's piano: you weren't caught.

By whom? Or, maybe, by what? I didn't know.

The strange ability vanished when I became a teenager, as if I no longer needed its protection, and it was smoothed away in my memory along with other oddities and fantasies of childhood.

I recalled it when I was twenty-five. When I was first summoned to the house that stood on the square directly opposite the red-and-white church. I had not noticed or feared it as a child. I knew that there was an evil house somewhere in the city, where people vanished, but I thought it was a different building in another neighborhood, beyond the river. At twenty-five, I knew exactly where it was.

It happened again on the square: a random pedestrian, sudden fear, the attraction of strange, invisible tracks. The setup seemed to repeat what had actually happened in my life: I had followed someone else's footsteps, pulled by the fate of another person—which was why I was called to the house on the square.

My childhood fear was deepened by a new, adult fear. I thought that I had been doomed to evil from my early years and had eluded its snares by miracle. Now it was too late to turn to the back courtyards, hide, or squirm. There would be no postponements and I had to peer into its jaws. No other way.

I would have arrived at the house, docile and ready to surrender. There was a short distance left, maybe two hundred steps. But a huge white gull, one of those that fly into the city from the sea and sit, stupidly significant, on the domes of the shuttered church turned into a warehouse, took flight and squirted yellow excrement in my face, cementing my hair and dripping inside my collar.

I vomited. Not so much from the stink as the unexpect-edness and the suspicious horror created in people like me who lack confidence and compensate with a marked display of fastidiousness and order when life plays its nasty tricks. However, as I did my best to clean up with my handkerchief, I sat on the bench and laughed. They were going to press my face into crap where I was going—and I got it here. Messy and smelly, I laughed uproariously.

I appeared before them in that state. Unapologetically, I handed the reception desk my summons, marked by a blotch of yellow. I was received with repugnance, they took me to the washroom, offered trite sympathy: it happens. But they could barely contain their laughter. All their usual methods and tricks became ridiculous and harmless. They couldn't pull themselves together, they were thinking about how they would tell their colleagues about summoning this guy and a bird shat on him right on the doorstep, and so they didn't manage to work me over. I didn't give them a second chance.

Now I go to that house.

The office where they interrogated me was now part of the archives. The walls were the same, uneven and bumpy, with leaks and swirls. Back then I imagined the plaster was imprinted with human suffering. Now I saw it was merely shoddy work. They learned how to torture people, but not how to plaster walls.

From the reading room on the second floor you could see the square, the red-and-white church, and the bench close to where the gull had soiled me. The corridor windows open onto the enclosed courtyard of the former internal prison, a square of ocher walls.

It didn't look malevolent at all, that courtyard. It was part of the museum now. Tourists entered the barred cage and ambled about, attempting—at least this was the museum's plan—to try on the despair of the prisoners.

Alas, I did not believe in this well-meaning pedagogy, even though I knew it was justified. In my experience, you could not prepare or train for a genuine meeting with evil. It always caught you unawares. The miracle, the true miracle was that there was always a person just as bewildered as the rest, a peer of peers, brother of brothers, or sister of sisters, who was not branded by evil, no matter how hard it tried.

That, as you understand, was not me.

Yes, I returned to the city I left twelve years earlier. Our place had been sold long ago. I took a long time choosing a place to stay, scrolling through Booking.com and Airbnb, but every address elicited memories. I wanted to find a secluded place, removed, a temporary home for a visitor.

The city insisted there was no such place. Then suddenly, when I refreshed the search page, this apartment popped up. I didn't recognize the street name, Lipovaya. I looked on Google Maps to see how long it would take to walk to the archives. I recognized it on the map. In my days it was called Communard Street.

The building?

Number 21.

The very one.

I looked at the photos of the apartment. Everything was different. Violet walls. Pink ceiling. White leather armchairs, puffed up like silicone lips. It was as if someone as zealous as a child with his first coloring markers had tried to paint over the past of these rooms. I recognized them by the view from the kitchen window: the brick boiler room chimney with rusted ladder brackets rose right in the center of the frame.

Building 21, Apartment 14.

The person who was the reason for my archival work had lived there. I tried not to think about it. I hadn't even planned to walk down that street. I wanted to be impartial. But someone had canceled their reservation, and the apartment called out to me: come.

The one who had died in it had no legal heirs. After the funeral I was requested to the notary's office, and in the presence of two officers in civilian clothing the deceased's will was read to me: he left his property and works to me.

I almost cursed him at that moment. Because he had—literally—cursed me.

State security knew well that he had longtime friends. Like-minded thinkers. Why not them? Why the young man he barely knew?

They had the power to overthrow the will legally. Or hide it, destroy it. But they preferred to play an operative game. First of all, they were forced—the times were different, not like the past—to follow some rules. And second, the suddenness of the will indicated a secret. A connection they had missed.

They latched on to me.

After the reading of the will, they brought me to his apartment; that was the first and only time I was there.

The apartment was being searched. They were shameless, of course. Probably, I was supposed to ask about a warrant. But I was too angry with him, my unsolicited benefactor. Angry and frightened. I spent six hours in the kitchen. They wouldn't let me leave: these things were mine now.

Late that evening, they drove up in a truck and took away all the furniture.

"Simply a formality," the officer in charge of the search explained in a paternalistic way. "We will seal the apartment. It belongs to the state now. The things can stay in our ware-house for the time being. We know you live in straitened circumstances. You decide where you will keep them. And we will hand them over according to the list."

Amazingly, I really did believe that it was a formality. The search was over. They didn't find anything. Let the things stay in their warehouse. I had no place to take them. And no reason.

However, just a week later the officer called me and asked ingratiatingly, "Why aren't you picking up your property? You know, we're not a left luggage depot. It's not nice."

"I need a truck, and I can't find one," I said, trying to rebuff him.

"Well, we'll help you with transportation," the officer announced. "A car will come for you tomorrow."

They took me to the state police garage. I felt calmer; where else would they keep the things? I calmed down and relaxed. We had made plans to bring the furniture to a friend's empty house in the country.

That's where they caught me. They led me into a hangar and turned on—after a second's pause—a bright light.

The furniture was there, arranged in the same way as it had been in the apartment, just spaced out a bit more. Next to each piece of furniture the contents were neatly displayed.

Everything had been butchered. Sawed. Carved. Gutted and turned inside out. I imagined them bringing it all here, setting it up as on their sketch, numbering and photographing the pieces. They took out knives, hacksaws, scissors, hammers, and crowbars. They started dismembering clothing, taking apart and battering the furniture. Cutting up the armchairs and couches into a flattened pulp. Tearing apart books: Was it really Arthur Conan Doyle under the Arthur Conan Doyle cover?

I felt sick. I had not fully understood how important it was for them to know whether he had written anything or not. I realized that right now at the apartment they were stripping wallpaper, lifting up floorboards, jackhammering walls.

After that, they would start on the inheritor. They had brought me there to show me what was in store for me. I would have given them his manuscript, gladly. If only I had it.

To show them I understood, that I was in the clear, I said, "Tell me, please, how do I renounce my inheritance in favor of the state?"

You could say that I renounced it.

Yes. You could say that.

They watched me anyway. Now I know that was called COS, a case of operative surveillance. It was to be conducted for three years and extended if necessary. Mine wasn't. I think that over three years even they, so suspicious, realized that I didn't know a secret hiding place in the woods to which his manuscripts were removed from the apartment just in time.

They knew there were no manuscripts. They did everything possible to keep words from appearing on paper. Yet they believed that a text could be written under their noses. Written and hidden.

Well then. It turned out they were right.

My COS was not kept. I was small fry. The storage period expired and they destroyed the file. There was a notation in the register, with start, end, and destruction dates.

My benefactor had a different file. Not COS, but COD: case of operational development.

Thirty-four volumes. With exactly three hundred pages in each volume.

From a writer's point of view—an entire collected works.

The volumes were what I was reading in the archives.

He has a name, but I will use what I first heard my father call him: Titan.

For my father, the nickname, the inside-joke, was ironic. Certainly, when they were young: they were almost the same age.

For me, it was a full name: a passionate password—a sign of disappointment—a symbol of faith.

Notably, they, the occupiers and spies, in defiance of their own conspiracy rules, used the code name Titan in their files, as if admitting that his person could not be hidden.

Of course, it was simply laziness.

But it turned out to be an admission.

My father was a composer. Author of two symphonies, never performed by anyone, and the tango "Love Incognito," a saccharine prewar tune that contained an ingratiating horror and trembled like lemon gelatin about to be eaten.

Titan, the nephew of a member of parliament, a popular poet and writer, was arrested right away in 1940 when Soviet troops entered our country.

Father was not touched.

He saw alien officers dancing with their ladies to his music.

Then Nazi officers danced to "Love Incognito."

And then the dancers were Soviet officers once again.

Music is a slut, Father used to say.

I think he was pleased when "Love Incognito" was banned as a "bourgeois perversion."

Father could have died in the war, could have been arrested later, but he died his own death in 1963.

He taught in a music school. When he came home from work, he went into the bathroom and spent a long time cleaning his ears. He thought he was going deaf rehearsing the loud marches of the conquerors with his students.

I did not blame him for the marches. But I did not tell my friends about them. A secret group had formed at my institute. We didn't do anything underground. We didn't say anything really treacherous. We got together, looked at old prewar books and felt that one day we would do something. That "something," vague and far-off, hypnotized us.

The name Titan, banned in print, was our beacon. We didn't read his books. We hadn't even seen his photograph. The war had destroyed the libraries. Much had been burned in stoves for heat. What wasn't burned was scrupulously removed by librarians appointed by the new authorities. We couldn't even find out what it was he had written about; the newspapers and literary journals of those days were also gone, and the adults either kept silent or said commonplace things. That inflamed our desire, each of us expected to find something personal in his texts.

We shared rumors that he had died in a Soviet camp in the far north. The inaccessibility of Titan's books wreathed him in a romantic aura, turned him into a banner and symbol of resistance. His terrible fate endowed him with a prophet's significance.

We looked. Made friends with booksellers. Tried to worm our way into gaining the trust of owners of private libraries. In vain. His only novel, *Summer with Avgustina*, and the collections of poetry remained elusive. No one trusted us small fry; you could get a prison sentence for owning Titan's book.

Father guessed about our meetings and searches, even though I was sure I was a good conspirator. One windy spring night, when the wires hummed and whined outside, Father called me into his room, a cubbyhole with cotton batting on the walls, an upright piano taking up a third of the space. This was where he gave music lessons, and where he composed. The music pages on the piano were reflected on the windowpane, as if the notes were black frost, mysterious signs of destiny.

I think my father was afraid that we fools would come across a snitch, who would sell us Titan's book, and the next day the police would come to search. That confirmed the boldness of the act.

"This is for you," he said, taking down a worn copy of *Piano Lessons* with a keyboard on the cover.

Father never tried to teach me music. I didn't inherit his ear. I grew tense.

"Open it," he said gently.

I opened it.

I flipped the cover, turned the flyleaf.

The title read: *Summer with Avgustina*, 1939.

That night I started reading.

We thought of Titan as a warrior. A prophet of resistance. A secret hero, general, leader. We were not put off by the novel's title, we imagined that Avgustina was probably a comrade-in-arms, a messenger, a member of the underground. Summer was the time of green forests, the time of war and struggle, which he had probably foreseen.

Instead, he turned out to be a lyric writer, a hymnist of quotidian feelings and sensuality.

Of course, I was stunned.

I thought that I had been tricked, that my father had given me a fake book! It couldn't be that they had arrested, tortured, crossed Titan off the list of the living for this! A trifle! A harmless love concoction!

I had expected to be initiated, to find the recipe for the sacrificial "something" that we wanted to perform, and I would be the apostle of our common endeavor. Instead I was reading, wading through complex syntactical filigree, a novel about unrequited love.

I quit reading five or six times. I returned as if by accident, unwilling to admit that I was captivated by the text.

No, it wasn't about the romance, even though I was at a ripe age, and I was in love with K., who was a year ahead of me and part of our group. You would think that *Summer with Avgustina* would have fed and heightened my sense of being in love. But no.

The novel about love was not really about love.

It was about time. The future that was already here even though we did not notice it.

In the text that Titan wrote from 1935 to 1938 the terrible imminent war had already begun. Its messengers and agents were already among the people. The invisible, ethereal cataclysm, the break in connections, the growth of wormholes and cankers had begun. People's faces were already darkened by shadows of death and marks of grief, branded by future losses, betrayals, redemptions.

An impossible photographer had captured it all with a clairvoyant's impossible camera lens.

Now I understand that Titan had not been arrested for his novel. No one in the new regime had ever read it. They just had lists of every more-or-less notable person, compiled with the help of our Communists. His books were expunged and destroyed not because they were considered particularly dangerous. It was a punishment.

But then I thought that Titan had incurred their wrath by the depth of his genius. I wanted to explain it to my friends, mustered my arguments, but I could not admit to having a copy of *Summer with Avgustina*. I feared their lack of understanding and disdain. Their disappointment.

The novel separated me from my friends and brought me closer to Titan, who I thought was dead. Probably that was my father's long-range aim: to ensure my safety, cut off or weaken dangerous friendships, temper the fever of youth.

Well, it was a good move. Father was wrong about only one thing, as were we all: he believed that Titan was dead.

Yet Titan came back.

I met him on the day of his return without suspecting that it was a meeting, since I didn't know his face.

I had a nose for the returnees. In those years, they no longer shot prisoners in the forests. Red flags were hung the night before holidays, and most of them were untouched and not torn down. Surviving prisoners began appearing from the North. The Soviets could have left them to die there in the taiga and tundra, but they allowed them to set foot on their native soil again, so that they would submit and accept the inevitable. And so that we young people would see their capitulation.

I quickly learned to note them, blindly wandering down long-abandoned sidewalks. Crushed, cut down by the camps, the way no locals were. Torn off and unable to grow back, to become part of the crowd again. They were thin and compressed, low to the ground like northern vegetation. They always opted for the sunny side of the street, instinctively seeking light and warmth. However, they still seemed taller than we were. As if we had grown smaller while they had been there.

That day I saw an unusual man near the train station. Not a local, not a returnee. Not old, not elderly; his age was immaterial.

He was short. Not a dwarf, of course. But clearly an extremely small man: one who hadn't eaten his porridge. A grown boy, a runt, a walking misunderstanding who could barely reach the ticket window. Anyone seeing him would smile and think what luck that nature didn't make the same mistake with me!

The small man stood by the lamppost and crumbled a piece of white bread for the pigeons. I paid no attention to his clothing or facial features, so amused was I by the ceremony with which he broke the bread and tossed it to the birds. What enormous self-importance, I thought, he's a little Napoleon. Yet his small body elicited unquestioning respect, as if . . . as if he were a conductor before a huge orchestra, a circus performer before an enormous lion; an animal tamer, yes, a tamer always looked weak and insignificant compared to what he was taming.

I walked past, putting a mental mark on the little man. I was a budding writer who collected people and things, listing him in my register of types—and never thinking for a second that I myself might be marked in response.

I don't remember exactly how I learned that Titan was back from the camps. There were whispers, voices in the air: he's alive, he's here.

The city, domain of devastating winds, capital of those who left forever, was waking up, anticipating the miracle of life's triumph.

Everyone who was told that Titan was alive immediately felt certain that he would write a book about his camp years, would speak for our entire wretched country that had lost so many sons and daughters.

Oh, he will definitely write it, said both the intransigent and the conformists. That's what kept him alive! Saved him! A holy duty! A calling! Since he's been through hell and back, just give him time and he will create it, he can do it! It will be the voice of freedom! This book will bring us all together! The book! Oh, that book!

I waited. I believed. Perhaps I believed more than others, for I had read *Summer with Avgustina* and understood his talent, his perceptive gaze.

Of course, no one who passed along the rumors had spoken with Titan. No one could name the person who had met with him and was the source of information. But the arguments grew more heated: Would it be a novel? Autobiography? Did Titan write it all in his head, in the camps, from first line to last? Or had he made notes on random and precious sheets of paper hidden from the searchers?

Many people believed that the book's magnificence would save Titan from another arrest. The times were different, people said to their friends. They won't kill him now. Won't throw him in the camps. They won't permit publication, of course, but . . . here the speaker would wink and add that there will be reliable people with typewriters at home, people with access to a printing shop.

Such stupidities annoyed me. Fools! Dolts! What did they know about how writers work? They expected the book in a year's time. It would be years before the book would be ready. By now, he must have started work, seen his remaining friends, who found him a room in someone's hospitable home with good paper and pencils.

Somewhere on the periphery of this imaginary world, I was lurking. So I was sent to Titan with a message—I didn't bother figuring out what or by whom. The iron old man greeted me gruffly, unhappy to be distracted from his manuscript, but learning that I had read *Summer with Avgustina* switched from wrath to kindliness and allowed me to read a page of the new book. I understood that in the future I would appear in its pages: the young friend of the main protagonist, a kind of Eckermann to his Goethe, symbol of the succession of generations, upon whom the aging singer would bestow his lyre when the time comes.

Time passed. The rumors about the coming book slackened. They began saying that Titan's health was undermined in the camps and he needed a year or two of rest and recuperation by the sea, far from the new hotels and the noise of unwanted but inevitable tourists. Others claimed that the text was almost finished, Titan had worked through the nights, and now his vision was damaged, and he had to wait until his optic nerves were healed.

Notes of early disappointment and edifying sobriety began to sound. What did you expect? He's an old, sick, and exhausted man. He's not the Titan of old, talented and bold. Then came the first skeptics: He's not going to write anything at all. If they let him out, he must have promised not to pick up a pen.

Unable to bear that vileness, I always rushed to defend Titan. I must have seemed like his page or squire. People thought I knew him, that my father had introduced us, since he had entrée into Titan's artistic circle in the past.

I understood that Father would never have approached Titan and certainly would not have introduced me. He would fear for the family. I began seeking a meeting myself. I was stupid and persistent, I had read *Summer with Avgustina*, and

I knew that Titan was my writer and I was his reader, that we were tied by word and fate and I wanted to learn from him.

I pestered people, begged for promises, and did not notice right away that certain people, old men of past prominence, were avoiding me, playing hide-and-seek: busy, not home, just left, on the phone long distance . . . An old friend of my father's, a bookbinder and used bookseller, the one who must have hidden *Summer with Avgustina* within a piano textbook cover, a straight and honest old man, asked me not to visit him anymore.

I stared without understanding. Was I scaring off his clients? He looked back at me as if I was a stranger.

It was only then that I realized what they took me for. An informer assigned to reach Titan.

I choked on outrage, I wanted to scream: How dare you! But I feared that would be the wrong reaction, it was what a real informer would say if he were exposed, howling in indignation that he was pure and good. I did not scream, I searched for the right and sincere words. The old man took my bewilderment his own way. And shut the door.

My father fell ill then. Caught a cold at a friend's funeral. His ears were blocked with purulent edema. He couldn't hear a thing and lay tossing and turning feverishly in his cotton-battened room. Unwritten and unperformed music shook his body, echoing in his trembling joints, in his muscles. Then it stopped.

Many people came to the funeral. The old men still avoided me politely and implacably. I thought that my father had learned of their suspicions and could not bear it.

Not knowing how else to show him that I had been unjustly accused, I decided on a sacrifice. Let him see that I was giving up my desire to find Titan. I took *Summer with Avgustina* in its fake cover down from the shelf and went outside.

At home I thought I would throw the book into the garbage or toss it into the river from a bridge. But out on the street I imagined attentive eyes everywhere. If I dropped the book or made a strange gesture, the spies would pull the volume out of the garbage or out of the water. I wandered indecisively through the city, fear growing with every step that the walk itself could appear suspicious. Just think: the son of a departed father just wandering around aimlessly! He must have found something seditious in the deceased's things and wants to get rid of it, looking for a place and opportunity.

Lord, it was just a small book, three hundred pages on thin paper. But it seemed so heavy and enormous! Thrown into a bin, it would be noticeable. Stuffed into a crack in an old wall, it wouldn't fit. Pitched into the bushes, it would get caught in the branches. Torn up and tossed away page by page, the wind would pick them up. Burnt, the smoke would attract attention.

Shamed, I relived my father's death, the vulnerability of his body compared to imperishable paper flesh. I brought *Avgustina* back home, no longer pursued by imaginary spies.

At home, I opened it to read a few pages in memory of my father, to honor the bravery of his gift. I realized I was reading a completely new text. What had seemed like background before, just details, now appeared with new significance.

Now this was a book about a father. About fathers. About elders who do not yet know that soon the occupation and war would disgorge them from their seniority and turn them from being their parents' children and their grandparents' grandchildren into the stepchildren of history.

Titan visited my father's grave on All Saints' Day, when every cemetery was filled with people and even the innumerable spies could not catch every conversation.

By the way, at the time I hadn't learned to notice spies. All I saw was the little man from the train station standing by my father's grave with a bouquet of narcissi. He turned when he heard my steps.

I always had a son's face, a replicated face, a clear sign—this is his father's scion. I had dreamed of being freed of that, to wipe away the brand of duplication, but that day it served as a password.

He offered me his hand and politely introduced himself by Titan's name.

The unseen Titan had been huge, a monolith, in my imagination. Here was a sparrowlike man with an infant's pure face extending his hand. I was confused, and he looked at me with kindly amusement: I understand, he seemed to say, and I would have been confused, too. In that easy and simple gaze I sensed hidden light and power, the animated meaning of All Saints' Day, a reflection of fiery tongues that descended to the apostles in Jerusalem.

I knelt before him. Before the higher spirit that lived in

an adolescent's body. I remembered how he fed the pigeons, giving away his first bread in his hometown, and I dreamed that I, too, would be eating a different bread from his hand, from the hands of my teacher. I could see no other meaning in our accidental meeting.

Titan laughed and said, "Get up, get up. Enough. You should bow to your father."

He hummed the first few bars of "Love Incognito," recognizable, treacly, inappropriate at the cemetery. I shuddered, knowing how hard it was for my father to be known solely as the composer of "Love Incognito." People asked him to play it, to sign a copy and add a few words as a souvenir. His acquaintances were certain that he was incredibly proud of the tango known throughout the republic, to the extent that nightclub musicians still played it, in a slightly updated arrangement, on Lithuania's former independence day.

Titan drummed the rhythm on the burial plot fence and said, "That last summer, 'Love Incognito' was my torment. It was played everywhere by everyone. At every party. At every café. You couldn't get it out of your head. As if your father wrote it so that it would spin in your brain forever. Not music, but a cheap trick. Oh, how angry I was! How I blamed your father! I knew what a great composer he was.

"But years later, in the Far East camp . . . During the third camp winter hunger destroyed my memory. It consumed itself. Memory needs energy to function, even though we don't notice that in ordinary life. In the camps, memory becomes a cannibal. In order to remember one thing, you have to forget another. Then a second, a third . . . I no longer could remember where I was and what I was.

"Suddenly I heard something familiar. A tune. Memorable. Persistent. It had crept into my brain deeper than I could imagine. It was the foreman's assistant, one of many of our countrymen in the camps, humming 'Love Incognito.' He was the only one with enough spirit left.

"Those notes, a few bars, the tune . . . I, who was nonexistent, insignificant, I recognized it. 'Love Incognito' revived dead connections, restored lost images . . . Every moment of that last summer was marked and imbued with those notes. That summer when I finished my novel was the summation and reflection of my entire life. Thanks to 'Love Incognito' I got it all back. I deciphered it and restored it out of those notes. So, in a sense, I am now your father's creation."

Titan looked at me, then at my father's headstone. He nodded barely perceptibly. I decided then that it was a promise to meet.

Now I know for sure: They spotted us at the cemetery. It's all in Titan's case file. A report from the surveillance about contact. With a special note to establish my identity. The data: my address, name-patronymic-surname. On the back, in the paragraph on "compromising data," a line about my father: former member of a counterrevolutionary party.

Next paper: direction to call me in officially for a prophylactic conversation. A report on the conversation, without mention of the seagull crap. They were too embarrassed. They reported that I wasn't fully sincere and tried to convince them that the meeting was accidental, that Titan had simply come to visit my father's grave.

Resolution: start a case of operative surveillance and give it the code name Mosquito.

Love Incognito—Mosquito: they rhyme.

I couldn't resist telling my mother about my conversation with Titan. I wanted her to have this message of grace because she had spent her life telling Father that his music should be performed in bigger concert halls.

She listened in silence, remotely, as if I had not been talking about Father, about music, but some childish pranks. I realized she considered Titan one of the people who thwarted Father on his path, who did not let him become like other composers who composed suites and symphonies about the peaceful life of labor and ripening harvests, to have the opportunity to hear his own work, free of ideology, performed in the orchestra pit.

They had argued about this when he was alive. Father knew how to charm her, to persuade her that he could do it without compromising, without traps, just by waiting, waiting just a bit more . . . And now, after his death, she was looking for people to blame. And she found him.

Four days later I looked for *Piano Lessons* on Father's shelf.

The book was gone. Mother had visited her friend's dacha on the weekend. She had a bag of groceries. *Avgustina* must have traveled with her. There was a kilometer-long path through the woods from the bus stop to the dacha. She must have buried it along the way. Knowing my mother, I knew she would never tell where.

On the fifth day, she brought the summons for me in from the mailbox.

She simply laid it on the table before me and left without a word. Then came the seagull shit.

After our meeting at the cemetery, Titan lived another fifteen years.

At first, I waited for a sign from Titan, for I passionately wanted to learn how to write, to receive the torch of expression from his hands, in order to write a novel about him and my father and about us, the mutes who followed. I did not understand that I was hiding behind the notion of a mandatory apprenticeship; I was putting off what only I could discover and do myself.

Titan behaved like the most perceptive of teachers: he would not take me on as his student.

Talk about his new book persisted, changing only in formulation. Expectations, initially frantic, died down. More moderate reasoning had it that this great work required time, was a heavy burden, everything had to be considered carefully, such books emerged once in a century... Faith in a quick miracle vanished, leaving only bitter anticipation and no certainty whether there was still hope or just an empty specter.

Some of our previous pundits began publishing in Soviet magazines and newspapers. Oh, they were treated carefully, not forced to renounce or stigmatize. It was enough to have a story appear about the beauty of our native land. Without Marx, Lenin, or Communism. But printed in the magazine or newspaper of the occupiers, in vile proximity to their hectoring editorials. Some readers searched the texts for coded meaning, Aesopian language, hidden messages of resistance. But these pieces were only reprehensible flags of capitulation.

Then Titan got around to it. He was given the entire page below the fold: Go ahead! He wrote about village celebrations, just what the editors liked, neutral, praising national traditions and stressing the importance of peasant labor.

I didn't want to touch the newspaper. I couldn't believe that Titan would behave this way. Someone else must have written it and they used his name without his knowledge, such things were known to happen. People crowded the kiosks, buying and reading the article, but no exclamations or mockery were heard.

Yes, it was his style without question. His text. An article on village celebrations and nothing more. Yet every word shouted something different. "Haystack." "Houses." "Riga." "Well." They spoke of burned haystacks, emptied houses, barns that became places of execution, wells from which no one would ever again draw water. It was greater than mastery and art: the silent voice of the departed.

The newspaper sold out in Vilnius in a few hours. Then the authorities seized the rest of the edition from the regional centers and libraries—unheard of!—and never offered Titan a chance to write for them again.

However, no uncensored text appeared in *samizdat,* either. Then it became known that the authorities had given Titan an apartment, the one in the writers' building on Communard Street where I was living now. He accepted it.

What could he have offered in exchange? Only not to write. Of course, people said that was just a trick, after all, he was not young, he needed his own place and he would write the book, definitely he would . . . but they were just fooling themselves.

The apartment had convinced me: Titan would not create anything. He was broken and resigned. He was like my father: bits and snatches, notes, ideas for symphonies, never written.

When news came that Titan had dementia, I was horrified that the world of his memory, restored by three notes written by my father, would once again fall apart, this time for good. I was quick to judge: that was for accepting the apartment. For his betrayal.

The dementia was followed by a year in a coma.

I did not understand then who had organized Titan's funeral, hired the hearse, arranged for a plot at the old city cemetery, where Father was buried, too. I didn't pay attention to people then. I looked at Titan's cold white brow and thought that they were not burying him but an unwritten book, imprisoned in his dementia-destroyed brain.

I was sorrier about the book, the miracle that could have illuminated and roused my life, than I was about him.

Now, thanks to the COD, I knew that they had arranged everything. The grave site and the hearse. Dressed in civilian clothes, they made up a fourth of the crowd at the funeral. They walked behind the casket, strolled along the lanes. It was their triumph.

Naturally, they had feared excesses and unrestrained protests, which was why they brought in so many operatives: dozens for one little man in a coffin.

As I studied the COD I had the feeling that they had come to make certain that Titan really was dead and the book would never be written. To see off the victim who had for decades provided them with work, awards, medals, and special food parcels for holidays and gave significance and meaning to their service.

When the state notary public read out Titan's will to me in the presence of two officers in civilian dress, I rejected him a second time; I rejected the man who did not wish to be my teacher when he was alive and who had left me an absurd, dangerous, and meaningless inheritance when he died.

Of course, now I understand why he had chosen me, my father's son, to be his executor. With an easy, evasive, dilatory personality. Why he had left me that strange mark of inheritance. A scar of shame.

Because I would come afterward. In that free "after" that he had sensed would be. The one I would never have believed would happen.

I would come and read his book.

His text.

His novel.

I had been reading the COD for months. Volume by volume. Other cases were microfilmed, but Titan's file was too large. It was given to me to read as an exception.

The file reflected his life week by week. I tried to detect the precise moment when he realized that they would never let him write his book.

When the first draft vanished? When the second typewriter broke? When some drunken toughs beat him up in the alley, breaking his fingers? When an old friend, who had served time, too, started telling him maybe it wasn't such a good idea, why take the risk, why not be careful? When his room burned completely—the firemen said it was a short circuit—and another draft turned to ashes?

I couldn't guess. I do understand that when Titan accepted the apartment on Communard Street where I was living, a gift, a golden cage equipped with lots of hidden microphones, he had decided on how he would write his novel, the only possible way.

They became the paper.

He became the pen.

He used the microphones' ears and the agents' eyes to write his magnificent and strange text, a story for no one. But they, the eavesdroppers, the informants, wrote it down because they had to. He turned his old man's life and bitter days into living breathing clay.

He went to the store, worked, made phone calls—but God's hand moved him. The reports of outside surveillance, transcripts of conversations, summaries from the post office of his mail, memos on the events compiled by those who listened to and searched his apartment, notes on his conversations with friends and dialogues with himself, the plans of the operatives' work, denunciations by agents, and reports on meetings with them all secretly gave birth to a text, fragmented and yet whole.

The spies were stupid. They did not understand that he was creating by using them, their fingers, their paper and typewriters, their trained eyes and ears. They were following orders, doing their trade. They documented their own villainous acts, great and small, their tricks and meanness. They deposited them in the archive because they thought their work was exemplary and could teach others.

Then he was paralyzed for a year. They continued surveillance of the apartment, sent agents to make sure it really was paralysis. They looked for the book; they sensed that he was writing it. They did not see it in front of their noses.

He died. They finished his text. Added the ending. They scrupulously gathered rumors. Was anyone saying he was killed? They sent agents to sow seeds of posthumous humiliation: Titan never had been a real writer, he was a failure, a burst bubble.

He died. They wrote down his tale of pain and perdition

in the faraway northern camps. I, dummy and failure, student who learned nothing, wept when I read the familiar words:

Suddenly I heard something familiar. A tune. Memorable. Persistent. It had crept into my brain deeper than I could imagine. It was the foreman's assistant, one of many of our countrymen in the camps, humming 'Love Incognito.'

WHOOOO

Kasatonov's guardhouse stood in the middle of the steppe pitted with indistinct sinkholes. Kasatonov liked it: it was as if during a war here, artillery had been fired from a distance. War had in fact passed through here in 1942, but it left no visible traces. A column of German tanks had driven through, throwing up clouds of chalk dust, but nothing more. Nothing more had happened here since time immemorial. If not for the sinkholes, there would be nothing to catch the eye. Besides the guardhouse and the semaphore, of course.

The limestone covered with steppe grasses was unstable. Rainwater seeped in and undermined it. The embankment was prone to collapsing or sliding sideways, which would make the rails crooked and the switch jam. That meant supervision was needed. An attentive human eye was needed.

A post at any other switch would have been removed long ago. A team would arrive on a dilapidated, oil-stained repair trolley, oil the mechanism, regulate the automated settings, and that would be it. The watchman would have been sent off to the city to retire and do crossword puzzles.

But here, Kasatonov had a special switch.

An H-hour switch.

One day, multistarred generals in underground bunkers would break open special seals, or whatever it is they were supposed to open, they wouldn't tell Kasatonov what, and military siren alarms would blare throughout the country, in all the barracks. Armies would move into staging areas to escape the enemy's missiles. And then Kasatonov's switch, which connects the single track with the main one, would join the points to the mainline rails. They would connect, without question. Trains carrying tanks and armored personnel carriers would pass over it.

It's far to the cities from here. Even to the stations. Barren hillocks, you wouldn't even run into a gopher, there was something they didn't like here, the bastards: maybe the chalk in the ground was wrong. Sometimes in the distance, at the boundary of your vision, a deer would flash by in the haze of overheated air. But you couldn't get it with a carbine, you needed an optical sight.

It was far, remote. That was why Kasatonov was stationed there, a skilled and proven man. He was repairman, lineman, and sentry. The guardhouse was an old freight car taken off its wheels. Post No. 4367STR.

Water was stored in a cistern, hauled in by a shunting locomotive once a month, along with food. In the winter, snow could be melted. There was never a lack of snow here.

Kasatonov tried planting potatoes, but they wouldn't grow. And it wasn't really suitable, it's not a summer house, it's a guarded site, and Kasatonov had the right to take the first warning shot, and then to shoot. He was given an SKS, a self-loading carbine, the weapon of the Soviet rear guard, military builders, warehouse watchmen, and prison guards. Kasatonov had asked for an automatic rifle. Still hadn't gotten one, they kept dragging their feet, saying it wasn't in accordance with the rules.

The rules called for two men to serve here, alternating twelve-hour shifts. One would rest, the other staying by the communications console, going out every two hours to check the switch and do the rounds. Those were the instructions written on a steel plate. Neither fire, nor water, nor a distant shell explosion could harm it. The instructions, embossed in metal, would survive a fallen watchman and be used by the next one.

Kasatonov respected that steel plate affixed above the console. He wiped it carefully to keep the paint from peeling. It was no toy, it was factory-made, stamped. Yet it seemed to speak to him directly: be on guard, Kasatonov, transmitting directives from the top, from the very towers of the Kremlin.

He was from a faraway forest region, forever beyond the reach of the railroad. They kept extending it, both tsars and the Soviet regime, but they couldn't overcome the swamps. At the southern edge they established the Zelenoe station, but from there you had to transfer to river transport. It was there at Zelenoe that he saw his first train, when he was a conscript.

Yes, there were supposed to be two men. In the first few years they kept promising that his partner would be sent any day. They've already selected him, he's coming, being trained, filling out forms, getting access, obtaining clearance for access to the instructions on the steel plate that Kasatonov put into the fireproof cabinet when the train engineer came for tea in the winter. It was a special post, and that meant the man assigned to the switch had to be checked up and down and inside out by the authorities.

He took inordinate pleasure in the words *register, record, document*. Registering meant seals and signatures, papers filled out, involving a person who was proven, trusted, verified, unassailable, subject to the Code and secret clauses of secret statutes, entered into the staff roster, allocated a salary, assigned to a numbered post, attached to a unit, a military unit, and through the unit to the whole, to the army, subordinate to command, required to maintain loyalty to his oath, guard the post, and be given a personal weapon—with the right to use it, *if*.

Except that no one was registered, no one was dispatched, even though Kasatonov had truly waited at the ready in those early years. He imagined his partner as a younger brother, the one he had never had. He would teach him the ropes, make sure he didn't laze around, went out on time to check the switch, and memorized the instructions perfectly, because there could be a surprise inspection, which happened sometimes.

Then that passed. Instead he developed a suspicious, worried fear—don't let them send someone, some slacker, some dolt who will need to be taught how to swat flies, while they pension off Kasatonov.

"You're joking!" he would say to an imaginary fat lieutenant in the personnel department. "That won't work. Kasatonov will continue serving." And self-assured and relaxed, he would go out to the switch, his steady companion, and sit on a piece of the wooden tie. He would sit looking at the distant mountains beyond the steppe. The peaks matched up, snowy, jagged battlements; the Caucasus.

Kasatonov did not like mountains. You might think, what were they to him, let them just be, they're beautiful. But they infuriated him. Who set them there across the flatness? The mountains didn't let railroads through. They didn't make room for trains. They had power over space.

Kasatonov would sit until twilight, and then pick up the long-handled hammer used at stations to check train wheels and brake boxes. He hefted it and eyed the spot and carefully beat out a ringing rhythm on the switch, gradually accelerating like a train.

Overwhelmed by loyalty and delight, he could feel the iron body of the railroad awakening, the railroad that exists in all parts of the country and in all its time zones. He struck one little railway joint, one hard bone sticking out, yet the response was from the whole, as if his insignificant tapping pleased it and he was allowed to place his ear on the rail as a reward. The echo of his hammer receded in the metal and then returned, transformed, from afar, having run thousands and thousands of kilometers across the great country created and bound by rails. The rails sang to him about everything that is and was.

About trains of soldiers that traveled from all regions to the west. About trains of prisoners that traveled from all regions to the north and east. About how you couldn't trust land. It was cunning and unfaithful and that was why you had to load its back with heavy embankments, rails, and ties, and drive spikes into the ties—only then could the land truly be conquered.

In the cursed August of 1991 the radio informed Kasatonov that there was a state of emergency in the capital. Then it fell silent, as if the receiver had broken.

He spent three days at the communications console, waiting for the green call key to light up, for the bulbs on the train map to blink, for the trains to start rolling, for a surge of the power that had been accumulated over decades and written about in newspapers and celebrated in songs.

The air rustled with the frightened whispers of mainline dispatchers. Three times the apparatus came to life, the yellow key lighting up: expect a call. But the green never turned on. The order did not come. The military trains did not roll.

On the third day Kasatonov, disillusioned and desperate, barely able to stand on his feet from exhaustion but not allowed to sleep, pushed the call key himself. For the third time in his life.

Twice before, the blizzards had blown snowdrifts the height of a man across the line and he needed a snowplow train. Kasatonov—following the instructions—had made the call, and a clear voice responded instantly.

"Duty officer. I'm listening."

Now, there seemed to be contact, the connection was on, but no one said anything.

"This is four-three-six-seven, over," Kasatonov repeated.

On the other end, it was as if kids were fooling around: picking up the phone and breathing into the receiver. Someone seemed to be walking, breathing, smoking, sighing heavily, unhappily.

Kasatonov could not believe this kind of negligence was possible. He decided it was an error, the signalmen had messed up, and there was no connection with the control point at all. He ran his eyes over the metal plate with the instructions. If there is no connection with the control point, you must sound the alarm. He tore off the stamped lead seal from the red key and pressed with all his heart.

Jiggle, jaggle, and then nothing.

The sound in his earphones was harsh, like a strong wind blowing over an empty bottle.

"*Whoooo* . . ."

Kasatonov tried again: *crack, clack, snap*.

And in the earphones, "*Whoooo*."

Third time: *click* and *pop*.

He shouted: "This is four-three-six-seven, come in!"

There was that sound again: "*Whoooo*."

Kasatonov suddenly realized that in many thousands of guardhouses and cabins, booths and compartments, cipher posts, offices, and bunkers, frightened servicemen were shouting into microphones, zero one and zero two, sixty-nine and eight slash seven, secret and super secret, all trying to shout their way to the top. And the response was the monotonous, terrifying "*Whoooo . . .*"

Kasatonov flew out of the guardhouse. Silence.

In the distance were the mountains bathed in light, their broken lines, crooked battlements, battlements, battlements.

Far in the distance, space sang along with the airwaves, the wind playfully roaring among the stones: "*Whoooo . . .*"

Oh, how he wanted to kill, shoot that *Whoooo*, tear it apart with explosions of shells, cut it to shreds with sprays of automatic fire! He grabbed his carbine and shot into the air.

"*Bang! Bang! Bang!*"

From the steppe the thrum settled around him: "*Whoooo.*"

He dropped the carbine, picked up his hammer, readied himself, and then banged out a melody on the rail, the secret code.

Nothing. The railroad was silent. Dead.

Kasatonov threw the hammer aside. Rushed to his bed, covered himself with his military coat, and stuffed cotton from the first aid kit into his ears so he could not hear "*Whoooo.*"

Only on the fourth day did *Whoooo* disappear from the airwaves. The voices of his superiors returned. But they no longer had their previous power.

Their military service was put under civilian command. He still served: wearing the insignia of a nonexistent country, with its military ID, with its bullets in his carbine. Kasatonov sensed that he could leave his post and nothing would happen to him for that. Many left; no wonder the rails were silent and did not respond to the hammer.

But where would he go? What did he have besides the guardhouse, besides the instructions on the steel plate?

Kasatonov believed that one day, not tomorrow, not in a month, but maybe in a year or two, the green call key would light up on the dead console, and a firm young voice would say, "Four-three-six-seven, do you hear me? Over!"

"Loud and clear, control point, over," Kasatonov would reply, straightening his uniform.

"Check the points, four-three-six-seven," the control office would order. "Readiness for twelve oh-oh. Tomorrow special trains will pass through you."

"Will check the switch, over," Kasatonov replied.

He would adjust everything, oil everything. In the morning, he would connect the side rail to the main line. The consists of trains would roll, the army would return, and the cheerful soldiers under the red banner would catch wind of *Whoooo*, chase it into the mountains, and kill it in the dark ravines.

During the day, Kasatonov hunted, setting snares in the steppes. In the evening, in the cooling twilight, he smoked the dried steppe grasses and stared at the distant city at the foot of the mountains.

They spoke a foreign language there, related to the language of mountain rivers, avalanches, and landslides. Even the dogs barked differently than in Kasatonov's homeland.

Long, long ago, when he was a young conscript, a soldier in a railroad convoy, Kasatonov transported those local residents to the hot deserts, from the Caucasus mountains to Asian Kazakhstan, to a place where there was nothing taller than a camel. Hundreds of train consists traveled east, leaving the dead at wayside stops. The engines' black smoke covered the rails. Kasatonov sensed that this was forever, there would be no return. That was what made convoy work magnificent and terrible. Not just a few Chechen prisoners here and there, but an entire nation, from young to old, was in its grasp.

And with this disorder—they were back. Once again, they were drinking the waters of their rivers, breathing the air of their mountains, when they were supposed to have rotted in the sands.

Before, when the highest command was in power, Kasatonov did not let himself ask why they had returned. Who let them? Now he began pondering: How was this possible? By what right? Was this how the disintegration of a vast empire had started? Were the mountains beyond the city, the alien and insubordinate mountains, the source of that devilish sound? *Whoooo.*

Kasatonov expected the call keys to light up in spring, when the snows melted. He remembered what he was taught: war sleeps in winter, the troops burrow into their dugouts, the weapon lubricants freeze. In spring, the roads open up and the generals lay out fresh maps atop their desks.

The keys lit up in the final days of November, in a snow-less period when all steppe creatures, now in their white winter coats, were helpless before hunters.

Kasatonov brought a white hare into the guardhouse, a huge one. The console was ringing, buzzing, *ding-dong*. His first thought was that it would freeze, just a click, and then nothing.

The green key was lit up.

Kasatonov turned it on cautiously, afraid he would hear that horrible *Whoooo*.

There was a loud voice: "Four-three-six-seven, respond!"

No *Whoooo*. He could hear other command voices, dispatchers calling other posts.

Kasatonov barely managed to respond, almost mixing up his own number, "This is four-three-six-seven, over!"

The speaker barked: "Battle ready! Four-three-six-seven, the password is APATITE! repeat, password APATITE! Do you read me, over?"

"Confirming APATITE, over," Kasatonov gulped and answered firmly.

The connection broke.

The instructions Kasatonov had showed the passwords BIRCH, TORCH, CORRIDOR, CORDON. No APATITE. He didn't even know what apatite was. Maybe they meant appetite? Did his nerves make him mishear?

He could have honestly replied that he did not know this Apatite-Appetite. He had not been informed. They had not updated his code tables. But what if the dispatcher had hung up on him? Sent the trains through a different switch?

"Battle ready, battle ready," he said to himself, tapping and greasing the switch. "Battle ready!"

His heart rejoiced.

"Apatite! Appetite! Appatite! Apetite!"

He wanted to stay up all night awaiting the signal, but fell asleep, exhausted, right at the console.

A horn blast woke him in the morning.

Kasatonov ran out of the guardhouse.

At the semaphore, at the switch, stood a consist of trains. Its end was invisible in the gray morning mist. His eyes scanned the cars and platforms: one, two, seven, eleven, twenty-two, he couldn't see beyond that. A regiment, maybe even a brigade. All its tanks, armored personnel carriers, trailers, tech vans, antiaircraft installations, camp kitchens, tankers, tractors, repair shops—in one formation.

Wrapped in tarps, the tanks and armored personnel carriers poked at the fabric with their gun barrels, as if they had a soldier's morning hard-on. The soldiers smoked and pissed from the train doors, the steam of urine mixing with cigarette smoke.

Kasatonov, moving the railway points, prayed for the diesel locomotive, rails, tanks, and cannons to depart, to pepper them with TNT over there, shoot, mutilate, clobber, wipe them off the face of the earth; crush them, bomb them out, so that the whole world would be brought to life by the shooting, and no one would ever dare say *Whoooo* on any speaker again.

The consist started moving heavily, crawled onto the main line, and set off in the direction of the mountains.

Days passed: as if the trains had not been there.

The communications console was silent again.

There still was no snow, as if winter was not prepared to come down from the whitened mountains to the plain.

Kasatonov began to think that it had been a dream: platforms, tanks, machine guns, quadruple barrels of antiaircraft guns, the evening call, the password APATITE or APPETITE.

Yet he knew definitively that the military trains had not been a mirage. The ties in the places where the zealous soldiers had urinated copiously still stank. He walked there, like an old hound around new markings, sniffing, where were they, the dogs, where did they go, why weren't they raising their voices?

On New Year's Eve, bare, black, terrible, the sky cracked open over the city in the distance, at the foot of the mountains. Pounding, roaring, yellow explosions, and red lightning bolts raced across the sparse clouds. He recognized the voices of tank cannon, the voices of artillery, and he danced in the icy wind and shouted into the darkness, laughing and mocking: "*Whoooo! Whoooo!*"

In the morning he was felled by a fierce fever, and the guardhouse was snowbound for days by blizzards. He didn't hear them. Then Kasatonov began getting up. He had strength enough to heat the guardhouse and boil water. His ears were swollen, as if from the shelling, and he could not hear the sounds of the world, the inflamed echo of the nocturnal cannonade traveling through his body.

One icy morning, as if to restore his hearing, a diesel locomotive sounded at the guardhouse.

Kasatonov crawled out, dragging a shovel to dig out the snow-covered railway point.

The train was on the main line.

There wasn't a single person on its platforms.

Only tanks and armored personnel carriers, dead, smashed, illuminated by the sun rising from the winter darkness.

They were poorly cleaned, like discarded tin cans. Like tin cans, they stank even in the bitter cold, reeking of rotted meat and cinders.

He stared in disbelief at the fractures of split armor, scorch marks, cuts, dents. At the black, human cracklings stuck to the slopes of torn turrets.

He heard the mountain wind howling in the dead metal, blowing into the blasted hatches and twisted barrels: *"Whoooo."*

190

Cyprus.

Troodos.

Way up high on the mountaintop, the white dome of the radar. It pulses invisibly, responding to space, taking in millions of cubic kilometers of sky. It sends tracking waves out across the Mediterranean, to distant deserts and mountains, keeps military planes on dispatchers' paths: transporters flying precisely along air corridors and pairs of fighter jets scanning the hostile soil of Asia.

The jet-powered birds weave a hunter's net over it. Their fierce speed daubs them in the air; they are above every crevice, empty space, village, river, and oasis. They have eyes that see at night and carry winged death—missiles. Sound follows. Sound is slower than death.

It is a new Olympus, from which the modern gods fling new spears. The road to the peak travels between mountain spurs overgrown with resinous firs and amid waterless valleys where neither river nor stream is heard. If the limestone cliffs do manage to expel a weak stream that hides from the sun in the sand and gravel, even the smallest drop of water yields oaks, knobby as if they take their stature from the stones, oaks that shield the rill from the sun with their impenetrable shade. Life here is the twilight of crowns, the finest perspiration on the stones; life is shadow, cover from the eagle's gaze, the vole's scurry, the snake's slither, the quiet flow of water feeding the thirsty cool roots.

Along the broad slopes, in their free folds, are monasteries. Grapes do not grow at that height, but the monks own vineyards below in the foothills, bathed in the sea's warm breath. That is why the monastery cellars are filled with dark bottles of wine, as thick as blood. In the dark of church vaults with narrow windows that protect against the molten weight of the sun, behind thick glass panes, lie reliquaries, glowing with the dull, underground light of silver and gold, the light of ores taken from mountain veins, encrusted caskets and trunks preserving the relics of saints.

Bone and metal. Here is a silver hand with soldered bones, the phalanges of three fingers. Here is a skull, gathered and wrapped in gold foil; only the forehead is open. And here is a totally unrecognizable piece of flesh that resembles a dried fig—you won't want to buy candied fruits in a village shop after seeing that.

It seemed as if a diabolical force, comparable to the force of the earth awakened in an earthquake, tearing plains apart, had torn apart the martyrs, shattering every joint, every articulation of the body, and tossed them into crevasses, animal dens, the deep seas, home of shells and fish, into the icy tundra and broiling volcanoes. I, an atheist or rather an agnostic in the Christian sense, thought that I recognized the characteristics of their death: it was what an air-to-ground missile does to the human body.

Still, I ascend Troodos, go up the mountain on foot with my backpack or on my borzoi-like bike, its tires thinner than a razor blade. Not by car, not by bus, I need to feel my muscles strain, my blood boil, the labor of the climb.

It is my temple, my throne, my altar.

My sensorium, tip of the tongue, tender nipple of my lover's magical breast.

My limit projecting into the sky.

My altitude point.

Here I feel—experience—sense—the sky.

From which I am excommunicated.

* * *

Up, up, along the corkscrew road, the sunbeam, past steep drops, pedaling, squeezing out the last drops of sweat. A pair of Falcons from the RAF Akrotiri Base pierce the sky over the sea and foothills, fledglings that are not yet allowed to fly free and are kept tethered.

They arouse memories of the engine noise, the silhouettes of fighter jets; that instant memory that separates us from others.

There is another memory connected with the Falcon. The memory of a courtly flying joke that should have become a squadron legend repeated in military bars at the height of the evening. Instead, it led to separation.

Standing up, I push, press, pound the pedals, hammering them like nails. I remember how Margarita, the light and joy of my past life, flew to her family in Germany from Cyprus.

We said farewell in the morning, and she took a taxi to the airport, always running a tight schedule.

She flew on an Airbus, an old hauler. When it landed in Frankfurt, I was at arrivals with a bouquet of her favorite white roses.

It was impossible. Margarita thought she was seeing things or that I had a double. But it was me. She thought she had been speeding along, flying as fast as possible. I hadn't told her that I was bringing over a jet to the base at Ramstein. After I landed, I had time to take a shower, change clothes, call a taxi, and buy flowers; the supersonic Falcon beat the slowpoke passenger Airbus in a breeze.

I felt uncomfortable, as if I had deceived her, done something forbidden and shameful, performed a stunt that mocked the reality of our separation. Mocked the order that guaranteed the true value of distance and the impossibility of falseness in relation to miles and gallons of fuel.

That must have been the start of the end of our love. A lover of solitude and travel by nature, she no longer felt completely alone anywhere. She kept thinking that I might appear at any moment, slip through secret passages in time, pop up on a street in Cairo or Barcelona like Hermes the winged god. I understood, I apologized, but apologies meant nothing.

High up on the hill stood the white radar dome.

So much like the dome of a parachute.

* * *

What really annoyed me on that island were the birds.

Local urban birds, sea and mountain birds, I was able

to make peace with them. Sparrows that pick up tourists' crumbs, warily watching cats, didn't seem to be birds at all, they spent too much time on land, in branches. Their bodies were too fat, with big bellies, and their wings were too short and insubstantial.

Seagulls, cormorants, pelicans, and other seabirds had specially shaped bodies intended for landing on water, and those shapes created a specific dynamic line to their flight that did not impinge on my feelings.

I was forced to accept the birds of prey: eagles, hawks, golden eagles. Here, where the fiery breath of winds from the stony desert of the east and the sandy deserts of Africa met, the two great climatic ovens baking the Mediterranean, there was less foliage and grass and the soil was tougher and harsher, filled with dens and holes. The sun exposed this land, tearing off the covers and giving its small inhabitants up to the Accipitridae, the various raptors. Some could carry off a lamb, others could barely handle a rat; some ate whatever creature was available, others ate only mice or just snakes and vipers. But the Accipitridae were predators, which meant they were stealth machines, appearing and instantly vanishing.

The famous pink flamingoes in salty swamps were just a cheap carnival sideshow: necks too long, legs too thin. Awkward creatures, Mother Nature's joke.

My island lay at the crossroads of great bird migration paths, ancient heavenly routes connecting north and south, the first regular itineraries of life on earth as we humans know it.

The island was a layover, a stop, a beacon. The birds that do not land to rest still use it as an orienting marker, pushing away from its mountains and turning to new paths. The island connects all their flight formations, their echelons, like an avian airport.

I was tormented by the instinctive geometry of those echelons that existed before humans invented the triangle. I envied the tested aerodynamics of those bodies created for rapid flight. Not for swooping in search of prey like dry-land predators. Not for a steep dive, like cormorants. Bodies made for a lengthy mastery of space, for flying between continents.

For the duration of the migrations, I spent weeks underground, living a twilit terrestrial existence until the calls of migratory herds finally ceased.

Yes, the life of the land was now closer to me. I greeted hedgehogs and foxes in my neglected garden, I welcomed the wild boars and mouflons that came to the hidden watering hole. I learned their habits, the tricks of earthly inhabitants who had no wings, who were doomed to limited freedom.

A scorpion, an old fellow with just one claw, lived under the limestone paver in the middle of the garden. I called him Harry. Why Harry? Because my F-16 Falcon was called Harry. It was its work name and call sign.

When Harry and I were shot down by a ZRK missile, I was turned into a land creature. I hid in the stony hills that had no plants and where shade existed only in caves. I saw no one but scorpions. I got water that remained from the spring rains in the washouts in the granite resembling tall-necked pitchers by lowering knotted strips of cloth cut from my underwear, sucked the moisture and left a drop for the scorpions. I ceased being a military pilot there, because I lived the life of a scorpion under the stones.

Now I was Adam in an undesired Eden. I tried to fertilize the land and plant cereals, grow flowers, but the soil did not respond to me. It was not my element. My element, the sky, rejected me, and not because I had been shot down or had killed others from on high. The sky did not punish you for that, for if it did no country in the world would have military pilots.

Troodos, the peak crowned with a radar dome! Only here, standing on tiptoe and reaching up with all my soul, could I experience the ghost of my old feeling, the pilot's most important feeling.

The feeling of takeoff, being airborne.

* * *

You will come across us without knowing who we are among spotters, the photographers who take pictures of takeoffs and landings, the aviation voyeurs who measure themselves by the length of their lenses. Among the habitués of cafés with a view of the airport, gritty dives serving oversalted and overcooked burgers and cheap diuretic beer, their walls covered with pseudovintage photographs of the first airplanes, ridiculous shelves of wood and canvas, places frequented by airport workers, mechanics, loaders, as well as tourists spending the night at the airport and killing time before their flight. In aviation museums, among the machinery of ancient wars, the great-grandparents of today's interceptors and attack aircraft, or on windy-day excursions when the guide doesn't bother to hide his frequent sips from the metal flask in the inner pocket of his jacket. In a cool amusement park that has a flight simulator. Among the anonymous visitors to Flightradar who spend nights watching yellow Xs of passenger and cargo flights moving across the screen, following each other along highways and clustering around major transport hubs like mosquitoes around a lamp. At public ceremonies with balloons and champagne to celebrate a new terminal opening or the unveiling of a renovated one. In places likes Berlin's Tempelhof, the Nazi temple of air travel that became a field for parties and picnics. At closed local airfields turned into, say, racecourses where the roar of engines and the smoke of overheated tires awaken the ghosts of prior takeoffs and landings.

We are drawn by the idols and temples of our profession, like birds sucked into a turbine. But we, a caste of pariahs, outcasts, don't mix with honored veterans and retirees, with those who were written off for health reasons or fired for violations. They are simply forbidden to drive planes.

No one has forbidden us—but we can't do it anymore.

The sky is closed to us.

* * *

There are pilots and there are aviators.

For the pilot, the machine comes first.

For the aviator, the sky comes first.

A pilot steers the plane. He is in it, in a duralumin capsule.

The aviator is steered by the sky. He is in it, and therefore in a plane.

Most fliers are pilots.

There are very few aviators.

I'm an aviator.

I was an aviator.

*   *   *

I always descend Troodos toward evening. There are fewer cars on the road, and I race the bicycle on long stretches until it seems about to soar. These are almost flying speeds: the pioneers of aviation started at less. The thin frame vibrates, turning into a contour of pure energy, I speed and turn into motion, into a flash; I metabolize and dissipate the stormy milk I drank from the cloud's nipples and once emptied, roll onto the hilly plain with grazing herds of goats and sheep with heavy udders full of the milk of the land, ordinary milk that gives aromatic cheese.

Beyond the plain, at the very edge of the waves lapping up in measured rows, the civilian airport is a flickering oasis of light. At that time of day, just before sunset, there is a traffic jam: from Europe comes one medium-size liner after another, weary workhorses that have flown tens of thousands of hours, having undergone major repairs and changed two or three brand uniforms before ending up in the fleet of low-cost airlines. I can clearly picture their hardened plastic, clouded portholes, a fuselage exhausted by metal fatigue that sometimes groans during takeoff, making passengers shudder and break out in goose bumps; worn padding of the seats, and, most important, the smell: that particular smell of an old airplane.

Old liners make passengers worry and encourage superstitions. The passengers think back on the trip to the airport: Had there been warning sign? Almost unconsciously, they weigh the balance of good and evil that all people assign themselves. The old liner rolls toward the runway, serving at these moments as a silent confessional, a kind of saucepan for evaporating sins and fears. And the vapors seep invisibly into the walls and upholstery, eat into the plastic and carpet, creating this stigmatic aroma of an old airplane.

I ride down without pedaling, pulled by gravity, and watch the planes land.

It was from this island, from the Akrotiri base, that I made my first flight as a military flier. And it was also from here, from the civilian airport, that I flew for the last time, as a civilian pilot.

The island seen from above resembles an amphora on its side. But in my life, it is a point. The starting point and the end point.

* * *

I have a professional digital telescope in the extension to my house. I can afford it. My airline paid me a large severance package in exchange for my silence about certain inexplicable changes in my organism that the press could have misinterpreted and made the company look bad.

The island has a perfect theater of sky: cloudless weather, weak ambient light, thin mountain air. Like many people who loved Arthur C. Clarke as children, I use the telescopic eye to follow distant galaxies, dreaming of being in space.

Beyond the atmosphere.

Where there is no sky.

As if in mockery, I was left with the light, muscular body of a fighter pilot. It cannot be explained only by working out and sports. On the contrary, I think my ability to work out and play sports is due to the fact that my body never changes, does not need repair, does not gain weight, burning calories rapidly, and does not succumb to alcohol.

But as soon as I get behind the wheel or in a passenger seat, stand in the gondola of a hot air balloon, fasten the belt on a hang glider, get up into a helicopter——that same body, dry as cypress, suddenly leaks: tears, mucus, saliva, sweat. It turns into jelly, paralyzed pulp. I feel like a plane that has lost control. Liquid pours out of me as if I contained a vat, a cistern, a snot volcano, a sea of saliva. I pee in my pants like an infant, I ejaculate without orgasm, I turn into a soggy mollusk unable to move arms or legs. But when they carry me out, my body's orifices and pores close up, strength returns to my muscles, with the habitual and obedient drives of desires.

Control returns.

Back then, the very first time, two weeks after the incident, when the internal investigation was finished and I, the copilot, received access to flying again, I humiliated myself and was unable to fly. Everyone put it down to psychological trauma, a rare form of stupor accompanied by a kind of physiological hysteria. The fact that the captain, the pilot, experienced the same reaction was attributed to stress, and to the special and profound emotional tie we developed, like twins.

They took us to doctors and physical therapists for six months, for examinations and procedures. It was very important for the company to get us back into shape, to show journalists that we were flying, that everything was fine. But from my body's very first refusal, I knew that the path to the sky was closed to both of us. I knew it with my heightened fighter pilot intuition that had let me down only once, back there over the Asiatic desert in my duel with a surface-to-air missile.

*　*　*

I now understand that I should not have returned to aviation and certainly not switched to civilian flight.

I wanted to fly. But the explosion of the missile deafened me and threw off the delicate tuning of my reactions. I was no longer a fighter pilot. But I was still good enough to be the co-pilot in the cockpit of a commercial liner.

Civilian airlines don't like hiring former military men. We have different reflexes, piloting skills, and risk criteria. We are hawks, not doves. We are solitary.

The head of Salut Airlines training center, himself a former military pilot, incidentally, who flew as a young man in Korea, did not want to take me on, despite my excellent results on tests and retraining courses. He probably sensed that I was an aviator and not a pilot. That I had returned to the sky so that I could overcome the misery of the explosion that had engulfed and entangled me. Get over it with the stubbornness of daily exercise. I recognized the sense in his rejection. But the temptation of the sky was more powerful.

I remember my puzzled annoyance in the early training flights. I feared that I would forget my former lightning speed, the sense of being an arrow, and become a mere tributary of autopilot. I promised myself that one day I would return to fighter jets, that I would break through my inability; I had forgotten that the sky had been returned to me. The sky remembered.

* * *

The sky is what is left when you remove all materiality: weather, light, color.

Not the stars.

Not the clouds.

Not the air.

What is in them, but not them.

* * *

I was teamed up with Captain McGee, a veteran of long-haul lines, a longtime employee of Salut Airlines. He was considered their best pilot; not a single mistake, not a single fine in over thirty years. His planes always took off and landed punctually, as if he were in cahoots with the capricious and vengeful spirits of time. There were occasions when he hit an air pocket or lost an engine, but no passengers were ever hurt, as if McGee had golden insurance, more than plain luck— the patronage of Aeolus, the master of the winds, or a gift like that of the Phaeacians from Homer's *Odyssey*, whose ships never sank as they delivered travelers unharmed.

The youngsters idolized McGee, hoping to inherit his success, but never thought about who he really was.

Yet I sensed in our first flight that McGee didn't have luck. The misfortunes that befell him did not require the highest level of luck. All it took was discipline, using the controls properly, and following instructions—the plane saved itself. His perfection was the perfection of restraint, accuracy, rigidity—and fear.

McGee was secretly afraid of the sky and its unpredictability. That was why he was a specialist in regulations and instructions, an expert in a liner's technical capabilities and the physics of flight and weather. He had five months left before retirement age: an ideal career. But with each flight, McGee worried more, as if he sensed that the postponed vengeance for perfection was nigh, perfection that others lacked through the saving penalties of flaws, small sacrifices, mistakes, the daily taxes of existence.

At the hearing, one psychologist said that we had too much experience for two people.

* * *

On the anniversary of that day, I rent a sailboat and go out to sea. The first few years I stayed on land. At night, half-asleep, I felt the clear sensation that I was falling. Through the limestone of the island, through the granite lying beneath it, pulled by the dead weight of my body into the hot darkness, the toothed crevices of the nether world.

It was the only flight left to me.

Not flight, but falling.

On the sea beneath the sails, I don't feel it.

On land I sometimes think that I have been falling all these years, falling through beds, floors, stories, roads, everything horizontal and hard meant to restrain bodies and objects. The fall is slow, like a house growing into the ground, but I feel it with the instinct of a man of the air; I have been given over to gravity, to its iron law.

* * *

I don't remember the sky that day anymore. Sun? Wind? Clouds? It's closed to me. I only remember how we began the descent—the bottom, the land, pulled the plane powerfully toward itself, and the top, the sky, became spectral, distant beyond reach.

We followed all the instructions. We could not risk the lives of the passengers. We were later praised at internal hearings: they were the correct actions.

* * *

It was an ordinary shuttle flight from north to south and back, bringing white-skinned tourists for a late vacation at the end of the season and taking the previous bunch back home. Easy work, ordinary work: connect two ends of Europe, two of its seas: the blissful Mediterranean and the gray, foggy Baltic.

Full flight; not a single empty seat. Good forecast: light turbulence over the Alps and nothing more. No one was late, there were no problems with luggage or customs. Takeoff on the dot, in the McGee style. A two-and-a-half-hour flight, a nice walk, as smooth as if we were on the street, there was nothing at all over the Alps.

We were getting ready to start our descent when Ground Control demanded an emergency interim landing. Suspicion of a bomb on board. Next to us, adjusting its speed, was a fighter jet, an old Soviet machine, whose silhouette I had learned as a fledgling flight school student. The sight of it brought back all my former reflexes in a flash.

We both knew that something was wrong. Something bad. Stunned, McGee wanted to give me the controls. I didn't take them. We were both frightened by the same thing: responsibility for the passengers.

McGee obeyed the order. He announced that he had to land.

* * *

Of course, I know his name. But I still call him by his seat number, 19D: my mind's pathetic attempts at evasion. He might not have considered the fact that the flight path went over a country he had fled to avoid arrest. Or perhaps he had the sentimental idea of looking down at his homeland, seized by a dictator, where he could not set foot.

McGee did not explain to the passengers why we were landing. Just an extra landing. Nineteen D probably did not guess right away that it was because of him. He thought it was just an evil jest of fate, a technical problem, and summoned the stewardess, screamed that he couldn't land, he couldn't, they would arrest him, he was political, a refugee . . . And then he must have noticed the fighter jet.

I can imagine how his heart fell. How the land grew larger in his window.

That last landing stands between me and the sky. It was like a staircase you can descend only once.

I'm at the bottom.

THE SINGER ON THE BRIDGE

Once a week, Lt. Colonel Lu, an officer of the embassy of the country of Khitan, took the S-Bahn to work.

When he first started working, he did this on Monday mornings, when Berlin got going, having switched back to a work rhythm after the relaxed weekend, and the city's musical measures, the melodies of its human flows and industrial cycles were easily heard; its long songs of roads and rails, stone, asphalt, and water in the locks.

Lu arrived on the platform at exactly 7:36 a.m. for the train from Pankow. Punctuality was a form of calibration, a mutual matching up of details, and he slowly adjusted himself to the city, learning to hear and join its tempo and pulse. This was the teaching of his master, Colonel Ho, who had guarded Khitan's embassy in Moscow in the most dangerous years when soldiers of both countries skirmished along their common border.

"The first line of defense takes place far beyond the embassy walls," Ho explained. "The first line is the foreign capital itself. The capital is the country's heart. Listen to the heart. It will tell you if evil is being planned."

Lu learned to listen to Berlin. To hear it more precisely than any other graduate of the special department in the military engineering academy that accepted only students with three gifts: painting, music, and poetry, the three highest arts of harmony. Even though it was not said officially—for superiority is not harmonious—Lu knew that he was the best of his generation, bearer of the rarest and most noble sign on Earth; chosen guardian.

That was why he was sent to Berlin in the early 1980s. It had not yet fully put itself back together, but was seeking to mend itself after the war and heal the cut made by the Wall. Sensitivity, foresight, and strength were needed. Here East and West faced each other, the energies of political tensions and friction simmered; weapons sensed the proximity of enemy counter armaments, thousands of ears and pieces of surveillance equipment listened to the alien ether, hundreds of hands dug tunnels to the other side, to plug into a communications cable or to discover agents. The fates of the world argued in Berlin, holding one another in a seemingly everlasting, hostile embrace.

Lu learned to hear. But in his heart, he feared Berlin. With his perfect inner pitch, he sensed something in the city that he could not hear. Something tensely and heavily silent. Eternally vigilant in wordless wakefulness.

Lu felt that something even when he was in the very heart of the embassy, in the secret room where the sacred fir from the Fadan Mountains grew, with a special plane arriving weekly carrying rainwater from the Fadan slopes and compressed air from its protected valleys.

He had considered it for decades: What was it? What was its essence? Its force?

The Wall had fallen many years ago. The cross traffic of streets and trains had been restored. Torn fates were rejoined. The city was healing. But the silence, the something, had not vanished. It lay deeper than the postwar past.

Who was it that was silent? Ancient victims of war? Jews deported to the East to die in ovens? Soviet or German soldiers who perished in the forests outside the city, in the city's yards and parks, streets, tunnels, and alleys? Civilians who died in bombings and gunfire? Alas, the silence did not point to anyone. It seemed to belong to no one.

Sometimes Lu thought that the silence was within him. It was a restless soul afraid to betray itself, a shard of the war—those were as plentiful as spawning fish here—that had settled inside him when he had been too open, listening to the city.

At other times, he imagined that it was a material object holding its peace, staying silent, small and huge at the same time, having become and not become part of the city, local and alien, like a meteorite fallen to earth.

Lu thought that it was the crafty city itself tormenting him, hiding its secret.

Berlin—divided and united—was always a city of disorder, endless delays, missed connections, bypasses, switched flights; an unreliable and treacherous city. The map of intertwining S-Bahn and U-Bahn lines reminded Lu of a natural hieroglyph that revealed not the intentions of city planners but instead the will of the place, arising from the swampy land, twisting and confusing the train tracks, breathing chaos.

There were times when Lu thought with regret of the

Moscow Metro; he had interned at the embassy there. The marvelous underground palaces of the stations. The simple and comprehensible route map. The clear rhythms of movement that revive the pulse of the Supreme builder, the late ruler slandered by revisionists, who had ordered the Metro to be dug in the deepest depths, down in the limestone, so it could be built without a backward glance at the old capital, at its crotchety bad temper.

After three decades of service, Lu continued his tradition of riding the S-Bahn once a week. That morning he sensed a higher blood pressure, even though the barometer had not risen. The city was preparing for an event that related to him, Lu, and the embassy he guarded.

At 7:33, Lu entered the station's brick vestibule filled with the fragrance of baked goods and coffee. He passed the flower shop, where his fellow countryman was putting white chrysanthemums into vases. The elderly seller, of course, did not know Lu. But the lieutenant colonel knew that stall and dozens of other diaspora-owned strongholds in the city where he could find shelter or help.

Lu sentimentally appreciated these people, seeking in their faces the features of his native fields, mountains, forests, and village groves. They reminded him of his own fate: growing into hard alien soil, penetrating but not integrating, not changing, becoming not one iota different.

At exactly 7:34, Lu checked his simple mechanical watch, he did not use electronics, and went up to the platform. The morning passengers were waiting for the train. The signboard showed two minutes until arrival. But Lu, as if the platform had gently pushed underneath the soles of his shoes, sensed that the train would not come: the event he had foreseen was beginning.

Yes: The signboard flashed—the train was delayed by five minutes. Then loudspeakers came alive with a metallic voice, a voice from the old Berlin, created to announce evacuation orders and air strikes: The line had been closed. A bomb was discovered during track work.

Well, Berlin had always been a city of bombs. The city of an ongoing war that still imperiously broke into the world of the living. However, the news took Lu by surprise. The speaker did not say exactly where the bomb was found, and the lieutenant colonel had the feeling that the city had thrown him a puzzle that hinted at the future.

While Lu took a taxi to the embassy, he recalled driving around East Berlin thirty years ago with an architect. The driver was an embassy security officer trained to take everything in stride. They circled the same streets, squares, and embankments day after day.

Selecting the place with exhaustive care.

They had carte blanche from the GDR authorities. The city was filled was empty lots, abandoned buildings, semiruins, patched sites of old bombings. They found a spot that was almost ideal. The best of the possibilities.

Embassies are special worlds. Islands, or rather, shells in a foreign realm. They are a living paradox. They must see, feel, and be open—but never allow anyone or anything alien inside.

The ancient tradition of his country teaches that embassies are not built as much as they are grown. They are created around the guardian, a man of harmony who is the only one capable of maintaining the balance of openness and self-containment. To be a diaphragm. He, officially a security officer, was that guardian.

His word was final on where to build. The architect created a building that echoed features of the ancient fortresses that had protected the country from raids by nomadic tribes. He built hidden bastions, defense belts to surround the inner point of tranquility, the secret garden where grew the sacred pine from the mountains of Fadan: an altar that did not demand material offerings, a source that offered the true spirit of the homeland.

Lu's real name had been sacrificed to the embassy, replaced by a pseudonym. That was the start of the perpetual ritual of fusion between man and building. Not the forced, crude magic of objects requiring flesh and blood, a literal sacrifice. It was something much more complex and intuitive, like art.

Lu, artist and officer, by his life maintained the essence of the embassy in two contradictory states: openness and self-containment. Protecting the source of the homeland, the essence of Khitan's existence, he supported keen attention to the alien surroundings, but it was attention without acceptance, without adaptation, without the loss of even a particle of Khitan.

Yes, the place was chosen almost impeccably. Khitan embassies in every country of the world are situated by running water so as to dissipate and weaken hostile emotions. They set the building on the embankment of a canal carrying water from forest lakes in sandy hills left by a great glacier. Lu traveled to those lakes, rented a rowboat, swam in one lake feeling the peaceful, gentle character of the water, replete with the cheerful and agile life of fish.

The embassy terrain opened onto the canal, leaving a small road on the side. There was no room for hostile crowds to demonstrate against Khitan's policies; the other bank of the canal was occupied by an S-Bahn line.

Yes, Lu was proud of his choice.

Until the Wall fell.

The taxi was just driving past the part of the Wall where there used to be a checkpoint.

Lu recalled that autumn when they started destroying the Wall, and even he, master of guarding harmonies, had not expected the cyclopean scale of the consequences. Lu pitied the Wall, inevitably comparing it to the Great Wall of Khitan that had lasted for centuries. The lieutenant colonel would spend long hours in the woods near the forbidden zone, meditating, learning from it what it meant to be a wall.

However, as if the storm caused by the cheering crowds had weakened his ability to hear into the future, he did not grasp the providential significance of what had happened, which soon touched him, too.

The taxi stopped near the S-Bahn station across from the embassy, on the north side of the canal. Lu always walked the last two hundred meters.

Over the bridge.

Over the hated—even though the guardian must not hate—bridge.

The bridge appeared four years after the destruction of the Wall. After the diplomats from Bonn, from the Khitan embassy in the former West Germany, had moved to Berlin.

The new authorities just went ahead and designed a broad, long street that could not have existed in the divided city.

Lu tried to protest the construction. Asked them to move the bridge farther away from the embassy. Change the street's geometry. Stop the construction. Bribe the contractors, threaten the workers. But nothing worked.

He was met with a superhuman stubbornness. The divided city was restoring itself; reconnecting what was thought to have been divided forever.

Lu met the overriding force of someone else's harmony—and lost. It was a painful lesson.

Once the bridge was built, the old gardener, Master Fu, who took care of the pine from Fadan, told Lu that the tree had grown a new branch: inappropriate, ugly, destroying the tree's balance and aura. Yet neither dared to get rid of it, and the bent branch stuck out sideways, like an unfinished span.

The bridge was wide enough for six car lanes. He couldn't even get them to make it narrower! The bridge was like a theater stage erected before the embassy windows, before Lu's own office in the center of the façade.

And the pedestrian path and bike lane! All together they formed an elongated plaza! Lu understood from the blueprints that it could hold five or six hundred people. He tried to persuade the building bureaucrats to narrow that, referring to agreements reached with the previous authorities according to embassy security standards. But he heard the same answer: "The project envisions a combined pedestrian path and extended two-way bicycle path."

Lu understood there was no hidden agenda. This wasn't a special operation. Not a counterintelligence plot. It was Berlin itself that pulled a mean trick on Lu. Berlin and its silence.

Lu managed to fix a few things. He planted trees to cover the façade. But the trees, as if to mock him, did not take well and grew badly. He concentrated on the internal: He spent years healing the ruined pine branch through meditation, teaching it harmony with music. But he succeeded only halfway: the branch was ennobled, but it never became one with the tree.

Lu wished he could ignore the bridge. But he never learned to ignore it completely. Lu was too hurt.

Ambassadors came and went. Personnel changed. The newcomers, alas, took the ugly bridge, which distorted the harmony of Lu's idea, as a given. A bridge was a bridge.

A trusted ally of Khitan's intelligence, a wonderful cook, opened a café on the corner. Sometimes émigré dissidents who picketed on the bridge had lunch there. Young low-ranking embassy staff also dropped in there. Once as Lu walked past, he heard one of them say that the bridge—just think—was beautiful!

The lieutenant colonel stepped onto the bridge.

His unobtrusive clothing did not attract attention and no one would have suspected he was an officer. He walked in the stream of workers, as if in a hurry, but he did not hurry, and people passed him without noticing.

Lu crossed the hated bridge not for the sake of the morning clerks.

Lines of people had formed on the pedestrian path. Three hundred, as usual. Similar and faceless in toxic yellow hoodies that covered their faces.

Children of the Moon.

After the construction of the bridge, the embassy lived happily for many years. Of course, there were occasional demonstrations, pickets, hunger strikes. Twice émigré madmen set fire to themselves on the bridge. But Lu did not allow the living torches to shake the spirit of Khitan in the building or its people.

Seven years ago, the Supreme Party had banished the Children of the Moon sect from the country. The ringleaders were shot. Rank-and-file members were sent to labor camps. Lu read the counterintelligence circular: "Pseudoreligious group denying the values of the Party, undermining the unity of the nation . . . The sect is destroyed and no longer presents a threat." Well, counterintelligence was unpleasantly surprised when the Children of the Moon arose in Europe.

The embassies in other capitals guarded by Lu's brethren were built so that only a few dozen people could gather at the main gate, by the façade. His embassy in Berlin was the only one where you could seat a symphony orchestra with an accompanying chorus on the bridge opposite its entry.

One morning they showed up, three hundred people. In yellow jackets, the yellow color of the moon. And until noon they sang dreary mantras, like wind howling in ruins.

After that, they came every day. The counterintelligence chief, Colonel Yu, tried to stop them. He scared off some, but others came in their place. Three were kidnapped and interrogated.

Lu saw the transcript. The Children replied readily.

"We pray for the destruction of the walls and retribution for the murderers," the Children said.

"Why aren't the walls falling down?" Yu asked mockingly.

"We accelerate the course of time. But not hundredfold. We do not have that power," the sectarians replied.

Then the city police made it clear that it would not tolerate any more kidnapping. Active opposition had to cease. Khitan counterintelligence decided this was a CIA operation using complex technologies to manipulate minds.

But Lu did not believe that. It was a commercially oriented sect. Their "faith" was nonsense, fairy tales about lunar cycles, a special race of moon people, the true ancestors of the human race, with Moon the mother goddess.

Lu knew how to listen. He heard in the consonances sung by the Children of the Moon an echo of true power, which he was taught could come only from a great and ancient tradition, a culture nurtured by generations of wise men, mystics, and artists who understood the harmony of nature and the mysteries of might.

He recognized such a tradition in the monuments of old Europe, in the vaults of its emptying temples, in the music of its departed geniuses. But for this mystery, the gift, to be passed on to sectarians, ridiculous fools?

However, Lu had heard it. So he ordered a check of the embassy's engineering systems.

Everything was in order.

The ambassador, a newly promoted technocrat, was cool toward Lu. He made it known that he considered Lu's service to involve outdated ritual, a stage set. Sometimes Lu wondered: Had adopting digital technology changed Khitan too much? These were dangerous thoughts.

The ambassador visited the secret garden and the Fadan pine with inexcusable infrequency. Once he even wanted to hold a private reception there. Lu had to send a dispatch back home. The ambassador was reprimanded, and severely so. He did not retaliate, but he kept his distance. And so the first notes of discord resounded at the embassy.

Three years later, Lu noticed that the Fadan pine's growth

was slowing down. Only the new, unharmonious branch grew quickly, as if sucking up all the juices. The new gardener sent to replace the late master Fu, whose body was brought to the mountains of Fadan to rest in the sacred grove and feed new trees, was himself a green shoot unable to treat the tree's terrible disease.

It seemed to Lu that this branch presaged an evil future. He sang hymns of nobility and honor for it. He played melodies of enlightenment on the *krua-di*, a water harmonica. But the branch shamelessly flaunted its foreignness, and it seemed to Lu that the pine, the sacred tree of Fadan, the mountains of the three hundred and thirty deities that encompass all the entities, hierarchies, and phenomena of the middle world, was afraid.

In the fourth year, Lu felt the first breath of decline. It began with trifles.

The embassy bought nothing local. Everything it needed, including groceries, was delivered by air and sea from the homeland, so that every object, every piece of food, contained the beneficent spirit of Khitan.

However, the staples started rusting, the stationery pins began bending. Stickers came unstuck. Paint peeled from the walls. Dishes cracked in the dining room. Electricity went on the fritz. Computers and air conditioners broke down.

The head of the embassy engineering and technical service, Zhu, also a newcomer, a digital boy, smart, coming from high-tech industry, shrugged it off. "Don't exaggerate,

Lieutenant Colonel! Everything today is *Scheisse*. Nothing lasts a year. But that's as it should be. Otherwise, what would the world buy from us? The word 'quality' has no meaning anymore. And that is progress, Lieutenant Colonel Lu! Amazing progress to our benefit! Abolish the life span, the durability of a thing, make it short-lived, like a mayfly, and sell the same thing twenty times over! This is the basis of modern Khitan, Master Lu! It is the foundation of our growth, but we have to put up with forced expenses, even here at the embassy."

Lu listened and knew that he wanted to return to the past when things were things and not moths.

Life at the embassy gradually deteriorated. There were quarrels, intrigues, theft, important negotiations failed. The second secretary was filmed with prostitutes and the video was leaked onto the Internet. There were other minor "leaks," and counterintelligence began to look for a mole, giving rise to spymania and spiraling squabbles between departments.

Only Lu understood that there was no spy and never had been. It was the Children of the Moon and their singing, inciting bad resonances that methodically undermined the embassy's foundation. Others, including the ambassador and the chief of counterintelligence, had stopped worrying about the Children of the Moon, treating them like something internal, harmless, amusing, limited. The yellow figures became endemic to embassy life, and this surprised no one.

Even the incident with Captain Hue, a brilliant youth, star of the analytical section, connoisseur of music and opera, habitué of great orchestra concerts, caused no alarm. On a business trip with his partner to Cologne, Hue violated instructions and left the hotel on his own, was apprehended trying to get into the cathedral, skillfully escaped from the police, and a half hour later—this was seen by train passengers—threw himself into the Rhine from the triple Hohenzollern bridge. Earlier that evening Hue was at the House of Music, listening to Schoenberg's *Verklärte Nacht* and *Pierrot lunaire*.

Exhaustion, said the embassy psychologist. The young man had too much responsibility. But Lu knew overwork had nothing to do with it. Hue was more than an analyst, he was a potential guardian, a listener born under the Air sign. Hue had approached Lu twice, even though officially he had no access to information about what the lieutenant colonel did. He came over and casually brought up the Children of the Moon.

Lu walked along the bridge, listening to the viscous melody of the mantras and peering into faces. All these years he had been waiting for the melody to change. The Children of the Moon would take the next step.

On the hump of the bridge, at the very middle, he heard it.

A new voice wove into the chorus. It did not repeat the mantras, it seemed to be conducting them, changing their timbre and rhythm. A dramatic soprano. Professional singing, opera class.

The voice seemed to intensify the mantras, teaching and directing them; made them delve deeper and deeper into worldly matters.

Lu, despite his training, lost his step.

The voice seemed to address him personally, calling on him to cast off the guardian's armor, renounce service to the embassy and the connection to the sacred Fadan pine.

Lu understood that the voice was not using those words. They were his own. He took earplugs out of his raincoat pocket and inserted them in his ears. The voice softened and his blood pressure went down. Lu finally picked out its source, the new one, in the center of the phalanx of the Children of the Moon.

The girl was dressed in their uniform, yellow jacket with hood. She stood like the rest of them, unmoving, hands crossed over her chest, but Lu could see that she was different. The Children were mostly from the lower classes, but she had the ability to act on the stage. And the voice—it was worth millions.

Someone from the surveillance team, on Lu's orders, photographed her face with a powerful zoom lens. They ran the photo through their database and soon Lu was given a printed dossier. While waiting for it, Lu stood by the window and looked at the bridge. The embassy was soundproofed. No noise was supposed to enter the building.

But Lu imagined that he could hear her voice.

Marguerite Kireno. Opera singer. Illegitimate daughter of actress Elena Kireno and writer Su Fo, an émigré leader murdered a week before in Rome.

Naturally, such things were not mentioned even in top-secret orders and reports. But Lu understood that he was killed by people from Khitan's secret service. They had wanted it to appear the result of natural causes, a heart attack, but they left traces and were caught on camera. The scandal was huge. Diplomats were being expelled.

The scandal would protect her, thought Lu. They could not touch her now, right after this fiasco. The authorities would forbid it.

Lu imagined Marguerite coming day after day, month after month, as the Children did. Looking at her photograph and hearing the ghost of her voice beyond the high-security windows, he dreamed that the ban would be lifted and she could be carefully captured and questioned: Where did she get the idea of singing with the Children of the Moon? Who taught her the song that—Lu checked—had made the needles of the Fadan pine droop as if frostbitten? Did she discover the fatal melody herself? Just through her talent?

He felt sick, he had chills. He knew it was not a cold but the reverberations of Marguerite's voice. The voice of an opera singer who lived in an imaginary stage set world, where they swing swords and fence with foils, where spirits and gods interfere in the lives of mortals, and the word is stronger than steel.

That was the source of the magic of her singing, he thought. She was young. She believed in make-believe, and her naive faith gave her strength. All the operatic machinery of emotions, all the stage conventions, all that was sublime in old Europe, all the stories of revenge and valor, all the miracles and transformations that occur in auditoriums were now working in Marguerite's favor.

At noon the Children of the Moon left as usual for the S-Bahn, and Marguerite left with them.

Lu felt disappointment and the anticipation for tomorrow's meeting.

Marguerite would come, and he would begin a silent duel with her. That night he would write his own melody, which would turn the embassy into a musical instrument: all his guardian bells that scared off spirits, the doors, pipes, flags, windows, and voices of the staff. The main note would be led by the water harmonica fed by a source flowing past the roots of the sacred pine, a source with the recycled waters of Fadan's mountain streams.

Lu decided to spend the night at the embassy. He had a private spot in the depths of the cellar, closer to the pine's roots. The builders left old masonry of ruined houses exposed there instead of walls: a display of the city's underside, its very guts.

He meditated, lying on a reed mat, but the future melody did not respond. Lu heard only Marguerite's voice and could not banish it. He was covered with sweat, as if a fever was beginning. His joints ached, and his muscles were tight.

Yet when the singer's voice grew quiet, relief did not come. Instead of a calming stillness he heard that strange and threatening silence that had been scaring him in Berlin. It was near. It was growing, preparing—he understood at last—to discharge, to explode with a deafening, thunderous sound.

After midnight, he fell into a light sleep. He heard the Children of the Moon talking in many voices about what they refused to disclose under interrogation.

"Man has two times. The time of the Sun. The time of being awake. And the time of the Moon. The second time. It flows while man sleeps. Ordinary people do not know it, do not live in it. It is like the force of lunar gravity, the tidal force. And it, too, moves fate. It, the lunar time, is what we, the Children of the Moon, conjure up . . . All your governments, ideologies, and political systems, religions and philosophical treatises, are born of solar time. Created by the heirs of those first humans who were afraid to step into the darkness away from the flames of their primitive fires. They chiseled flint for axes and kneaded clay for pots. They invented signs for fear of losing their wisdom, created embodied gods, and invented hierarchies of power.

"In the ancient night, in the hopeless darkness, there was only a disembodied sound, only the sounds of deaths and births, fights and hunts, roars and squeaks, screams and longing moans . . . And those who went the other way lived next to you. Who believed the night and not the day. Those who do not have a history, such as you understand it; their weapons are older than bone arrows and bronze axes. It was born in the darkness of the world, when the hands of humanity were still empty, did not know the tools, and the world responded directly to sound, the only instrument that man carries in himself."

Lu woke up. He was unbearably cold. The sweat had

dried, the chills stopped. His body tightened and hardened. He did not know whether he was awake or had plunged deeper into sleep and was only dreaming that he had awoken.

Suddenly Lu felt he was something enormous: a giant metal drop suspended in the belly of a flying machine. Now he was she, pregnant with explosives, with a name written in chalk on the fuselage by joking technical personnel: Daisy.

The engines roared, and the machine rose heavily into the sky and headed east. Nearby he could hear the sounds of numerous machines carrying other bombs. Daisy was the biggest and most powerful: the only one in this raid.

Close bursts were heard. The machine rocked, a small hot splinter of debris broke through the plane's plating and stung Daisy's metal body, gnawing at the tail, breaking something there and disrupting the connection of parts. The flying machine tilted, the hatch doors parted, letting in the roaring night air. Daisy was thrown into the darkness, where slanting ghostly beams of searchlights and dark clouds of bursting zenith projectiles roamed.

For a moment he separated his consciousness from Daisy and managed to see the "flying fortress" with engines burning on the right wing. He managed to understand that the pilots were wounded and would try to take the plane back to the West, but would not make it. The bomber was doomed, it rolled obliquely out of the sky over the fiery city, it was pulled, magnetized by the black swamps of Brandenburg, its last flight watched by the locator stations that stand on the sand hills above the Stone Age chapels.

The pilots dropped the bomb, six-ton Daisy, destroyer of bunkers, ahead of time in a vain attempt to lighten the plane. He managed to see the cloudless sky and full moon—a bad night for a raid, for the planes were clearly visible to the antiaircraft gunners and fighters, the meteorologists had been mistaken with their forecast—and here his consciousness was pulled back in toward the dropping of the bomb.

They rushed down toward the streets lit by blazing fires. Lu recognized the locale immediately: there was the canal reflecting the phosphorescent moon, there was the S-Bahn station, there was the destroyed building on the site of which the embassy would be built.

Daisy didn't realize that the explosive mechanism was out of order, and she rushed down with all the gravity of her intended purpose. The surface struck her face, but it could not resist the pressure. The soil dispersed, parted, letting the bomb pass deeper than sidewalks and foundations and sewer pipes, deeper than all the layers of the city—to a place where the earth knew neither shovel nor plow.

Lu woke again. Rose unsteadily as if he had suffered a powerful blow. He walked along the walls on tiptoe, carefully. He remembered the old German construction official who had helped him choose the site for the embassy.

The German had complained about the difficulty of building in this city, because it was littered with old bombs, many of which were still dangerous. He told him about the types of bombs.

Lu took his words seriously. Sappers checked, sniffed out the land, tracked the excavation work, and found nothing. The German, Herr Derenmeier, congratulated him.

Now Lu listened, holding his breath. He had been warned that morning: the announcement about the bomb on the platform, and he did not heed it! It was embassy land around him, sovereign territory blessed by the spirit of Khitan. But below, deep below the embassy, the land retained the past of this country, it was as alien as the moon.

Lu ran upstairs, to the office, to preempt, to order that the girl, no matter how, at whatever cost, be removed from the bridge, prohibited from approaching the building, gagged. Otherwise she would sing again, using the Children of the Moon as an orchestra, a resonator, and wake up the six-ton Daisy, designed to destroy bunkers, which had penetrated too deeply and therefore was not found by the experienced bomb squad—no one expected that Daisy, designed for the most protected targets, could be here.

He was too late: the Children of the Moon were on the bridge. Desperately, Lu looked at them, counted them without really counting, and realized that she, his rival, his enemy, was not there.

She had not come.

Staggering, paying no attention to the surprised stares, Lu went out into the garden in front of the embassy.

The Children of the Moon were droning their hymns, the usual ones, preserving an echo of power, but in the wake of Marguerite Kireno's operatic voice, they were not at all alarming.

Lu listened, smiling, almost believing that his evening meditations had frightened her away, made her change her mind: he listened with extreme depth.

Then he understood why Kireno would not be there.

She did not need a second time. She had accomplished it already.

Her voice was still there, in the stone, the asphalt, the steel bridge spans, the brick box of the S-Bahn station, the foundations and walls of buildings, the rushing water, in the concrete flesh of the embassy and the land beneath it. It resounded like an extended aftersound, rooted in matter itself; stroking, waking the queen bomb.

Kireno could not have known about its existence, Lu thought.

He answered himself: Fate was greater than knowledge. She called for it—and fate responded.

At that moment, Daisy woke up.

SERGEI LEBEDEV was born in Moscow in 1981 and worked for seven years on geological expeditions in northern Russia and Central Asia. Lebedev is a poet, essayist, and journalist. His novels have been translated into twenty languages and have received great acclaim in the English-speaking world. *The New York Review of Books* has hailed Lebedev as "the best of Russia's younger generation of writers."

ANTONINA W. BOUIS is one of the leading translators of Russian literature working today. She has translated over eighty works from authors such as Yevgeny Yevtushenko, Mikhail Bulgakov, Andrei Sakharov, Sergei Dovlatov, and Arkady and Boris Strugatsky.

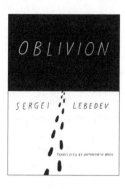

Oblivion
by Sergei Lebedev:

In one of the first 21st century Russian novels to probe the legacy of the Soviet prison camp system, a young man travels to the vast wastelands of the Far North to uncover the truth about a shadowy neighbor who saved his life, and whom he knows only as Grandfather II. Emerging from today's Russia, where the ills of the past are being forcefully erased from public memory, this masterful novel represents an epic literary attempt to rescue history from the brink of oblivion.

The Year of the Comet
by Sergei Lebedev

A story of a Russian boyhood and coming of age as the Soviet Union is on the brink of collapse. Lebedev depicts a vast empire coming apart at the seams, transforming a very public moment into something tender and personal, and writes with stunning beauty and shattering insight about childhood and the growing consciousness of a boy in the world.

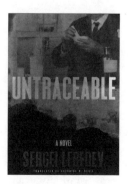

Untraceable
by Sergei Lebedev

An extraordinary Russian novel about poisons of all kinds: physical, moral and political. Professor Kalitin is a ruthless, narcissistic chemist who has developed an untraceable lethal poison called Neophyte while working in a secret city on an island in the Russian far east. When the Soviet Union collapses, he defects to the West in a riveting tale through which Lebedev probes the ethical responsibilities of scientists providing modern tyrants with ever newer instruments of retribution and control.

THE GOOSE FRITZ
BY SERGEI LEBEDEV

This revelatory novel shows why Karl Ove Knausgaard has likened its celebrated Russian author to an "indomitable . . . animal that won't let go of something when it gets its teeth into it." The book tells the story of a young Russian named Kirill, the sole survivor of a once numerous clan of German origin, who delves relentlessly into the unresolved past. *The Goose Fritz* illuminates both personal and political history in a passion-filled family saga about an often confounding country that has long fascinated the world.

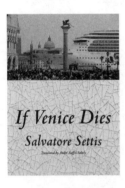

IF VENICE DIES
BY SALVATORE SETTIS

Internationally renowned art historian Salvatore Settis ignites a new debate about the Pearl of the Adriatic and cultural patrimony at large. In this fiery blend of history and cultural analysis, Settis argues that "hit-and-run" visitors are turning Venice and other landmark urban settings into shopping malls and theme parks. This is a passionate plea to secure the soul of Venice, written with consummate authority, wide-ranging erudition and élan.

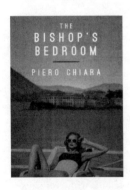

THE BISHOP'S BEDROOM
BY PIERO CHIARA

World War Two has just come to an end and there's a yearning for renewal. A man in his thirties is sailing on Lake Maggiore in northern Italy, hoping to put off the inevitable return to work. Dropping anchor in a small, fashionable port, he meets the enigmatic owner of a nearby villa. The two form an uneasy bond, recognizing in each other a shared taste for idling and erotic adventure. A sultry, stylish psychological thriller executed with supreme literary finesse.

THE EYE
BY PHILIPPE COSTAMAGNA

It's a rare and secret profession, comprising a few dozen people around the world equipped with a mysterious mixture of knowledge and innate sensibility. Summoned to Swiss bank vaults, Fifth Avenue apartments, and Tokyo storerooms, they are entrusted by collectors, dealers, and museums to decide if a coveted picture is real or fake and to determine if it was painted by Leonardo da Vinci or Raphael. *The Eye* lifts the veil on the rarified world of connoisseurs devoted to the authentication and discovery of Old Master artworks.

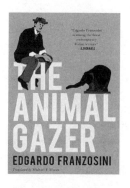

THE ANIMAL GAZER
BY EDGARDO FRANZOSINI

A hypnotic novel inspired by the strange and fascinating life of sculptor Rembrandt Bugatti, brother of the fabled automaker. Bugatti obsessively observes and sculpts the baboons, giraffes, and panthers in European zoos, finding empathy with their plight and identifying with their life in captivity. Rembrandt Bugatti's work, now being rediscovered, is displayed in major art museums around the world and routinely fetches large sums at auction. Edgardo Franzosini recreates the young artist's life with intense lyricism, passion, and sensitivity.

ALLMEN AND THE DRAGONFLIES
BY MARTIN SUTER

Johann Friedrich von Allmen has exhausted his family fortune by living in Old World grandeur despite present-day financial constraints. Forced to downscale, Allmen inhabits the garden house of his former Zurich estate, attended by his Guatemalan butler, Carlos. This is the first of a series of humorous, fast-paced detective novels devoted to a memorable gentleman thief. A thrilling art heist escapade infused with European high culture and luxury that doesn't shy away from the darker side of human nature.

THE MADELEINE PROJECT
BY CLARA BEAUDOUX

A young woman moves into a Paris apartment and discovers a storage room filled with the belongings of the previous owner, a certain Madeleine who died in her late nineties, and whose treasured possessions nobody seems to want. In an audacious act of journalism driven by personal curiosity and humane tenderness, Clara Beaudoux embarks on *The Madeleine Project*, documenting what she finds on Twitter with text and photographs, introducing the world to an unsung 20th century figure.

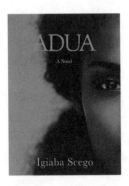

ADUA
BY IGIABA SCEGO

Adua, an immigrant from Somalia to Italy, has lived in Rome for nearly forty years. She came seeking freedom from a strict father and an oppressive regime, but her dreams of film stardom ended in shame. Now that the civil war in Somalia is over, her homeland calls her. She must decide whether to return and reclaim her inheritance, but also how to take charge of her own story and build a future.

THE 6:41 TO PARIS
BY JEAN-PHILIPPE BLONDEL

Cécile, a stylish 47-year-old, has spent the weekend visiting her parents outside Paris. By Monday morning, she's exhausted. These trips back home are stressful and she settles into a train compartment with an empty seat beside her. But it's soon occupied by a man she recognizes as Philippe Leduc, with whom she had a passionate affair that ended in her brutal humiliation 30 years ago. In the fraught hour and a half that ensues, Cécile and Philippe hurtle towards the French capital in a psychological thriller about the pain and promise of past romance.

THE MADONNA OF NOTRE DAME
BY ALEXIS RAGOUGNEAU

Fifty thousand people jam into Notre Dame
Cathedral to celebrate the Feast of the
Assumption. The next morning, a beautiful
young woman clothed in white kneels at prayer
in a cathedral side chapel. But when someone
accidentally bumps against her, her body collapses.
She has been murdered. This thrilling novel
illuminates shadowy corners of the world's most
famous cathedral, shedding light on good and evil
with suspense, compassion and wry humor.

THE LAST WEYNFELDT
BY MARTIN SUTER

Adrian Weynfeldt is an art expert in an
international auction house, a bachelor in his
mid-fifties living in a grand Zurich apartment filled
with costly paintings and antiques. Always correct
and well-mannered, he's given up on love until
one night—entirely out of character for him—
Weynfeldt decides to take home a ravishing but
unaccountable young woman and gets embroiled in
an art forgery scheme that threatens his buttoned
up existence. This refined page-turner moves behind elegant bourgeois facades
into darker recesses of the heart.

MOVING THE PALACE
BY CHARIF MAJDALANI

A young Lebanese adventurer explores the wilds of
Africa, encountering an eccentric English colonel
in Sudan and enlisting in his service. In this lush
chronicle of far-flung adventure, the military recruit
crosses paths with a compatriot who has dismantled
a sumptuous palace and is transporting it across the
continent on a camel caravan. This is a captivating
modern-day Odyssey in the tradition of Bruce
Chatwin and Paul Theroux.

New Vessel Press

To purchase these titles and for more information
please visit newvesselpress.com.